Praise for
OUT COLD

"*Out Cold* floored me with a quick one two of the serious and seriously funny. Schreck's unique blending of the absurd and the sublime along with his rather oddball cast of characters makes OUT COLD a great read."

Reed Farrel Coleman, Two-time Shamus
Award winning author of *Empty Ever After*

"…a fast, funny, rip-roaring read…wit and humor shines through on every page. But what I love most about Schreck's creation, Duffy Dombrowski, is the decency and dignity with which he treats the unforgettable cast of loonies, addicts, and criminals who parade through his office. I haven't cared this much about a protagonist in a good long while. Duffy is real hero and a true original."

Blake Crouch, author of *Abandon*

"As good as early Spenser and better than almost anything out there today, this series delivers."

Tim Maleeny, best-selling author of
Greasing the Piñata and *Jump*

General Duffy comments

"Fresh, intense and funny, Duffy Dombrowski packs a knockout punch."

Publishers Weekly

"…warmhearted, tough, funny…"

Kirkus

"The writing is seamless, true artistry and a joy to read. Forget Prozac, or even that double of Bourbon, this is what feeling good is all about."

Ken Bruen, author of *Once Were Cops*

OUT COLD
A DUFFY DOMBROWSKI MYSTERY
(ROUND THREE)

A NOVEL

BY

TOM SCHRECK

OUT COLD
A Duffy Dombrowski Mystery
An Echelon Press Book

First Echelon Press paperback printing / December 2009

All rights Reserved.
Copyright © 2009 by Tom Schreck

Cover Art © Gavin Dayton Duffy
w/ Nathalie Moore

Echelon Press
9055 G Thamesmead Road
Laurel, MD 20723
www.echelonpress.com

ISBN: 978-1-59080-622-7
1-59080-622-0
eBook 1-59080-623-9

PRINTED IN THE UNITED STATES OF AMERICA

10 9 8 7 6 5 4 3 2

For the two Mrs. Schrecks

My best friends and the loves of my life

Notes from Tom Schreck

Hanging out with Duffy and Al has been great. Because of them I've met some real life heroes I'd like to tell you about.

Part of an author's glamorous life is, of course, the book tour. Duffy-style that means my wife, Sue, and I throw my three hounds in the old Lincoln and drive to Southfield, Mi, Erie, Pa, Chittenango, NY, Ocean City, NJ or, any place else for that matter, for basset hound rescue events. You see, there are armies of people who just won't tolerate a houndie being mistreated.

This year some real-life puppy mill owner (my wife made me take out the other word I wanted to use) in Arkansas called a local rescue group and told them he was getting out of the business and they had a week to get his eleven bassets or he'd "take care of them" (meaning they'd go to a shelter and be killed or he'd take them out in the woods and do it himself.) The rescue group in Arkansas was overwhelmed and they didn't know what to do.

Then they called ABC Basset rescue in New York. Let me tell you something: ABC doesn't mess around.

In 48 hours a couple of guys were in a truck and on their way. They grabbed the "Arkansas 11" wrote a check for over $3,000 in vet bills and had all the dogs set up in foster homes by the time they got back to New York. Undoubtedly, every single hound was on the good furniture and counter, surfing treats out of the kitchen within an hour of their arrival.

My wife and I are proud to sell the Duffy Mysteries at basset events and give 100% of the profits to the organizations.

This past fall ABC auctioned off a chance to name a basset in *Out Cold*. Sherry Moore, herself an Arizona rescuer, bid $1,000 to put her houndies, Sally and Guffy, in this book.

Our tour also took us to the Michigan Basset Waddle, which takes over an entire hotel. You think you've seen it all? Go to this event and have a drink in a bar filled with hound dogs, or take a dip in the pool with a few bassets floating by. Jeremy Ruckhaber won an auction and became a villain. Ashley Amato also won and her own rescue Lola (who I got to meet!) got featured. Michael Levine bid the highest in the online auction and his basset, Maui, got fifteen minutes of fame. Bonnie Bostelman's hound, Louie, got a role too.

The nice folks at Droopy Basset Hound Rescue of Western Pennsylvania hosted us at their annual Slobberfest. Kristen Hathaway won the auction there and doubled her bid, so both of her hounds could make it in *Out Cold*. Blake and Sherlock were two very cool short-legged friends I made.

I couldn't make it to Maryland for the Basset Hound rescue of Old Dominion event but they sold the books and auctioned off a couple of characters. Marty Clark's hound, Sadie, and the Erickson family's guy, Arthur, are now immortalized.

You might have noticed a Maltese-Pomeranian named Tedward in the rescue scene. Well, Sissy Spadaro won the auction at Ryley's Run, a Golden Retriever rescue organization in Albany, NY and I decided not to be breed-centric.

Despite my hatred for the Red Sox, we love to visit the New England Basset Hound rescue and sell books for them. We've also done it for the Tri-State Basset Hound Rescue gang in New Jersey, who has a great boardwalk parade that takes over the entire town.

The folks in Arizona (who rescued twenty-two hounds from a puppy mill in one day themselves this year) auctioned off a couple of my books, I'm trying to get to see the folks in Alabama and would love to do the event for Belly Rubs Basset Rescue in Mississippi just a few miles from Elvis's birthplace.

If any hound people are reading this please, contact me. If there's a way you can make some cash off of me for the hounds let's do it.

I've had two rescue bassets myself. My first one, Buddy, became a therapy dog and spent his days with kids with autism and other developmental disabilities, and his nights visiting old folks. Buddy once ate my boss's lunch, took a dump in the CEO's office, and always verbally assaulted the water delivery guy. He rarely did what I asked, but he always did anything a kid or someone in a nursing home wanted. If I'm a good boy when I die Buddy will be waiting for me.

Riley is our current basset rescue and he's also a therapy dog. His original owner locked him in a cage all day long, neglected him, and called him "Rotten Riley." He was on death row when a nice lady named Heather saved him and let us adopt him. Riley volunteers his time visiting veterans in the behavioral health unit at the Albany VA.

We should all be so rotten.

My other two hounds, Wilbur and Roxie, make the trips with us and Agnes is always there in spirit.

Duffy has got some people friends, too. Elaine Woroby won the auction at the Wildwood Programs Spring Gala for the second straight year. She was bummed when I told her she couldn't kill her husband Mark again; so bummed she took her own life. Wildwood provides services for people with autism, complex learning disabilities, and developmental disabilities.

The Catie Hoch Foundation was founded in honor of a precious little girl who was taken from us far too soon. Gina Peca, Catie's mom, turned tragedy into triumph and began a remarkable foundation that is helping find a cure for neuroblastoma and does all sorts of cool things for kids and families who have gotten a bad break. Karl Bendorf was bidding like a crazy man at the auction and was rewarded with a role in *Out Cold*. Gina keeps getting outbid in the auction and says she wants to win someday and be described as an exact double for Angelie Jolie. I got news for you Gina—you're far more beautiful.

Lastly, I would like to thank my publisher, Karen Syed. Sometimes it can get pretty dark after midnight. It's good to have someone in your corner who can take your fight to a whole new echelon.

At the coroner's inquest after Sugar Ray Robinson killed Jimmy Doyle in their 1947 title fight.

Coroner Gerber: Did you know you had him in trouble?

Robinson: Mister, it's my business to get him in trouble.

1

"Duffy...Duffy...do you know where you are?" Smitty said.

"Shit, right on the chin. Did you see his head whip, around? Shit," some other guy said.

I went to sit up and felt my head slosh around like a bowl filled with some sort of goo.

"No, no, no, don't try to sit up. Lie back down," Smitty said.

They pushed me back down, but they did it gently and I didn't resist. I knew I was in a gym with painted red walls. I heard the sounds of the gym, though they were off a bit and the place had a hush to it. Things were happening and I knew what was going on–sort of any way. I felt removed from it.

"I want to get to the hospital. Which one should I take him to?" Smitty wasn't talking *to* me. He was talking *about* me.

I sat up straight fast and the blood rushed to my head with a gigantic throb. It wasn't painful in a sharp, burning pain. It was dull and livable.

"Whoa, don't get up," Smitty said.

I didn't like the sound of *hospital*. I got up from the sitting position to show everyone I was all right.

My legs buckled and I staggered into the ropes. I fell backward into them and went halfway through the bottom two. Smitty sprang up and hugged me awkwardly.

"Duff–shit. Somebody get me the stool." He sounded panicked. Smitty never sounded panicked.

My legs must've been on the same circuit as my mouth, because I kept trying to say something and my mouth wouldn't move. Things felt murky. Around the ring, guys stared at me. Out of the meshed conversations I heard something like: "Did you see that fuckin' hook?"

My answer would've been, "No."

<u>2</u>

I sat at my desk drinking the brown stuff the staff at Jewish Unified Services referred to as *coffee*. A Monday, and I had five back-to-back appointments this morning, because I had to catch up. A few sick days last week to go to Gleason's Gym and spar had put me behind.

I went to see Trina, the office manager.

"Who's my 9:15?" Before I could get an entire sentence out of my mouth, I tripped over something. I lost my balance a little and banged into the wall.

"Walk much?" Trina said. "Karl is your 9:15."

"Oh, very nice. I almost do serious bodily harm to myself and you find it funny."

"It was pretty funny."

I looked at the box that used to contain a case of Campbell's Chicken and Stars soup. Now it had cans of various meat and fish in it.

"The Mission looking for canned goods? It's August," I said.

"It's for the soldiers overseas."

I looked in the box again and saw cans of Spam, sardines, and Vienna sausages.

"Apparently, fatty foods loaded with salt are going to help the war effort."

"No, it's for the soldiers to have snack foods, and canned goods keep the best. They're calling it the 'Snack Attack'," Trina said. She checked the clinic's answering machine.

"Have you ever eaten Spam? Wait a minute. Can you

even say that to a woman and still be considered a gentleman?"

"When did you start considering yourself a gentleman?"

"You doubt my chivalry? By the way, who's my 9:15?"

"I already told you–are you gonna keep asking me all morning?" She feigned annoyance.

"C'mon, it's Monday," I said.

"Yeah, maybe you shouldn't take stupid pills for breakfast on Mondays."

"Hmmm….and you work in human services…"

"No, I'm the secretary."

I went to the files to get Karl's chart. His last name is Greene and it wasn't near the 'Gs'.

"Does Claudia have Karl's chart for signatures?"

"Duffy, you got that file fifteen minutes ago."

"That's right. I need more coffee," I didn't remember anything about getting the file. That felt a little weird. So did my head.

I got knocked out for the first time Saturday afternoon. I've been boxing my whole life and I've never been knocked unconscious. I've had my nose broken a bunch of times, I've been cut, and I have had my bell rung, but I never went out for a few minutes. It happens and it happens to the best fighters.

I'm not one of the best fighters and have almost as many losses as wins. I sparred with a heavyweight contender all last week and made an extra thousand bucks. I used eighteen-ounce gloves and he used fourteen, which is bullshit, but when they pay you to be cannon fodder, bullshit comes with the territory.

The buzzer on my phone jarred me out of my reverie. Trina announced Karl was here for his appointment. Karl was a tough session when I felt fresh and rested, but on an under-caffeinated Monday morning, it equaled torture. This was only his second time in, but his first had been a little, let's say,

16

out of the ordinary.

"Mornin' Karl," I said and extended my hand.

"Yeah, that's what you'd like, wouldn't you?" Karl said with a laugh. It wasn't a happy laugh, though I couldn't say if he smiled or sneered because his Michael Jackson style surgical mask hid his expression.

"Whatya mean Karl?"

"Don't play games with me. I get what's going on, you know."

I wasn't sure if he did actually. Karl and reality parted company sometime between high school and a short stint in the Marine Corps. That stint included a trip to Iraq.

"Well, whatya say we head into the counseling room then?"

"I'll follow you," Karl said.

I think they call it paranoid schizophrenia. Karl recently hit his mid-twenties and had started getting delusional a few years back, which is just about the typical age schizophrenia starts to develop. I'm guessing dealing with Parris Island, wacky military discipline, and RPGs, IEDs, and whatnot might have sped up the process a little bit. I didn't know much more because the Veterans Administration, that super-efficient federal organization, had yet to send me any info on Karl.

"How's the week been?" I tried to be casually therapeutic.

"The week has been just fine–for the NWO."

"The NWO? The angry rap group with the inappropriate name?"

"Don't play coy, Dombrowski."

"Coy? Me?" My head started to throb. I couldn't tell if it was from Saturday or from Karl.

"New World Order," Karl said and snickered.

"Not sure I'm down with what the NWO is about, there, Karl."

"Yeah–and the World Trade center collapsed when two hijacked planes flew into it. Ha! You people kill me!"

"Ah, Karl, have you been taking your meds?"

"That's what you want, isn't it? That's what they've all wanted since I enlisted. Keeps me in the program."

"The program?"

"Oh, you don't know about the program? Ha! When did they get you?"

I didn't remember getting into the program. I did remember Karl was just about due for a psych consult and I thought maybe we could put him number one with a bullet on the waiting list.

"Karl, how's your drug use been lately?" I said, temporarily trying to steer the session away from all things conspiratorial.

"The drugs have kept me a slave at times, but it's a slavery I welcome compared to the other choices," Karl said.

"What does that mean, Karl? The part about slavery?"

"As long as you're hooked they can control you. Shit, why do they introduce you to the stuff? It's just another way for the man to get you under his thumb."

"But Karl, it's your choice to use drugs, isn't it?"

"It is now, but it wasn't then," Karl said and punctuated it with a sneer.

"Huh?"

"Never mind, Dombrowski," Karl looked me straight in the eye. "Never mind."

My advanced psychological training, which amounted to my junior college diploma from an online school of higher learning, told me I should continue to provide unconditional positive regard to my client by moving to a subject we mutually agreed would be more beneficial.

That and the fact the current line of conversation drove me up the fucking wall.

"How's life at the Mission?" I asked, inquiring about

18

Karl's department of social services financed living situation.

"It's great because I left."

"Why? Does that mean you're out on the street?"

"I like the street. They can't keep such a close eye on you when you don't have an address. The man likes it when you have an address."

"Yeah, but isn't there something to be said for warmth, shelter, and three squares a day?"

"It's August. It gets a little cool at night, but it's worth the freedom."

It's sessions like this that make me question the overall utility of human services. I wasn't sure what exactly I did for old Karl except piss him off and make him more suspicious. I also wasn't sure what kept him coming, but I hazard the guess even Karl, despite all his talk, liked his monthly DSS check.

"Have you formed any positive relationships in the last week?" I hated asking clichéd human services questions, but Karl had me kind of stymied.

"Positive relationships," Karl smiled out of one corner of his mouth. "Counselor Dombrowski, do tell me what makes a relationship positive."

"You know, uh…relationships marked by…" He'd caught me spouting bullshit and he knew it. So did I. An awkward silence hung and Karl gave me a self-satisfied smile while I squirmed with really nothing of substance to say.

Finally, he broke the silence.

"Do you know about the fires? Or, are you going to play dumb?"

"What fires?"

"Yep, I knew you'd play dumb."

I looked at Karl and kind of squinted, which made my head throb a bit. I really wasn't up for another go around.

"You know Karl, we've probably covered enough for today," I said.

"Whatever you say commandant–I know better than to

19

disobey. I remember what you did last time I did."

I didn't.

I walked Karl out and went to see Trina about getting Karl in for a psych session with Dr. Meade as soon as possible.

Trina stood at the file cabinet, up on her tiptoes, trying to water her spider plant. She wore a pair of 501s and the denim hugged every turn her body took. Her stretching to take care of her plant gave me an extra treat for which I offered the good Lord gratitude. She had the radio on the FM classic rock station.

"Trina can we get Karl into to see Meade ASAP?" She recoiled from her watering position.

"ASAP is six weeks."

"Oh, come on–really?"

"You can get him in for a med review Thursday, but for only fifteen minutes."

We only had Meade, the shrink, one day a week. It wasn't enough, but that was the world of non-profit human services in Crawford, New York.

"I'll take the med review."

"Med reviews are not to be used as a substitute for therapeutic psych visits," I heard from over my shoulder.

"Good morning, Claudia," I said to the Michelin Woman. Claudia Michelin, the clinical director and my nemesis, who lived for the bureaucratic paperwork I detested. She had been trying to fire my ass for the last six years and had come close plenty of times.

"Trina, don't schedule Karl a med review spot. Give him the next available therapeutic session," Claudia said. Claudia, nearly six feet tall, with a black perm, was a rice cake shy of 250 pounds, hence, my private nickname 'The Michelin Woman.'

She turned and headed toward her office. Trina rolled her brown eyes at me and I shrugged my shoulders, which

20

made my head throb again.

"You all right?" Trina said.

"Yeah, why?"

"You just wobbled."

"Wobbled? I didn't wobble."

"You wobbled."

"Bullshit."

I didn't feel much like arguing about my gait, especially as the throbbing returned, so I turned to head toward my cubicle, when Clapton's *Layla* faded out, and the radio news came on.

"Six dead, twenty more hospitalized in a fire at ROTC training camp believed to be deliberately set…"

3

I started to think Karl might be on to something. Then I realized everyday there's a fire someplace, and mentioning a fire might occur somewhere in the world–with no other reference point whatsoever–didn't exactly put Karl on par with Nostradamus.

I headed to the Y for a quick workout and to blow off some steam. Still stiff from last week's work, but I knew if I got a workout in, the body would start to loosen up a bit. I had my sweats on and went through the process of wrapping my hands when the throbbing around my temples went up a gear. It didn't hurt a lot, but I did notice it. After a minute or two it subsided, or at least I thought it did.

The Crawford Y, built in the 1920s, remained an old time Y. No aquamarine colored exercise machines, no tanning beds, and generally a complete absence of fad-type stuff. On the other hand it had no shortage of the sort of stuff that made old time YMCAs creepy. It had too many guys in the health club who just spent too much time in the nude, walking around and doing nothing else. I'm not sure where they read watching TV with your nutbag on a vinyl couch for two hours qualified as good cardio work, but there was no shortage of guys who did just that every single day.

The Y also featured the dying breed of handball players. The same six or eight guys who played every day for the last 900 years and appeared to hate one another. The white hoop players and the younger black hoop players who, without really anyone saying anything, segregated themselves into two different courts like Selma, Alabama in the mid-'60s.

They played two styles of ball. On those rare occasions when the games somehow got integrated, the white guys tended to call more traveling calls and the black guys tended to call more fouls.

Then there was Fat Eddie, the old gay guy who passed out towels from a cage, located right by the showers. I'm guessing when he took his career aptitude test it recommended he throw towels to naked athletic men while sitting in a chair, eating Fritos all day. Fat Eddie had the perfect job. Recently, they added to Eddie's responsibilities and identified his station as the place to drop off the canned goods for the soldiers. So, in addition to getting the chance to dry off in front of the fat man, you could also hand in a can of Spam for his 'Snack Attack' collection. Some how it made sense.

I headed down the stairs to the boxing gym, a dank room with low lighting and layers of fermented BO from years of training. No ventilation in the boxing room meant the body funk had seeped into the concrete and leather, and permeated the atmosphere. All of this made it perfect for my sport.

I got in front of the floor-to-ceiling mirror to warm up with shadowboxing and danced around the crack that went straight down the middle of the mirror. The crack had been there as long as I remember, and if I ever had to throw punches into a mirror without a crack I think I would get confused.

It took a long time to get warm and I couldn't figure out why. I threw jabs and methodically moved to my right–what a left-handed fighter should do–but I felt awkward from the soreness. I started to pick up the pace to get a sweat going when I heard Smitty come out of his office.

"Duff–hold up," he said. He stood in the threshold of his little office with the plastic window so old it had yellowed. He folded his arms and scrunched up his forehead. Balding, his curly grayish hair framed his haggard brown face. He sighed and unfolded his arms and walked toward me.

"Go on home, Duff," he said without any expression or inflection.

"What?"

"Go on home."

"What are you talking about?"

"You ain't right, kid. You're balance is off."

"Just loosening up."

"Go on home, Duffy."

"I'm fine, really."

"Go on home. Now." He increased the inflection in his voice just slightly, but that's all he ever did. I knew not to question him, but I didn't understand what the big deal was. When Smitty said you had to do something you had to. He didn't see a ton of grey in life, and I respected him even when he was wrong. Besides, I had no fights on the near horizon, so there wasn't much point in arguing.

It's about ten minutes to my converted trailer on 9R and Elvis came along for the ride as he always did. I loved the King's early sixties period, and he went from *One Broken Heart for Sale* to *Please Don't Drag that String Around*–both songs by Otis Blackwell, the guy who did *Don't Be Cruel*. Or, come to think of it, maybe it was Leiber and Stoller, the guys who did *Hound Dog*. I always got that shit mixed up.

My domicile gleamed in the sun, as aluminum Airstream trailers tend to do. I had christened it the Moody Blue after the Elvis song, and also because I thought it lended some class to living in a trailer. It made it kind of yacht-like–in a white trash kind of way. The customized addition coming out the back of it gave it a special appeal, so please don't make the mistake of assuming it is just a trailer.

My girlfriend's…er…uh…my fiancée's–yeah that's right, the future Mrs. Duffy Dombrowski's–car was parked outside on the gravel. This hadn't been a four-star day, but there was still a chance to turn it around with a ninth-inning rally. Rene and I had been seeing each other for almost a year, and for a guy who has had a lifetime of bad relationships, she was a welcome relief. She wasn't diagnosable with any major psychiatric illnesses, she hadn't stolen anything from me, and she enjoyed sex. That put her in a very small percentage of the women I've gotten involved with.

Rene was a graphic designer, which made her a little artsy, but not enough to make her a whack job. I liked artsy-fartsy, I liked avant-garde, and I even liked a woman with a little bit of a dark side. Dark side in the sense she gave life some thought and didn't always see things as uncomplicated, easy to define, or static. She was also a hot redhead with green eyes, had an ample bosom, and legs that came all the way up to there. I guess you can tell a guy like me is in love when he chooses 'ample bosom' over 'a great rack.'

The best part was she was crazy about me. She knew the kind of money I made and it didn't matter. You see, she was brought up with money, but with a couple of emotionally distant parents who, honestly, just sounded like assholes. The fact I worked with poor people and lived in a trailer didn't turn her off; she actually kind of liked it. She said I was 'genuine.'

That's me, one genuine motherfucker.

It doesn't mean everything was perfect. Two things she didn't like at all—one was the fact I boxed. She saw it as crude and macho and a useless archaic way for two men to hurt each other. My esoteric and philosophical explanations didn't work and my references to Gene Tunney, considered a gentleman and a genius, Sugar Ray Robinson, a brilliant tap dancer and entrepreneur, and Hector Camacho, who liked to wear loincloths in the ring, didn't help. I figured she'd warm up to boxing after a while, or soon enough it would be time for me to retire.

The other thing she didn't like was my roommate, who,

unlike most male roommates, would come along with the marriage. Al is my roomie, and he and Rene just didn't see eye to eye on many issues. Actually, Al didn't see eye to eye with any body because, well, he's a basset hound and he's only about eleven inches tall. It wasn't really surprising she didn't get along with Al. Al barked all the time, and when he wasn't barking, he farted and when he wasn't gaseous, he smelled a tad houndy. He was given to fits of enthusiasm in which he would jump on people. This was more of a problem for men because at Al's height his attacks landed directly on the most sensitive area of a man's body. He also ate furniture; never quite mastered the whole housebreaking deal, and he never did anything he didn't want to do.

Al was a great pet.

I got him from a client who got murdered. 'Al' was derivative from a Muslim name that had to do with Allah because his original owner was in the Nation of Islam for a while. I said I'd watch him while she did a short stint in the county lockup, and she got killed. For that reason and for one other Al was staying.

The other was he's saved my life a couple of times.

When I pulled up, the fact the Blue was quiet was a good sign and probably meant the two creatures in my life were simply avoiding each other. I came in the door, toward the back of the trailer. I called it the front door because it sounded better than saying 'I came in the door toward the back of the old trailer I live in.' Renee was on the couch that had no upholstery on the arms because of Al's obsessive-compulsive relationship with fabric. Renee didn't bounce up to kiss me, which was her somewhat over-exuberant way of greeting me since we'd been seeing each other. Some people found her affection a little nauseating, but I didn't care. It was a nice ray of sunshine especially on days that were shit sandwiches.

"Hey, what's goin' on babe?" I said by way of greeting.

Her usually flowing red hair was tied back in a bun and she looked pale without any makeup. Frankly, she looked rough.

"Duff, we've got to talk," she said without looking at me.

Now, I've been dating long enough to know 'wanting to talk' wasn't a good sign.

"About?"

"I don't know. Something doesn't feel quite right"

I got that funny feeling in my throat and chest when something bad was about to happen.

"Something with us?"

"I don't know. I guess everything that has to do with one of us has to do with both us," she said and looked away.

Philosophically, I think that made sense, but it didn't do anything to that feeling in my chest.

"Hey, are you all right?" Rene looked at me for the first time. The look on her face was one part concern and a bunch of other parts anger.

"What are you talking about?"

"You're wobbling."

"I am not."

"Did you get hurt boxing?"

"No."

"You did and now you're lying about it."

"I got hit. That's not getting hurt."

"Oh bullshit, Duffy. You know exactly what I mean."

I got caught lying and I felt my face flush. The physical reaction to knowing I've done something wrong ran through me.

"I can't believe you. We're supposed to be getting married and you're lying to me." She stood up and headed for the door.

"Rene…"

She kept right on going out the door.

I followed behind her, but she ignored me.

"Rene…"

She started her car and pulled out with out looking at me.

Almost on cue, Al came around the corner and looked me up and down. It was the basset hound equivalent of saying, 'Is the bitch gone?'

I looked Al right in the eye.

"Yeah, she's gone," I said.

Al let out an audible fart.

It really, really stunk.

4

I didn't much feel like sitting around in the stink thinking about what had gotten into Rene. With the gym not an option and no prospects for a date, my choices were scaled down a bit. Hell, they were more than scaled down; they were eliminated. It was time to go to AJ's.

AJ's is the dive I hang out in. There are no ferns, no fake antique wall hangings, there are no cheery wait staff saying, "Hey guys, would you like to try a bloomin' onion?" Nothing close to that. There was AJ the Third, who inherited the bar from his father, who had inherited it from his father. It wasn't rustic, it was old, and it smelled of gallons of flat beer and the flat patrons who had been drinking it for the last one hundred years. No one ever described AJ as cheerful, but he stocked Schlitz and that was all I needed.

The ten-minute drive from the Blue got taken up with Elvis's gospel number, *I Got Confidence,* which considering how I felt, was pretty ironic. Just the same, AJ's and the boys were the electro-convulsive jolt of insanity I needed.

"It wasn't called 'Pig Bay'," Rocco explained.

"Pig Bay? Isn't that the Internet site where you can get livestock supplies on auction?" TC said.

"No, stupid. We're talking about Kennedy," Rocco said.

"Let's not forget Marilyn Monroe. She had something to do with the Cubans," Jerry Number One said.

"She was screwin' Kennedy and Sam Gandlefini," TC said.

"Gandelfini is the guy on the Sopranos. He's too young to screw Marilyn Monroe," Jerry Number One said.

29

"How old do you gotta be to screw?" Jerry Number Two said.

"Boy, it was DiMaggio getting screwed," Rocco said.

"Huh?" TC said.

And so it went. Meet Rocco, TC, Jerry Number One, and Jerry Number Two, otherwise known as the Fearsome Foursome. AJ's brain trust. They were always here and always engaged in inane conversation. Usually it was just them, me and my cop friend, Kelley, and once in awhile my landlord, Dr. Rudy.

AJ slid a Schlitz longneck in front of me before I opened my mouth. The TV was on Classic Sports with Bill Walton over-enunciating about how he's still depressed about losing to Notre Dame. The Foursome moved on to current events.

"Awful thing about that fire," TC said.

"Yeah, don't forget about the box and the cans," Rocco said.

"What the hell is it with every place having a box full of canned goods for soldiers? Are these guys really dying for over-salted canned meat?"

"I don't think you have the right attitude Duffy. I was in the service and I loved a can of Spam once in a while. Took my mind off the battle," Rocco said.

"That fire was college guys, wasn't it?" TC asked.

"Yeah, college-age guys at ROTC training–that's rough," Jerry Number One, said.

"Did they know what caused it?" I asked.

"Something about an electrical short or something like that, but some terrorist outfit has said they were responsible," Rocco said.

"One of my clients who's a little on the paranoid side told me there would be a fire today. He's into all the government conspiracy crap. Iraq left him a little fucked up," I said.

"You don't believe in government conspiracies, Duff?"

Jerry Number Two said.

"I don't know. I don't think about it much."

"You think Oswald acted alone? You think we didn't know Pearl Harbor was about to happen? You probably think we landed on the moon," Jerry Number Two said, pausing to sip his Cosmopolitan for dramatic effect. Red stains from the Cosmo dotted his tie-dye.

"I don't know, Jer. I'm just a guy with a headache, drinking Schlitz."

"That's exactly what they want, you know," Jerry Number two said.

I decided it was okay if I thought Neil Armstrong landed on the moon, at least for tonight. My head started to throb a bit and the Schlitz seemed to be hurting more than helping. I didn't want to make the shift to light-speed and start on the Jim Beam, so I thought I might cut my losses and head home early.

Before I could get up, the talking head on the TV started interviewing some guy through a split screen set up. The guy's name was Dr. Theodore Martin and he headed up the team of crisis counselors dispatched to deal with the stress of the survivors on the campus. I paused for a moment when the guy mentioned something about how important it was to ventilate the emotions involved in a trauma as soon as possible. He went on about how debriefing was crucial to dealing with such an event. I had let the Schlitz help me debrief my own stressful day, and now it was important to get home and process some sleep.

Before I could get away, the Foursome sucked me back in.

"What's an engaged lover boy like you doing out in the middle of the week?" Rocco said.

"Ah, no particular reason," I said.

"Sounds like trouble in paradise to me," Jerry Number One said.

"What's going on Duff, the wedding is off?" TC said.

"No, no, no…" I said.

"I never could see marriage," TC said. "I think the Mormons got it right."

"They're the ones who started that college, right?" Jerry Number Two said.

"Yeah, Oral Roberts," Rocco said.

"That ain't it," TC said.

"It is, too," Rocco said. "I think it has something to do with having more than one wife."

"What does that mean?" Jerry Number One said.

"You know, as long as you keep it Oral it's not cheating so you can have as many wives as you want. That's why he changed his name to Oral," Rocco said.

"It's Brigham Young," Jerry Number Two said.

"Yes, that was their motto. They encouraged it," Rocco said.

"Encouraged what?" TC said.

"Bring 'em young, bring 'em old—it doesn't matter. That's one horny religion. They wanted to make sure everyone knew to be, as they say, 'be like a fruit fly and multiply'," Rocco said.

I decided to be like a fruit fly and fly right out of AJ's. It was a long day and it wasn't a good one, so it was time to cut my losses. My '76 El Dorado looked almost surreal under the amber streetlights across from AJ's, next to the cookie factory. The cookie factory's silos must've been making that red goo that goes in the center of those sugar cookies because it hung in the air like some sort of fructose, corn syrupy fog. The 8-track played *It's Midnight*, which it was heading for, and the king sang about knowing it was late and that's when he's weak. I think I understood just what he was talking about, because I just didn't feel right. My head hurt, I felt a little woozy, and something felt weird with Rene. She's entitled to a non-bubbly day and it seemed needy on my part to read a whole lot into it. Just the same, there are times your instincts tell you something is wrong and you just feel it. Of course, having a love-life track record comparable to the '63 Mets didn't help one's sense of security.

Elvis was getting to the part about how things look brighter in the daylight when I saw a series of cop headlights up ahead, just outside Jefferson Park. Jefferson is Crawford's answer to New York's Central Park, and a poor answer indeed. The cop cars were by the area in the park with a stinky pond and a bunch of trees separating the bad part of the city from the less bad part of the city. At night it was the haven for teenage drinkers, the gay guys who rendezvoused with anonymous partners, and the ever-present drug dealers. Flashing lights outside the park were as common as they were on the Crawford city hall Christmas tree.

My curiosity got the better of me and I pulled over to the curb to see what was going on. There was an ambulance, and the cops and the EMTs were trying to subdue a guy who was getting out of control at the thought of getting strapped down to a gurney. In the small crowd of park regulars that had gathered, I spotted Froggy, a gay guy who's been on and off my caseload for years. We've done favors for each other over the years–not the kind that happen in the park–and even though he did very little of what I suggested to him therapeutically, he was a good man. I once helped stop some beating of the gay men in the park and Froggy never forgot.

"Yo, Froggy," I yelled.

He squinted through the flashing lights with a self-protective sneer before recognizing me.

"Mr. Duffy, how you been?" Froggy said. Froggy's blue-black complexion shined in the lights and his Caribbean accent set him off from the average Crawford citizen.

"What the hell happened here?" I said.

"Some crazy-as-shit street guy took a beating and it sent him off. I mean O-F-F."

"Anybody you know?"

"Not one of my types. He be shoutin' at no one, carrying on about people out to get him, the military stealing his brain and whatnot..."

I stepped away from Froggy without saying goodbye. I headed towards the commotion to get a closer look. Sure enough, the man they were trying to subdue was Karl. He was bleeding from a couple of spots on his face and his clothes were torn and dirty. They had him on the gurney, but he still screamed something about the truth setting him free.

"You getting rude, Mr. Duffy," Froggy said. It jogged me back.

"Oh, sorry, Frog."

"You know this gentleman?"

"Yeah, a little bit," I said.

<u>5</u>

The blood gushed out of both eyes. It was thick and came out with the force of a fireman's hose. It hit me in the face and splashed in my own eyes, making it difficult to see. I felt a piercing in my side and then two of them were at my sides throwing punches at me. The whole time I couldn't do anything to defend myself even though my hands were free.

The blood continued to splash on my face, the piercing kept entering my side, the two shapes whaled away at me, and I couldn't raise my guard. When my vision cleared I could see a teenage boy fifteen feet away crying for help. He's in pain, scared to death and he looks pathetic. He screams for me to help him and I can't move. Something awful is going to happen to him. Slow dribbles of blood start to run down the boy's face. When I look close I see the boy is me when I was fifteen.

The blood starts to run down his face harder, and the blood gushing from the eyes in front of me turns black. I look to my side; the sharpened steel point that is stabbing me in the side turns into a snake getting ready to bite. It's all happening at once and suddenly something wet and scratchy is dragged across my face...

A piercing sound shakes through my head, my eyes open, and I'm in that weird place between sleep and awake. I see Al sitting on my chest staring at me.

Fuck. The dreams were back.

I went to the bathroom, thought I was going to get sick, and held it off. It was a shitty way to wake up and I had thought these things had gone away. Awhile back I got involved in some violent shit and though I didn't really think it bothered me much during the day, I'd get these really fucked up dreams at night. It made sleep unpleasant and something I think I unconsciously avoided, which ironically, made the nightmares more likely to happen. The self-prescribed medication in the white bottle with the brown label slowed them, but didn't prevent them. Stress brought them on, but I wasn't entirely sure what I was stressed about.

Regardless, I was up and the day had started, so I made some coffee and tried to get normal. The headache had dulled, which was the only bright spot of the morning so far. That is, until Al started to object to the birds flying around outside the Blue. This offended him to his core and he wanted the sparrows to understand his objection. The sparrows seemed to take a special joy in pissing Al off and continued to flit around the window. Al balanced between the top of a set of shelves and the back of chair. In terms of equilibrium Al was no Alvin Ailey. One particular sparrow must've given Al the finger or the wing or something because Al growled and then let out this long baritone bay. The sparrows didn't like the baying and flew away, which brought Al back to barking. It also changed his body position abruptly and the chair tipped over, sending him ass-over-tea-kettle to the carpet.

He did a quick body roll, righted himself, and did that tornado basset move to clear the accumulated slobber from his jowls. Then he lay down and started to snore. With Al's morning exercise regimen complete and the noise reduced to his wood sawing impersonation, I was able to call the hospital. It was only 7:45 a.m., but I wanted to find out about Karl.

"Crawford Medical Center, How may I direct your call," the operator said. At first I was glad not to get an automated system with a menu longer than the Chinese take out place around the corner.

"Yes, I'm calling about a patient. His name is—"

"I'll transfer you to Family Services."

The phone began to ring. And ring. And ring.

"Family Services, Michele speaking, how may I direct your call?" the younger, but no more friendly, voice said.

"I wanted to find out about a patient admitted—"

"Hold on. I'll transfer you."

I never had time to object.

"Crawford Medical Center, how may I direct your call?" the first woman said.

"I just spoke to you and you transferred me and now they transferred me back," I said.

"How may I direct your call?" she said.

"I just want to find out about a patient."

"Hold on I'll transfer you," and she did before I could scream.

I decided it would be best if I showed up there in person, which would make me late for work, but I could couch it in the fact I was visiting a client. The Michelin Woman would smirk about something, but I had become immune to her bitching at me.

Besides, I always welcomed an excuse to go to the medical center, because it gave me a chance to visit Dr. Rudy.

Rudy was my landlord...well, sort of my landlord. An uncle of his died and left him the Airstream trailer I now call home. Rudy had no use for it and gave it to me. I knew Rudy because he worked the fights for the state boxing commission and we kind of hit it off. He wasn't your typical country club doctor—he was a regular guy.

At the hospital I stopped by Rudy's office before I went anywhere else. He had a small space in the office building adjacent to the hospital. When I came through his door, there he was, like always, hunched over his computer, next to a half eaten toasted coconut donut, and sweating. Rudy always sweated.

"Internet porn again, Rude?" I said by way of greeting.

"Oh good. I was hoping someone would stop by today and borrow money, get me in trouble, or ask me to do something illegal," Rudy said without looking up from the monitor. He did push up the glasses that had slid down his nose. He had deep pit stains soaking through his shirt even though the air conditioning seemed to be at around forty degrees.

"What are you doing?"

"It's called work, kid. You oughta try it sometime."

"That's just plain hurtful. I thought you took the hippo-crapical oath or something."

"Kid, let's get it over with. What do you want?"

"One of the guys got rolled in the park and I came to see him. Can you tell me what room he's in?"

"I'm glad I got a half million dollars in medical school loans. It qualifies me to be Duffy Dombrowski's personal receptionist," he said. "Give me the name."

"Karl Greene."

Rudy got out of whatever screen he was in and shifted to another. He exhaled heavily and muttered a few 'Come ons' to the slow hard drive.

"He left AMA," Rudy said when he found the name.

"What's that mean?"

"Against Medical Advice. He split even though we told him not to."

"*Hmm…*"

"Look kid, I love you to death and would love to chat with you all morning but can I get back to work?"

"Yeah…sure."

Rudy turned toward the computer and exhaled again. I stood there thinking.

Rudy stopped typing for a second and turned toward me again.

38

"Hey, kid, I almost forgot. Do you know any fancy caterers? I mean, who does the clinic use when they got a big deal fundraiser?"

"Caterer? What's going on, you stepping up from Dom's Sub World?"

"Well, sort of. Marie and I have been talking, and I want to throw a shindig at the house. I'm having a pool put in too," Rudy said in a different tone. Marie was Rudy's one that got away. She didn't like Rudy's devotion to the medical profession and tendency to overwork.

"Well, well, well..." I said.

"Well, well, well up your ass." Rudy spun around to the monitor again. I took it that he didn't want to take shit for Marie.

"I'll ask at the clinic," I said.

"Yeah, great," he said without turning around.

I headed out.

It was after ten when I got to the clinic. The Michelin Woman stood in the reception area hanging up a poster from the state about training on compulsive Internet porn addiction.

"You're more than an hour late, Duffy," she said, making sure the poster hung straight.

"I was at the medical center checking on Karl. He got beat up last night."

"We've spoken before about you becoming over involved with your clients."

"Yes, we have," I said and walked past her.

"I'm docking you an hour and eleven minutes."

"Swell..." I said. I headed back to my cubicle just to get away. By the time I got there Trina buzzed my extension.

"Your 10:30's here," she said.

"I don't have a 10:30."

"You're losing it Duff. You called Mr. Sprain yesterday

39

to have him come in," she said, not feigning or hiding her annoyance at all.

I told Trina to send Mr. Sprain, or as I called him, Sparky, into the multi-purpose room for a counseling session. Sparky was an unusual client in that he actually tried to improve his life, and he had succeeded to a degree. He got the name 'Sparky' because he's an arsonist who had a history of setting fires for money. He once explained to me when he got short on cash and wanted to get high he could always find a small business owner who looked for a little 'Jewish Lightning'.

Sparky's anti-Semitic but colorful euphemism for arson not withstanding, setting fires tend to get you in trouble in our culture. The problem was Sparky was damn good at it and his services were almost always in demand in Crawford's failing economy. Even with the temptation of easy money, Sparky had been able to put together seven months of sobriety and, how do you say this...adopt a fire-setting-free lifestyle.

"What's goin' on Spark?" I said by way of an astute counseling session opener.

"Mostly good Duff, mostly good," Sparky said. Sparky was a shifty guy–if not figuratively, literally. He never quite sat still and he had a tendency to try to crack his neck every twenty seconds or so.

"Duff, these twelve steps–do I gotta do them in order?"

"I don't think so."

"Some guy at an AA meeting the other night told me I hadn't done Step One and was trying to do Step Four already and if I continued to do that I was sure to get drunk. I didn't understand what he was getting at."

"Well, Step One is about admitting your life is out of hand and Step Four is about making an inventory of your life."

"The guy said I was a dry-drunk and that I was b-u-dding-building up to a drink–or some shit. He also said I wasn't keepin' it green enough and something about if I keep going to the barbershop I'm bound to get a haircut." Sparky looked confused. "Duff, what the fuck are these people talking about? I mean, I want to be clean, but some of this shit is a little wacky."

I resisted telling him to put 'principles above personalities' or 'to take what he needs and leave the rest' or even 'one's too many and a thousand's never enough'. Instead I said, "Ah, some of those guys are a little fucked up, Sparky. I mean, they may mean well, but some guys have never been good at anything their whole life but AA, and it gives them a chance to preach. Ignore it."

"Thanks, Duff."

Another existential dilemma with my fellow man solved.

We kicked around another couple of things, talked about the Yankees middle relief issues and whether or not their starting rotation could go into September and October. That was more than enough for the day and we agreed to see each other next week at the same time.

I headed back to my desk and I got to my cubicle just in time to answer my phone. It was Smitty.

"Duff, how you doin'?" When Smitty called me at work it usually meant a promoter had contacted him about a fight.

"We got something?" I said.

"No son, I just called to see how you were feelin'."

"How I'm feeling?"

"Yeah, the head, is it clearin' up?"

"What the fuck are you talking about?"

"Don't get upset Duff. You should get it checked if it's still hurtin' or if, you know, you keep repeating yourself."

"I'm not repeating myself," I said. It wasn't like Smitty to get overly concerned about this stuff.

"Look kid; just keep an eye on it, will you?"

"Sure, Smitty, whatever. I'll see you tonight."

"Son, take another week."

41

"No, you know me, I get buggy without the work."

"There's no sparring here for you son–take another week and we'll talk. Now, I gotta run." He hung up.

This day was shaping up as a real shit sandwich.

I checked the calendar for today and it was a beaut. The Abermans were due in, to continue their decade-long bitch session disguised as couples counseling. Then it was Eli, who had been coming for eight years with no more than a few days here and there without his daily dose of two or three forties of Olde English, and then, Sheila, my seventeen-year-old kleptomaniac who would come in if she weren't in jail. Then the day ended with Karl, which I figured was a long shot.

"Are you talking to me?" Monique, the counselor in the next cubicle said.

"Huh?" I looked around the partition. She had slid back on her desk chair and looked at me with her eyebrows raised. She had on a white jacket with a black shirt; it seemed to bring out her black skin.

"You're talking out loud, but I think just to yourself," she said.

"I was?"

"Uh-huh."

"Sorry, I didn't realize I was doing that."

"It's okay. I just didn't want you to think I was ignoring you. I heard Claudia say she was docking you."

"Yeah. I went to the hospital to check on Karl and I was late."

"What happened to Karl?"

"He got rolled in the park."

"That's some evil, isn't it?"

"Yeah."

"Are you okay?"

"Why is everyone asking me that? It's making me

crazy."

"You're wobbling a little."

"I am not. Shit." I felt my face flush. "I'm going for coffee."

I headed off to the break-room to get a cup of the shitty coffee. People got on my nerves a lot lately. Monique was almost never one of those people and it made me wonder if it was other folks pissing me off or something within me.

When I got back to the cubicle I looked at a couple of the files I had pulled out to see where I stood with my paperwork. I thumbed through Eli's chart, noting it had been six weeks since I put anything in it, which wasn't particularly good since he came in once a week for a session and once a week for group. Sheila's was slightly better because I wrote something in her file a month ago, but that was also her initial visit. The Abermans won the prize though, because it was a full eight weeks since I noted any of their sessions. If this was a representative sample, then things didn't bode well for my case load, and it was only a matter of time until the Michelin Woman caught wind of it and started to get up my ass about it.

Eli didn't cover any new therapeutic ground in today's session. He hit four NA meetings this week and got high after every single one. He reasoned hearing about drugs set him off, which presented a problem with going to NA meetings. He'd down-played his affinity toward the street prostitutes he claimed to be trying to help every night by giving them meal money. Eli didn't connect their affection toward him with his charitable efforts to keep Crawford's gals well fed.

Sheila claimed to have not ripped anyone off all week, her new, bright red Jordans and matching oversized red Ecko T-shirt not withstanding. Then the Abermans arrived and Mrs. Aberman chose that moment to confront Mr. Aberman about the stack of *Club International* magazines she found on a shelf in the garage. Mr. Aberman claimed he had found

43

them on the lawn and was waiting for the Crawford recycling night to dispose of them. Mrs. Aberman countered by questioning why the porn stash was sealed in a watertight bin and in chronological order. All of this was awkward enough for me, let alone Mr. Aberman, when Mrs. Aberman upped the ante when she asked why a bottle of her favorite extra extra virgin olive oil made it into the garage next to the bin. Mr. Aberman claimed he took a sip of it every day because he had read it would raise his good cholesterol. I had my suspicions that Mr. Aberman was raising something else in the garage with the magazines and the cooking oil, but I held my opinions to myself and mentioned something about trust and the need for open communication. The Abermans were just happy to be able to fight with each other and didn't really hang on every word I said.

I got up from the desk in the counseling room after they left and felt the blood rush to my head with a thick throb. It seemed to subside as I headed to the bathroom so I didn't give it a lot of thought. It was close to three, but I didn't have much faith in Karl showing–in fact, the more I thought about it, the more I was convinced Karl had left town.

I figured this was good as any time to get going on the charts.

As I opened Eli's file my phone buzzer buzzed.

"Your three o'clock is here," Trina said.

"Karl?"

"Yep, and Duffy you've got to see the get-up he's wearing."

I went out to the lobby. Karl stood with his back to the wall on the right side of the door like he was hiding.

"Hey Karl, how are you feeling, buddy?"

One arm was in a sling and he had three or four bandages on his face. When he shifted his weight he grimaced a bit. Oh, and he wore a Washington Redskins helmet and the bright yellow gloves housewives used to wear when they cleaned.

"Yeah, sure. As an agent with the NWO, I'm sure you give a shit," he said.

"Karl, I'm not with the NWO. I'm with JUS, Jewish Unified Services. Why are you wearing the Redskins helmet?"

"It's the only one Goodwill had. I plan to put some duct tape over the insulting racial stereotype image as soon as I get the cash."

"No, I mean why a helmet?"

"I was in the hospital."

"…and they told you to wear a football helmet?"

"No, but if you think I'm stupid enough to not realize what they were doing, you're the idiot."

"I don't understand."

"The tracking microchip? The GPS? Don't tell me you don't think they're keeping tabs on where I'm going."

I wasn't sure how to address that.

"You want coffee?" I said.

"Sure."

"Okay, c'mon back and we'll get a cup."

Karl followed along, albeit with his helmet and rubber gloves on. Right or wrong, sane or insane, this guy was in a fair amount of emotional pain and my job is to help him deal with that. Looney Tunes or not, I took that aspect of this gig seriously.

I let Karl pour his own coffee and we sat at the 'Staff Only' break table. I figured if we went into an official room Karl would pick up some extra secret radio transmission telling him Lee Harvey Oswald wanted him dead. This way we were just two regular guys enjoying a cup of awful coffee. It just so happened that one of us regular guys was wearing a football helmet and rubber gloves.

"So it must really suck having your own government after you," I said while stirring the non-dairy creamer into my

Styrofoam cup.

"You use that shit?" Karl said.

"What shit?"

"Non-dairy creamer. You know what's in that?"

"I thought it was, like, ground up milk or something."

"That's the problem, no one fuckin' thinks. That contains partially hydrogenated oil–geez…"

"Help me out here, Karl–I don't know what that is." The coffee was bad to begin with and I guess I was about to hear it was much worse than I ever dreamed.

"The powers that be found a way to fatten fat and put it in almost everything a kid eats from the day he's born–so much so that you miss it without even knowing what it is. They got you craving something you don't even know exists." Karl shook his head almost in pity. "Let me guess, you probably love chicken wings?"

"Yep."

"Potato chips?"

"Yep."

"Oreos?"

"Actually, I'm a Chips Ahoy guy."

"There you go. You're hooked and you don't even know it. They got you where they want you." Karl leaned back in his chair.

"Didn't you think I was part of *them*," I said.

"I did and you still could be, but you seem like one of us–the unenlightened lambs heading off to slaughter."

"Karl, just one thing: what does this fattened fat do to you?"

"That's the beauty–you have no idea. Seventy-two percent of America is obese."

"Isn't it because we're lazy and eat too much?"

"Yeah, that's part of it. Fat, lazy, Chips Ahoy addicts don't complain about forty-five percent of their income going to weaponry designed to eradicate the third world, but that's

46

only part of it." Karl sipped his black coffee.

"What else is there to it?"

"Fat people get sick and they get sick a lot. That means they need lots of prescriptions to control their blood pressure and their cholesterol and their heart disease and their joint diseases, because of the fat they're carrying. Follow the money my friend–there's lots of folks getting rich on your partially hydrogenated oils."

"I see." I sort of did, but I liked my Chips Ahoy. "Seems like something a whole lot worse than fat happened to you because of the government," I said and let it hang there.

"You don't know the half of it," Karl said and looked down at the table.

"You feel like telling me?"

Karl shook his head and took a sip of coffee. It wasn't easy to sip the coffee through the helmet, but he managed by lifting up the facemask. A single tear ran down the left side of his face. He didn't wipe it away.

"All I know is they fucked with me and they're not done fucking with me, just like they're fucking with a lot of people," Karl said.

"Karl, do you know what your diagnosis is?" I stood on shaky ground here, but Karl and I had connected at least to an extent.

"Schizophrenia with paranoid symptoms, Major Depression and Substance Dependence Unspecified. According to them I'm a real smorgasbord."

"You buy any of it?"

"Look Duffy, I know you think I'm a whack job. I got news for you: I know I'm a whack job, but there's an old saying. Just because you're paranoid doesn't mean they're not out to get you."

"I guess you got a point." I thought for a second. "Hey, the last time you and I talked, you mentioned something about a fire. That night there was a fire in the ROTC dorm."

47

"Yeah…"

"Did you know something?"

"Me? I'm just a chemically addicted, paranoid schizophrenic, depressed, nut job."

"And then you got beat up…"

"Just a coincidence, I'm sure." He winked at me.

"What could the two possibly have to do with each other?"

"Depends who you talk to doesn't it? I'm a semi-street person ex-vet. There are a lot of us bumbling around city streets, rambling. They like it that way."

"I don't understand, Karl."

"Most don't. Most don't even pay attention. Wait till the next bomb goes off in a federal building and no one will pay attention to that either. Everyone will get all up in arms and there'll be all sorts of attention paid to the cults and the cult leaders. No one will even notice the CIA connection."

"You lost me…"

"What's his name? Koresh? The Waco dude–Ex CIA– they had to get him out. Nice production. We're due for another of those real soon. Probably in the South–everyone assumes the South is full of extremist red necks."

"I don't know Karl, I just don't know."

"Of course you don't, Mr. Duffy. Enjoy your chips." He raised his cup in a mock toast and walked out. A pretty dramatic exit, except for the football helmet and rubber gloves.

<u>6</u>

I didn't get to any of the paperwork, so after four sessions I fell further behind. The Michelin Woman would go ballistic when, and if, she found out, because she couldn't stand it when all of life's ducks weren't lined up in rows. This duck almost never got into a row, so she generally hated me. Eventually she'd get around to checking the files and I'd get in trouble, but you know, the specter of getting in trouble never really was a motivator for me. If I could avoid pain-in-the-ass trouble I would, but I didn't spend my entire existence fretting about getting in trouble.

If avoiding trouble wasn't my thing, fighting definitely was. It's hard to explain to people who don't do it, but I need to fight–it's my Valium. When I don't get to fight, I start to get squirrelly and tense and I don't like the feeling. When you get to fight, your body relaxes, your mind has to get away from the daily bullshit to concentrate on protecting yourself, and you get to challenge yourself with a physical chess game. It didn't have anything to do with beating someone up–except for the fact I really like landing a good shot, not because I like inflicting pain, but because it's good to know my punches do what they're supposed to do.

Being told to take time off from the gym pissed me off. I knew when I felt all right and I knew when I needed rest. I knew I needed stress relief more than anything right now and it was taken away from me. Well, it was taken away from me at the Crawford YMCA boxing Program. There were other places to go where they knew me, and knew me well, where I could get some work in. Smitty wouldn't have to know and I could avoid an argument by doing what he said and stay away from the gym. Going across town to another gym was a win-win situation.

Just south of Crawford was Ravenwood. They had their own boxing club, so I drove the fifteen-minute ride. I wanted to spar so much I could taste it, and with Elvis doing *Trouble* from '68 on the way over, I was primed and ready to go.

Stan Cummings had run the gym for twenty years. As an amateur I regularly competed against his guys, so I was known and respected at Ravenwood. They had about a half dozen guys training in the gym, and from watching for a few seconds I could tell only one of the guys actually fought. If you've been in gyms most of your life you can tell almost instantly who fights competitively, who might be a sparring partner, and who just comes to hit the bags and feel like a fighter. You can tell by the way they carry themselves mostly. The guys who fight aren't posturing or strutting, their movements are natural and not contrived, because they're not thinking about proving anything. The guys who spar, and particularly the guys who come in and out of the gym with long periods of not sparring, are more herky-jerky in their movements. They're not as at ease and, though they don't posture all the time, you can sometimes pick them out because they're doing their best not to look nervous, which is, of course, a dead give away.

The final group is the guys desperately trying to fit in. They study how guys talk, how they move, and what kind of slang they use. They have the right equipment, sometimes the most expensive kind, but it's broken in differently because they haven't really programmed the body to do everything in an economical boxing style. When they hit the bag they waste movement, they wind up and over hit,–all things that would leave you open in the ring. After you did it once and got drilled in the ring you stop doing it in your shadow boxing and on the bag.

People ask me if I hate the whole boxing-as-workout movement that kind of peaked and since has sort of petered out. I didn't feel strongly about it either way, but I never considered it boxing, and no one who really boxes did. Sometimes guys got good at hitting bags and doing drills and they'd want to go to the next level and actually spar. They'd get in the ring with even the kindest of real boxers, and the realization that they knew nothing about what they were about to do would hit them. A decent guy wouldn't blast a newbie like this unless maybe they needed to be taken down a peg, but probably not even then.

Even though they didn't really get hurt, the boxercise guys would all of a sudden understand when someone else is in there with you it is a whole new thing. Boxing without fighting is kind of like masturbation is to sex–there're some similarities and it can make you feel good, but you should never mistake it for the real thing.

Cummings finished working his one real fighter on the pads, wiped the sweat off his own scar-tissued forehead, and caught my eye.

"Duffy…what brings you around?" Stan carried about fifty pounds more than he should, but his years as a middle of the road heavyweight were still there under the layer of hard fat.

"Just looking to see if I can get some work in," I said.

"Nobody at the Y?"

"I don't know. I just wanted to get some different work in." The real deal was if your trainer didn't want you sparring, another trainer wouldn't let you. I didn't want to lie so I let ambiguity do it for me.

"Smitty okay with it?" Stan said.

"Uh-huh," I said which felt damn close to a lie.

"Well, let's see, the only guy I figured on working was Stefon, the young heavy. He's got the Golden Gloves in a week and half. You wanna work with him?"

"Sure," I said.

I loosened up a bit, got my hands wrapped, and Stan got me laced up. When the round bell rang, Stefon and I touched gloves and went to work. A big and wiry kid, maybe six foot three, and around 200 pounds who clearly had strength, but like a lot of amateurs his footwork gave away his inexperience.

We exchanged some jabs with the neither of us landing. The punches slid off the 18-ounce gloves and I turned Stefon just by my positioning. Most people don't let footwork cross their mind when they think of boxing, but it may be the most important thing when you get up to the higher levels of the sport.

I kept moving to my left, planting and throwing my straight left—a very fundamental practice for a southpaw fighter. He blocked the punches easily and I was trying to figure out if the kid was quick or if I was telegraphing my punches. I could tell one thing for sure, my body wasn't in a hurry to loosen up. I felt stiff and a little slow. It was one of the reasons I hated staying away from the gym and out of the ring. It always seemed like it took a little while to get my reflexes back.

The kid doubled up a jab and they connected off the top of my headgear. The first one he just flicked out, but the second one he stepped behind and it thudded. He was a decent amateur and an athletic kid, but he shouldn't have got that in on me. I threw a right hook followed by a straight left and they both missed. I lost a little balance by missing. The kid leaned backed and countered with a straight right and a hook of his own. The hook hurt.

I got up on my toes to shake things out and work my footwork a bit. Stefon got a rhythm and now moved on his toes. He came in with the same double jab and I could see it coming a mile away, but for whatever reason I didn't get my hands up in time. The flicky one caught me on the bridge of the nose and the thudder thudded. I swung a hook and missed again and this time I was off balance enough to be embarrassed.

The kid waited, timed it until I stood up straight, and drove his right hand straight down the middle.

There came a thud, and then a flash of orange light inside my head.

That was all I remember.

7

"Duffy, you know where you are?" Stan Cummings said. My head felt soupy.

"Duff, you all right?" Stan said again.

I was on my back, squinting to figure out what was going on. The top left part of my head ached and I felt like I did when I came out of a deep sleep.

Maybe hibernation.

"Yeah, I'm fine," I said and began to sit up. When I did, it felt like my brain rushed to the front of my head and I felt like I wanted to throw up.

"You know where you at?" Stan asked.

"Sure," I said. I was at Gleason's but it didn't look right.

"You're at Ravenwood, remember?"

"Fuck you, Billy. I know where I am. I just got caught." I started to stand up. When I did it didn't seem like all the circuits fired. My legs were a little slow on the uptake.

"Easy, easy," Stan said.

"Oh fuck you, Stan. I'm all right," I said. "Smitty didn't call an ambulance or anything did he? Smitty! Where is he?"

"Duffy, Smitty ain't here."

"Huh?"

"You're at Ravenwood, remember?"

"Billy, stop the dramatics. I know where I am." A tall wiry black kid stood on the other side of the ring, looking at me like I just landed from Uranus.

"Nice shot, kid," I said and walked over to touch gloves.

"I hardly hit you, man," the kid said. He didn't say it to brag. He said it out of confusion.

"That's the way it happens sometimes." I stepped out of the ring and walked carefully down the ringside steps.

"Duff–You wanna go to the hospital?" Stan said.

"Stan, c'mon will ya," I said.

Instead, I went to my own treatment center: AJ's. I'm not trying to say I felt fine. There's no question I got my bell rung. It wasn't the first time and it damn sure wasn't going to be the last time, at least as long as I stayed a fighter. It's not as macho as it sounds, it's just something over the years you get a little used to, or your muscles and joints get used to it, and it's not a big a deal.

Big deal or not, I had a pretty good headache and it was starting to feel like a bourbon night. I'm mostly a Schlitz man, but when medicinally called for, I'll prescribe myself some of the brown elixir. Getting out of the car got it throbbing a bit, which wasn't pleasant. As I headed into AJ's, the Foursome were already throbbing about something else.

"What the hell are you going to do with a truck from World War Two?" Jerry Number One asked Rocco.

"It's not just any truck it's a *Deuce and a Half*," Rocco said.

"The Beach Boys had a song about it," TC said.

"No that was 'My Little Douche Cup'," Jerry Number One started to sing. "She's my little douche cup. You don't know what it's for…"

"I think it was 'My Little Deuce Coupe–Coupe, Jerry, Coupe," Jerry Number two said.

"You guys are assholes. The Deuce and a Half was the most versatile truck in World War Two. It could haul equipment, troops, equipment…you name it," Rocco said.

"What are you going to do with it?" Jerry Number Two asked.

"Refurbish it and restore to its original grandeur," Rocco said.

55

"Grandeur?" Jerry Number one asked.

"Yeah 'Grandeur.' You gotta problem with 'Grandeur'?" Rocco said.

My head really throbbed now. AJ slid the longneck in front of me without me saying a word.

"Had a few already, huh, Duff?" AJ said.

"No, just came from the gym."

"You sure?"

"What're you talking about?"

"I don't know. You kind of wobbled in and your eyes are glassy like you'd had a bourbon or two."

"I'm tired and I got a bit of a headache is all. You know what though, the bourbon sidecar sounds pretty good. Can you throw a cheeseburger on for me too?"

"Sure," AJ said without a smile. He was softly singing 'My Little Douche Cup'.

The carbonation in the Schlitz tickled the back of my neck and felt cool all the way down to my stomach. A hit of the bourbon brought a little warm glow on top of that and life seemed to be getting better.

Rocco was halfway through a knock-knock joke involving Oprah and forty pounds of crack when Jerry Number One shouted, "Yo, AJ, can we get some sound?"

The news was reporting on the nationwide drive to get snack foods and other items to the overseas soldiers. They showed several cut-aways to boxes at malls and schools and other places filled with snack foods, CDs, and books.

"AJ, you should set up a 'Snack Attack' box in here," Rocco said.

"A box of what?" AJ said.

"They're collecting Spam and whatnot for the soldiers," TC said.

AJ just stared at TC.

"Well, it's not just Spam. It's other shit. They got them Vietnamese sausages."

AJ kept staring.

"Vienna," Jerry Number Two said.

"She's the one on *Wheel of Fortune*," Jerry Number One said.

AJ continued to stare.

"Hey, AJ, I wanted that burger rare," I said.

He rolled his eyes, started whistling 'My Little Douche Cup' through his teeth, and got my very well-done burger. Accompanying it were the bottom-of-the-bag potato chip crumbles and a pickle from a jar as old as the Beach Boys' last hit.

"Yum," I said to no one in particular.

AJ disappeared into the kitchen and came back with an empty box that said on the side '124 count quarter pound hamburger. 72% beef'.

I said, "Yum" again.

"Hey, that place is only about thirty miles from here," Rocco said. The Northeast can depository, or whatever the hell it was, at a local farm that was also a dog kennel and rod and gun club. The guy talking on camera had a flattop and looked about as ex-Marine as you could get. He talked about supporting troops, loving America, and knowing what it's like. They were panning the farm and the cans collected when the camera abruptly cut away and the Special Report graphic appeared without sound.

AJ's stilled.

There was nothing the brain trust liked more than the drama of a special report.

"...Reminiscent of Ruby Ridge and Waco, an organization just outside Tuscaloosa, Alabama has been raided by U.S. Marshals. We are gathering information as we speak, but we do know this: The farmhouse you see pictured here is the home base for an organization known as The People of God's Kingdom. It is a fundamentalist Christian organization that takes in drug addicts, street people and the mentally ill, and rehabilitates them. The organization has come under criticism as cult-like and has been accused of brain-washing their members. Some have speculated they are supported by, and receive financial backing from, anti-US organizations outside of the country. The organization is now headed by Jeremy Rukhaber, an ex-Marine, highly decorated in Iraq, who was dishonorably discharged from the military following the Abu Gahrib scandal.

"You can see on your screen the U.S. Marshall special tactical unit, those large armed trucks, circling the farmhouse where Rukhaber and an estimated 17-20 of his followers are holed up. This stand off is now in its twelfth hour and..."

There was a large explosion and cascading dark gray smoke. The sound of rumbling came through the correspondent's microphone.

"Holy shit!" the correspondent screamed, unaware of still being on the air.

Holy shit was right.

8

The corpse is stuck in the door jam and I'm throwing punch after punch into his head. With each punch his head becomes more and more disfigured, like it's not human. There are little girls all around begging me to stop. I pay no attention and keep throwing punch after punch into the corpse.

I keep throwing punches over and over. As I do I realize though I'm punching the corpse, the girls bleed as if I'm punching them. Their screams and shrieks go right through me and I feel the nausea, but I keep throwing my combinations. Their screams get louder and more intense and still my hands go.

I feel the sickening vomit feeling and I punch through it until...

The wet scratchy feeling goes across my face, followed by an ear-piercing bark. Al is on my chest again, looking worried. I push him out of the way and run to the bathroom and throw up.

"Morning, Duff," Sam, from the business office, said.

"Good morning, Sam," I said.

"Duff, what's the name of the guy who works in the forest, wears a forest ranger's hat and carries a can of kerosene?" Sam never ran out of Polish jokes. I've gotten used to them like people get used to annoying ringing in their ears.

"Geez, Sam, I can't wait to hear."

"You sure, Duff?"

59

"Go ahead, Sam?"

"Stanislaus the Fire Prevention Bear of the Polish National Forest Service." Sam laughed way harder than what the joke called for and headed back to the business office.

Showing up at work wasn't a slice of heaven on most days, let alone days with a throbbing headache, but Sam's morning greeting made even the below average day much more below average. The Advil wasn't touching the throb. I reconsidered my previous night's use of bourbon as an analgesic.

I grabbed some files and headed to my cubicle. Just to sweeten the pot on this bright sunny morning, there was a note from Claudia.

Please see me immediately when you get in and bring the following records...

She asked for Eli's file and a few others, but Eli's alone was worth getting me in a shit load of Michelin Woman trouble. The woman lived for the by-the-book paperwork stuff I hated. It had been awhile since I had gotten in trouble for paper work negligence, not so much because I had got much more conscientious about it, but more because I had been lucky enough not to get caught.

I headed into Claudia's office, dreading what was about to happen.

"Please close the door," she said without looking up from her day planner.

I sat down, not saying a word. I wanted this to get over as soon as possible, and I knew talking wasn't going to slow it down, so I kept my mouth shut.

"I did my regular review of charts. I am dismayed at the state yours are in." She looked up at me. I just shrugged.

"Do you realize you haven't updated Eli's chart in six weeks?"

"I thought it was five."

"Five is just as unacceptable."

60

"Technically, five weeks late would be a little better than six weeks late, wouldn't it?" I said.

"No. You are either in compliance or out of compliance, and you are definitely out of compliance."

"Story of my life," I said.

"This isn't something to be flip about Duffy. You are getting a written warning. I insist these charts get updated within seven days."

"Seven days? C'mon Claudia, you know that's not possible."

"Well then, it won't be possible for you to work here," she said. She slid a written warning form, for me to sign, across the desk.

My head throbbed and I just wanted to get out of her office. I've been behind before–some might say perpetually– so I knew the drill. Staying up all night writing in files sucked, but it didn't suck as much as listening to Claudia.

I headed back to the cubicle and saw Monique busy writing away at her charts. She was a disciplined character, but she was in no way a goody-goody or Michelin Woman butt girl. She just saw it as something she was responsible for. Today she had her iPod ear buds in while she wrote.

"What are you listening to?" I said loud enough to be heard.

She finished writing a sentence, pulled the ear buds out, and rolled back in her chair.

"Stan Getz."

"Stan Getz? Wasn't he the white saxophone player? What about Bird or Coltrane?"

"It's music, not a painting. It doesn't have color. It has to have soul not dark pigment."

"Gotcha."

"What were you in the office about?"

"What am I ever in the office about…?"

"Duff, why don't you just do the notes every day? It

61

takes care of itself if you approach it that way."

"I don't know 'Niquey. I just don't have the discipline."

"Duff, you have discipline when you box."

"That's different."

"Only because you want it to be."

"You're right." And she was. She was almost always right, but spoke in a way that didn't make you resent it.

My desk phone rang.

"This is Duffy," I said.

"What's the guy's name you were looking for the other day here that went AMA?" It was Rudy and he wasn't big on 'Hello and how are you doing?'.

"Never mind, Rude. I found him."

"It's was Karl Greene, wasn't it?"

"Yeah."

"He's in here again. Someone tried to cut his throat."

"Is he dead?"

"No, no, no. Actually he got barely cut," Rudy paused for a second, and spoke like he didn't quite believe what he was about to say. "He wore a football helmet and they couldn't get a good angle on his throat, but they still beat the shit out of him. Any idea why the guy wore a football helmet?"

"To render the governmental homing device, placed in his brain the last time he want to the hospital, ineffective."

"Seriously, Duff. Why'd the guy have a helmet on?"

"I was serious."

"This guy's nuts, huh?"

"The helmet saved him, right?"

"Yeah, but Duff…"

"Nuts is a relative thing," I said.

I finished up with Rudy, decided I would start getting disciplined on files tomorrow, and headed to the hospital. On my way out, the lobby TV was replaying the explosion at the People of God's Kingdom.

9

Karl lay in restraints in his hospital room. His Redskins helmet sat on the vinyl chair, with his rubber gloves neatly folded, next to him. His eyes were closed and a bandage stuffed with gauze wrapped around his neck. The TV was fixed on CNN and the coverage was all about the People of God's Kingdom, although now it was being referred to as 'Massacre at God's Kingdom'. Ironically, the post-traumatic stress-debriefing guy was going on about the same shit he spouted about at the ROTC fire.

I whispered Karl's name to see if he was aware of my presence and got nothing. I put my hand lightly on his wrist being careful to avoid the IV tubing taped there. I whispered again while I slightly tightened my grip. Nothing.

"Kid, he's out of it. They got him on Haldol," Rudy said, from the doorway. He sweated and he had deep pit stains under his arms. He always did. He also had his customary stains down the front of his shirt made up largely of the menu of his last meal.

"Haldol? That's pretty heavy duty in the tranquilizer family, isn't it?" I said.

"Yeah, from what I heard it was warranted."

"Why?"

"He wouldn't let anyone touch him; he was flailing around so bad. He was mostly incoherent and getting dangerous."

"Dangerous?"

"He was throwing karate kicks and what not. The first orderly that came near him wound up in some sort of hold and got a broken wrist."

"Score one for the underdog,"

"Yeah, except this was an innocent orderly making about eight bucks an hour trying to help a guy with a slit throat."

"Probably not in Karl's perception."

"True. 'Course Karl believed he was with the government and wanted to check on the chip that was already implanted in his brain."

"Yeah, he talks a lot about that shit."

"He keeps up with current events, though. I'll give him that." Rudy took a second to wipe the sweat from his forehead with his tie. From the looks of the tie I could tell it wasn't the first time.

"Current events?"

"Yeah, he talked about this shit," Rudy said and pointed to the TV and the CNN coverage.

"Really, how so?"

"He knew it was coming, the CIA, same story as Waco…that kind of shit."

I didn't say anything. I just thought about things for a second. The room got quiet except for one of Karl's monitors and it beeped continually at three-second intervals.

"Hey, kid, you all right?"

"Huh?"

"You're swaying back and forth."

"Just tired."

"What do they have Karl on that makes him so out of it anyway?"

Rudy just looked at me. His face lost expression and he walked over to me.

"What?"

He took out that little pen thing with the light on it and shined it in my eyes until I pulled away. I hate that thing.

"You get knocked out recently?"

"What?"

"Don't bullshit me, kid. When did it happen?"

"When did what happen?"

"Fuck you Duffy. When did it happen?"

"I took one last night over at Ravenwood. Got me on the point of the chin–nothing really, just one of those shots."

"Uh-huh. And at Ravenwood–why were you at Ravenwood and not at the Y?"

"I don't know."

"Was Smitty there?"

"No, I–"

"So you got knocked out before and Smitty wouldn't let you spar…"

I didn't say anything.

"Stupid ass. Duffy, you ever hear of post-concussive syndrome? You know better than to mess with this shit," Rudy was pissed. "Now, you're standing there all wobbly, eyes fucked up, and repeating yourself like a mental case. Damn, you piss me off."

"C'mon Rude. I've been doing this for years…"

"Exactly. Who would ever think getting hit in the head over and over could be bad for you…" Rudy shook his head. "Get your head out of your ass while you still can." Rudy walked out of the room.

Rudy knew me and he knew boxing. A lot of people don't get boxing, but Rudy did, at least on some level. It got me thinking.

10

"They got to me," I heard Karl rasp. It brought me back out of my head.

"Easy Karl," I said.

"They got to me."

"Who are they?"

"The usual. Call them what you want."

Before I ran out and got my own Redskins headgear, I reminded myself Karl was schizophrenic, fried from years of drug use, and was currently on painkillers and the massive tranquilizer Haldol. It kind of made me pause before I went with his theories.

"Take it easy, Karl. Does it hurt much?"

"Not physically. What hurts is they get away with it, over and over and over."

"Yeah," I said, without really knowing what I affirmed.

"You don't believe me. You think I'm a doped up whack job."

"How could you say that Karl?" The word hypocrite came to mind.

"Because I am a doped up whack job. I know it; we don't have to pretend I'm not."

"Karl…"

"I wasn't always though. You can look it up." Karl raised his eyes and grinned a resigned smile.

"Karl, take it–"

"Remember Duffy. Just because you're paranoid doesn't mean people aren't out to get you." He closed his eyes.

"Karl, take it easy. Just get some rest. It's not worth…"

He was already asleep. I touched his hand and said goodbye.

I drove back to the clinic knowing I was in Michelin's shithouse and it probably wasn't the time to start blowing off work. A cruise around the parking lot, though, told me her car wasn't in. That's when I remembered she had her monthly podiatry appointment and the county planning meeting. I thanked God for Claudia's recurring corns, and decided to find out a bit more about the shit Karl was going on about.

It was Wednesday afternoon and the day Kelley, my cop friend, got his haircut. I had a few cop-type questions for him. Even though he wasn't always thrilled to be answering them, he eventually did.

"You know what I'm fuckin' sayin'? You know what I'm fuckin' sayin?" Junior, the young barber, was sayin' when I came in. It wasn't a coincidence because Junior punctuated everything he said with 'You know what I'm fuckin' sayin?'. After awhile it became the white background noise of Ray's.

Kelley sat next in line. Before I could speak to him barbershop protocol demanded the exchange of inane conversation with both barbers before addressing others.

"Hey, Duff," Junior stopped cutting some cop's hair. "We got the new Penthouse in. It's got some real fuckin' snatch in it. You gotta check that shit out. You know what I'm fuckin sayin'!"

"Junior, you know I can't look at that shit in the middle of the day. Next thing you know I'll be borrowing some hair gel and heading off to your bathroom–then my day is shot."

"Duff, you're a pisser, you know what I'm fuckin' sayin."

"Hey, Duff," Jackpot, Ray's other barber, said without looking up from the racing form.

"How you doin' with the trotters, Jackpot?"

"I hit the superfecta at Vernon Downs--a nice pot."

"Wow, again?"

"No, that's the same fuckin superfecta he told you about

67

two months ago, you know what I'm fuckin' sayin'. Fuckin' Jackpot keeps bringing it up like it was this morning. You know what I'm fuckin' sayin'?" Junior said.

Jackpot rolled his eyes and shook his head without saying anything.

"Duffy you here for a cut?" Jackpot said.

"No, I'm just here to see Kelley."

I sat down next to Kelley, who was reading an article about the Yankees latest losing streak and why it spelled the end for life as we know it.

"Not looking at *Penthouse*?" I said.

"Why don't you borrow some of Junior's hair gel," Kelley said without looking up.

"Hey, let me ask you something," I said. Kelley didn't look up from *The Post*. A lot of conversations with Kelley started out with me doing all the talking.

"One of my guys has gotten beat up twice in the last two days or so. One time it was in the park and this last time I'm not sure where, but someone tried to slit his throat."

"Guy's name is Greene?" Kelley said. He read about the Yankees woeful middle relief issues.

"Yeah, how'd you know?"

"A guy gets his throat slit, it draws attention."

"What do you know about it?"

"I just told you all I know about."

"Is it weird the same guy gets rolled in such a short period of time?"

"No–maybe someone out on the street is pissed off at him. Maybe he owes money or stiffed someone on a deal. It could be a whole host of things."

"He's also paranoid schizophrenic," I said.

"Here we go. What does that mean in cop terms?"

"Well, for instance, he wore a Redskins helmet and rubber gloves the last time he got attacked."

Kelley laid the paper down in his lap and looked at me

68

for the first time.

"That'll get your ass kicked, just on general principles."

"He also tends to go on and on about conspiracies and how the government is always doing things to us, and we have to wake up from our ignorance."

"So this guy is hangin' on the streets of Crawford sportin' Redskins gear and calling everyone ignorant. Hard to figure why some of Crawford's citizens might find that offensive."

"The thing is, Kell, in his ramblings, he's kind of predicted a few things that have come true."

"Here we go…"

"I'm serious. The ROTC fire and that WACO thing in Alabama."

"He said they were going to happen?"

"Well, sort of. He said something like it would happen."

"Duff, something like that shit happens every day."

"I probably should mention he is paranoid schizophrenic."

Kelley looked at me for the second time in the conversation. He didn't say anything–just looked at me.

"What?"

"You just said that."

"So"

"I mean you just repeated yourself."

I didn't say anything. I had gotten a little tired of people pointing this sort of thing out to me.

"Look, Kelley, I guess what I'm asking, is there any chance some bigger force is out there against Greene, and they're making it look like random street beatings?"

"There's a chance there's a Bigfoot."

"Never mind," I said.

"Kelley, you're up. How about those Yankees?" Junior snapped the apron from the last guy's cut. "They gotta get some relief, you, know what the fuck I'm sayin'?"

I started to feel like the Yankees weren't the only ones.

11

I got back to the office a little after lunch, and, lucky for me, the Michelin Woman remained at the County Planning meeting. It was one of the myriad of meetings she went to on a daily basis with a host of other social workers cut from the exact same cloth. I had a vision of the group of them sitting around a table eating donuts and drooling over the chance–and the power–to create a new form.

In the parking lot I tried giving Rene a call and her voice message immediately picked up. I left a message for her to call me and I got a creepy feeling something wasn't right. Rene was one of those people who almost surgically attached herself to her cell phone and if you got her voice mail she'd always call right back.

I sat in the car for fifteen minutes listening to Mad Dog Russo go on and on about the Yankees overpaying for players and how it was bad for baseball. A caller from Yonkers countered with the fact the Yankees were good for baseball no matter what and the Dog should understand that by now.

Fifteen minutes went by and there was no call from Rene.

I headed into the clinic, comfortable in knowing Claudia was out, and I beat this system once again.

Back at the office, at least Trina noticed my absence.

"Where the hell have you been?" Trina said when I set foot in the door.

"The hospital," I said.

"Thank God. It's about time you got that head thing checked out."

"I visited Karl. What head thing?"

"C'mon, Duff."

"I'm serious—what head thing?"

"You're wobbling around, complaining of headaches, you lose things, and you repeat yourself."

"C'mon..."

Trina just looked at me. Our eyes locked for just a couple seconds longer than usual. I couldn't say for sure, but I thought she welled up a little. She shook her head in disgust.

"Why?"

"Why, what?"

"Why do you insist on doing something that hurts you so?" She looked away.

"Because I can't sing or dance..."

"It's not funny—and aren't you supposed to be getting married? I mean, doesn't that change anything for you?" Trina busied herself with stuff around her desk. I got the message women are so good at sending, that the interaction was over.

Back at my cubicle the voice mail left me four messages. Two from the Department of Social Services, most probably looking for some documentation I hadn't sent them, and one from the probation department also probably looking for documentation. There was also one from the Veteran's Administration medical records department. I called the VA

"Medical records," the voice droned.

"Yes, I'm returning a call. My name is Duffy Dombrowski. I had requested the record of Karl Greene. I'm a counselor at Jewish Unified Services in Crawford, New York," I said as officially as I could muster.

"The file you requested is currently under review at another site and there will be a delay in getting it to you."

"Isn't there a copy you can send or a summary?"

"We don't keep copies, sir."

"Can you just send me the discharge summary?"

"The discharge summary is with the chart, sir."

"Can't they send me a summary?"

"They don't do that, sir."

"Well, when can I expect the chart?"

"I have no way of knowing, sir."

So it went, a shining example of government efficiency.

I looked in my appointment book. I saw my first appointment of the day was with Sparky. I look forward to meeting with him because he was really trying, and it is energizing to do that kind of work. I mean Eli was great and I felt for the Abermans because they were chronically unhappy, but honestly, they weren't going to change. Eli liked getting high and running the streets. It was what he was into, and playing the clinic so he would get his welfare check was part of it. He wasn't mean or obnoxious about it, but I knew the role I played with Eli.

The Abermans somehow either enjoyed–that seems too strong a word–maybe they bonded to being unhappy. Mr. Aberman is stupid enough to keep his porn stash out in the open and he uses his wife's status olive oil for lubricant. If I was Freudian trained, I could make some sort of inference about the role of Mrs. Aberman's olive oil, but the more I thought about it, the more the mental image of Mr. Aberman in his cold, dank garage rubbin' one out started to bother me. I guess my point is, if you don't want your wife finding your stroke mags, hide them better like the rest of us do. Don't put them in Tupperware with the extra extra virgin olive oil on top. I think Mr. Aberman sent a message and I think the message said something along the lines of 'I resent having sex every solstice, and so you'll feel bad, I'm heading out to the power tools to grease up my tool…, and by the way I'm using the goddamn overpriced oil you buy instead of the generic!'.

I had difficulty shaking the visual associated with Mr. Aberman and became worried a particular mental image would be stuck in my consciousness forever. Thank God, Trina buzzed me to let me know Sparky arrived.

I met Sparky in the multi-purpose room. I could tell right away something wasn't right. Rail thin and fidgety to begin with, today somehow he had ramped it up a notch. The circles around his eyes were darkened and when he blew into the room so did the smell of cigarettes. It hit me like a jab, almost like Sparky himself morphed into one giant cig.

"Duff," Sparky looked over his shoulder and then at me. "I need a favor."

"Shoot, Spark."

"I ain't never told you this." He snapped his gum, looked over his shoulder and back again. "I got a kid."

"Yeah?"

"Yeah, a five-year-old little girl. I ain't never married her mother, but I used to stay in touch until I went in the joint."

"So, what's keeping you from getting involved with her again?"

"Well, after I got out, I fucked around with the drinking, you know the whole bit and now the mother has a restraining order on me." He looked over his shoulder and back, and wiped the corner of his eyes before he spoke again.

"Duff, I love that girl, and I know the kind of man I've been, but I want to be in her life. I want a chance. A chance I know I probably don't deserve." He sniffed real hard, hung his head, and cursed.

I sat silently, pretending to be naturally therapeutic. That sounds better than being naturally without-a-fucking-clue what to say next.

"Duff, I've been good with the AA. I've been tryin', I've really been fuckin' tryin'..." He stopped, sniffed, wiped his eyes and looked away to try to hide it.

"There are channels you can go through with family courts. You could get a lawyer," I said.

"I tried that shit, but who's going to give me a break? I'm a fuck up. I know that."

This might be the space where you think a super

competent counselin' guy might say something along the lines of 'Don't give up! The system will help you out!' I've worked in that system. It won't help you out, especially if you're Sparky and you're a drunk, a firebug, and a guy with a history. That's the truth and if you're in the real world you know it's the truth.

Still, I kind of felt like I played out the therapeutic silence thing, so I found myself saying, "You can stay with it, man. Work the system and don't give up. Don't let it make you drink," I said, like an asshole. There's something about being a counselor that forces bullshit out of your mouth even when you don't want it to.

"It's tough, Duff, I feel like drinking. I'll tell you, but not being able to see Kristy would be just an excuse. I know."

"I guess it's an acceptance thing," I said. One of those things I said instead of saying 'It sounds like you're shit out of luck to me.'

"What's the ex's name. I never hear you mention her."

"Paula Bentley, she's a Crawford girl; we met at McDonough High. She lives out in Vorhees Park and works at the high school as a school nurse. She's all right–the whole shit's my fault."

"Yeah, I'm sorry, Sparky. I'm not sure what you can do except wait it out."

"Yeah, I know, Duff."

Later we talked about AA and what it means to get a sponsor. I let Sparky know it's best to find someone he could relate to, who has at least five years clean and who isn't a woman. The Sparkman nodded and acted like he gave a shit, but I knew he got stuck on seeing his daughter. It got me thinking guys who have to quit drinking don't have the luxury of taking little mental vacations like I do when I visit AJ's. The booze causes more trouble than the little vacays and it just doesn't work for them. Consequently, they're left with having to think their thoughts and figure shit out.

That didn't sound like any picnic and it made me wonder if I'd be stuck thinking about Mr. Aberman with his pants around his ankles misusing his wife's cooking oil.

Thank God I could drink.

I finished up with Sparky and had kind of a shit feeling. I know things don't get better just because a guy gets better, but it seemed like Sparky could use a break. Maybe it just wasn't to be.

12

I called Crawford Medical Center and found out Karl hadn't gone AMA. A call to Rudy informed me he suspected even if Karl wanted to split he probably wouldn't be up for it. He also went on to say the guy got more depressed and barely spoke to anyone–even about conspiracy theories.

Trying to figure out how to cheer up a guy who believed everyone was out to get him was tough. I figured I'd pop in on him so he'd have someone to talk to, seeing as I was about the only guy in his life. He didn't trust me, but I think he had begun to feel he was letting his guard down with me, even if it was just a little bit. Whether that assumption was correct or not, I just wasn't sure, but I felt like I had to go check him.

I didn't want to get to the hospital right at the confusion of dinnertime and shift change, so I headed home for an hour or so to check on Al and to grab something to eat.

When I came in the door Al had climbed up on the back of the chair and was arguing with the sparrows again. His excitement over seeing me threw off his equilibrium and though he tried to get the last word in with the sparrow, his split attention twisted him up and he fell over backward. This time he had a soft landing into the seat of the chair and just sort of slumped off of the chair on to the floor. He ran over to me and jumped up and yelled his enthusiasm and affection for me as I tried to make it through the house.

I cracked open a Schlitz, hit the remote, and eased back on to my couch to watch a little TV. My arm rested on the plain wood of the arm. I noticed bite marks on the wood, though not many. Apparently, Al didn't need to add wood fiber to his diet at this time.

CNN was still breaking down the 'Massacre at the People of God Church' and profiled their leader Rukhaber. They went over his history as an Iraqi vet and his career as a 'private contractor' in a private security force. The news people discussed the role of private security in relation to the army. The best I could figure, they were mercenaries doing pretty much the same thing soldiers did, only for a lot more money. At some point Rukhaber had a falling out with his employers and turned into the fanatical, nut-job, church guy.

Al sat at my feet staring at me without blinking. He hummed progressively louder in a way I've come to know builds to a crescendo—the kind of bark that goes through your head like an ice pick. I hated that bark and did whatever I could to circumvent its occurrence. The Schlitz was cold and the couch felt good, but no amount of denial could prevent the oncoming barking, so I knew time had come to give Al what he wanted.

The building urgency from Al meant he wanted either to eat or walk. The fact of the matter was he always wanted to eat, but sometimes he needed to walk. 'Walk' is actually just a polite euphemism for taking a shit, but society frowns on the use of that terminology in social conversation. Nonetheless, Al's walks often looked like crawls where he slowly sniffed the ground looking for the exact right spot to leave his fecal calling card. Al put it in his day planner every morning, with an A2 priority. Eating got an A1 for first priority, while A3 penciled in his twenty-two hours of sleep. The rest of the task list items were minor activities centered on annoying me.

So, despite how comforting the Schlitz-couch continuum, it was time to let Al lead me down Route 9R in search of the ultimate canine crapping experience. I got up from the couch, which signaled to my friend a walk's eminence. I put on my sneakers and he went off, not being able to control his glee at the thought of taking a crap in tall grass. When I got the leash it sent him over the top, and he jumped up and kicked me in the nuts.

I don't like getting kicked in the nuts.

I doubled over in pain and repeatedly yelled the word 'fuck' which I believe Al mistook for 'walk' This got him even more excited and he jumped up and headed-butted me which sent a thick throb through my cranium. I followed that action with more 'fucks' and Al got even more revved up. Before I could get the leash fastened Al took a leak on the carpet in front of the door.

I love the company and unconditional love of a pet.

Al waddled his way down 9R, busily searching for the exact ideal spot to do his thing. His waddling got more pronounced and the telltale back arch seemed to indicate something, but he wasn't quite ready. It took another half mile before he went all the way and left a fifteen-pound prize on the side of the road. I did my best to imitate a Sea World deep-diving showman by not breathing. I didn't time my exhalation correctly and my respiratory system forced me to do a gigantic inhalation. I snorted like I was in the VIP room of Studio 54 in '77. Al's essence filled my sinus cavities until my body rejected it and I went into a coughing spell. Al ignored me and lay down next to it and closed his eyes. The whole curved back, muscle contraction thing involved in this bodily act had made him sleepy.

I wasn't ready to stand in the funk watching Al go into REM, so I began to walk, pulling him. I don't know if you've ever taken an 85-pound Basset out for a drag, but it isn't a lot of fun. I've always thought they should add it as an event in that bizarre *World Strongest Man* competition you see on ESPN late at night. It could be put right after they make the Bulgarian guy carry an AMC Gremlin on his back while he walks through molasses. They'd have to cover the basset in Vaseline or something to prevent road burn or put him in a spandex suit but I'm sure they could work it out.

Al began to come to about twenty yards into our drag. He stopped and did the tornado-basset thing to clear his jowls and then reluctantly joined me in the walk. Because there are no sidewalks and because there aren't many humans inhabiting the region, I reasoned it was permissible for me to leave Al's biodegradable contribution to the eco system in its natural state and not pick it up.

That, and the fact I found it disgusting.

We made it back to the Blue. I grabbed the Caddy keys and went to head out to the medical center. Al beat me to the door and got between me and the knob. When I'd go to grab the knob he'd jump up and knock my hand away. This was his subtle way of letting me know he wanted to come along.

I knew better than to fight with Al, so I opened the passenger side of the El Dorado and hoisted him up. His tail wagged; he knew he had conned me into giving him what he wanted. He gave me a look that half said, 'Thank you Duffy, you're a kind and benevolent master' and 'Duffy, you're a sap'. Shortly after he proceeded to commence drooling on the orange velour of the passenger seat. He started a fresh spot, of course, because it just isn't any fun drooling into an existing and crunchy old drool spot. Other than the drool oozing from Al's mouth he remained motionless on the trip.

We pulled into the medical center parking lot. I cracked a couple of the windows and headed to the entrance. Al did not accept this move. He began to bark in rapid-fire progression, then alternated the bark riot with long *Ahoooos*. People started to stare and a security guard began to walk toward me, so I headed back to the car and got him out. He cheerfully plopped down on the pavement and looked up at me as if to say, 'What next?'.

Next was how to get Al into the hospital and up to Karl's room. I had been caught trying to pass Al off as a therapy dog at a nursing home. Suffice it to say I didn't convince anyone there, and there were probably posters of him and me all over nursing stations in Crawford. I decided to take my chances.

We headed in the main entrance past the reception desk. At the desk sat a woman of maximum density, wearing a headset and a thin, but very visible, black mustache and a dress resembling something you might throw over your boat to protect it in the winter.

Ironically, a big sign hung next to her desk. It said 'Snack Attack Collection Site: Bring in Canned Meat!'. I knew it was for the soldier thing, but it was an odd juxtaposition of messages next to this particular receptionist.

"Oh, a new therapy dog! Isn't he precious!" she yelled to us across the desk.

My therapy dog is a sap for affection and charged the receptionist with a forceful gusto that broke him free from my grasp.

"Oh, what a sweet boy. You're a good boy!" she said. Al stood on his two back legs, his front paws resting on the receptionist's ample bosom, licking her face. She had her eyes closed and was taking it all in.

It was like a car wreck and I couldn't not watch.

"What's his name? He's gorgeous!"

"His name is Al," I said. Al dropped down to all fours. "He's a good boy."

Al had worked his way in between the woman's thighs. She tried unobtrusively, to nudge him away, but he resisted and stuck his nose right between her legs.

It was a socially awkward moment.

"Al is a basset hound." I heard myself say. The receptionist looked at me, strained to push Al's nose away.

"Basset hounds are scent hounds and they are bred for hunting and tracking small animals like rabbits, gophers, or woodchucks." I had no idea why I went on like this, but I felt I had to say something.

Al sneezed and the receptionist yelped

He went right back to where he was.

I reached in with the leash to try to get him hooked up again but the positioning of her thighs and Al made it impossible. Al sneezed again.

This time I got him hooked. I pulled as hard as I could and got him out of there. I didn't get a chance to say goodbye.

The rest of the walk to Karl's room was mostly uneventful. Al pranced along at my side, getting smiles from the cute nurses, who seemed appreciative of his volunteerism as a therapy dog. Al started to pant partly from the exercise, but also from the sheer joy of interaction in the world. It was Al's world and the rest of us just lived it.

Karl was sitting up, staring at the TV when we came in. He didn't turn our way when we entered. I let Al walk over to him and surprise him. Al was good in new situations, and he was cautious in this new environment filled with new smells, lights, and gauges.

"Whoa, looky here. Hey there hound dog!" Karl snapped out of his trance and bent over to rub Al's ears. "Hey fella, what's happening, my man!" It took a full moment or two before Karl noticed me in the room.

"Hey Duffy, who's this?"

"That's Al," I explained to Karl it was short for his hard to pronounce Muslim name.

"Hey man, Assalaamu alaykeum! My brother," Karl said rubbing Al behind the ears.

"Ahooo, Ahooo, Ahooo," Al said.

"Why does he have a Muslim name?"

"He was in the Nation of Islam security force as a man trailer and bomb sniffer, but he got asked to leave on account of hygiene issues," I said.

"That's it Al–stick it to the man!" Al jumped up on Karl's lap and started to lap at his face. Karl smiled from ear to ear. I had never seen him so happy.

"Karl, how are you feeling?"

"Great, now. I love dogs, man. They're pure, you know. They ain't about fuckin' with you and manipulating you with some silent agenda."

I thought about Al eating my couch, kicking me in the nuts, and waking me up every morning at four a.m. for his breakfast. It didn't seem all that pure of heart to me.

"Good boy, good boy," Karl said.

Al growled.

"What's a matter, what did I do Duff?"

"He doesn't like being called 'boy'. Comes from back in his Muslim days."

"Oh. Sorry my brother. Good dog, good dog!" Al went back to licking his face.

I wanted to talk to Karl and didn't know how to broach it, but I had never seen him in such a good mood. I didn't want to waste it.

"Karl, who beat you up this time? What happened?" I said.

He kept playing with Al and began to talk without looking at me.

"Whatever happens, man? I was in the park minding my business when I get grabbed from behind and a knife is put to my neck. Next thing I know its lights out and I'm in here."

"Were you going on talking to people about conspiracies and that shit or were you really minding your own business?"

"The conspiracies ain't shit. That's what they want you to think. Look at all this shit here." He pointed to all the medical equipment. "Who's paying for it? I sure as hell ain't. So who's paying for it? Who paid for it to be here for a guy like me to use? Who benefits? Follow the money, Duffy."

"That's the kind of shit. Were you yelling that in the park and getting on people's nerves?"

"It's too bad if it gets on their nerves; they need to be enlightened."

"Karl, people hate to hear this kind of shit. That's what

keeps you getting your ass kicked. Don't you see?"

"And I suppose you just want to sit back and let shit happen. Just like this massacre bullshit. Massacre at People of God. What a crock!"

"Now, right there–cut that shit out. You keep saying this ambiguous shit and then acting like you knew it all along. Did you know anything about this before it happened?"

"How could you not know? This Rukhaber, you'll find out sooner or later he was CIA, FBI, Secret Service, or something. Then whoever claims that will get discredited, caught with child porn or they'll just disappear. Watch–"

"What the hell are you talking about Karl?"

"It's like the black man. Every time we get a black hero they seemingly fuck it up. King, Malcolm X, Ali–you name them. If they're not homogenized like Michael Jordan they get destroyed. That's why you get fools like Sharpton as spokesmen. It's an automatic discredit."

"Karl…you've predicted, at least sort of, two events. Do you know they're going to happen?"

"Duffy, Duffy–I'm a whack job, how would I know?" He went back to playing with Al's ears. Al went back to ahoooing.

"So tell me what's happening next?" I stared right at him.

He shrugged and smiled a crooked smile.

"Let's see, we've had the act of God with a fire, we had the bogeyman getting blown up…*hmmm*…I'd guess it's about time for some sort of poison scare. You know, something in the water, some senator gets some white powder, bad Tylenol…that gets the ignorant masses petrified."

Al lay on his belly all spread out and snoring. I didn't have any idea what Karl raved on about, and I thought, maybe, I really had gotten hit on the head too much. CNN showed a collage of Rukhaber's photos on the screen. It ended with him in his desert khakis in a shot from Iraq.

Karl laughed out loud.

13

I got to the office the next morning and checked out Karl's file. The only information in it was the info I had put in it, which, by the way, meant there wasn't anything in it at all except names and addresses. Karl had refused to give me much personal stuff, because of his New World Order bullshit. I knew his folks were dead, he lived at the Westview Apartments–or at least said he lived there, and he had been born thirty miles away in Vorhees Park.

I checked with Trina, but nothing had shown up from the VA. The prospect of getting some worthwhile info on Karl didn't look bright. I didn't really care, clinically, about getting information, because all it tended to do was make a file really fat. We had plenty of records weighing twenty pounds because of the amount of useless counseling the client's had had over the course of their lives. It didn't really improve their treatment outlook much.

Monique walked back from the kitchen with her customary cup of chamomile tea. She wore a throwback baseball cap from the Negro League team, the Pittsburgh Grays.

"Nice lid," I said.

"Thanks, Duff."

"Satchel Paige's team, right?"

"Actually, no. Josh Gibson's."

"He was like the black Babe Ruth wasn't he?"

"Babe Ruth, isn't he in second?"

"Now he's in third. Bonds broke Aaron's record."

"Don't get me started," she said.

She placed the tea down, rolled in her desk chair, and got out her first file. She did the same thing in the same way everyday and never looked under pressure.

"Hey 'Unique? You ever have to get VA records on a client?"

"Sure, all the time."

"Why does it take forever?"

"What are you talking about?"

"I asked for Karl's info weeks ago and I've gotten nothing."

"That's weird. Usually the VA gets stuff to you for the first visit."

"When I called, they said the chart was out and wouldn't be back for awhile."

"I suppose that's possible."

"Great."

I guess it didn't matter much in regard to Karl's treatment. I mean, the guy wore a football helmet and rubber gloves, and took all sorts of drugs, prescribed and unprescribed. A bunch of Army hospital gibberish would only bore the shit out of me if I ever read it.

I decided before I began the day's procrastination in earnest I needed some really bad lukewarm coffee to get me going. I got up from the Duffy's Cubicle of Love and came face to face with the Michelin Woman.

"Good morning, Duffy," she said through a grimace. At least that's the way I interpreted her non-verbals.

"Hey Claudia."

"Duffy could you do me a favor today?"

"For you, Boss, anything."

"Vorhees High School has a computer they want to donate. Could you drive out there and get it?"

"Sure."

"This won't be an excuse for not having your paperwork up to date. I trust you've gotten caught up at this point."

"Of course," I said. I never passed on a chance to go for a ride and get out of the office. I wasn't in the mood for paperwork anyway. It was also, maybe, a chance to snoop around about my buddy Karl.

Vorhees High is in the hills about 20 miles away, and I took the nice drive. Vorhees is one of the small villages people escaped to when they left Crawford. More and more Crawford was starting to feel like a northern borough of New York City and the Crawfordians weren't pleased with it.

Going into a high school is always a trip. It surprises me just how young the kids are and how much skin the girls show on the average school day. I don't know if that's Brittney's, Paris's or Lindsay's fault, but I knew if I was fourteen and had to sit around all day and pretend I wasn't looking at the half-naked girls around me, I'd go out of my mind. I remember keeping my hands in my pockets to hide my day dreams enough back in McDonough.

McDonough was what I pictured a high school should look like. Old, made of concrete and smelling of disinfectant and whatever it is they season schools with. McDonough was probably a modern school when it was built in the '40s, but the '40s happened a while ago and it wasn't modern anymore. They had a few computers around, but not as many as you'd think in today's high school. When you did see a computer, the off-white plastic looked like an out of place anachronism, as if they didn't belong there or at least not yet. McDonough was dark, not very friendly, and it carried the weight of the years it spent in the worst section of the city.

VHS gave off a much different feel. First of all, it was bright with a forced cheeriness that didn't fool me for a second. It had a smell to it that was probably newer more eco-friendly disinfectant and different type of floor wax. The kids looked different than the kids at MHS. These kids were almost all white. There were a few Indian kids whose dads, I guessed, were doctors, and just one or two black kids. The place reeked of Abercrombie and Fitch, and the girls went to tanning salons and got their nails done. Somehow it seemed a meaner, more exclusionary place even though it was far less diverse than its inner city counterparts. Maybe McDonough had more skin colors, but fewer classes of people.

I had to buzz my way into the school, sign in, get a big orange badge, and be escorted to my destination. I know about Columbine and all the other high school dangers, but the whole system struck me as bizarre. As if I came to the place with some sort of high-powered assault weapon, a buzzer, a badge, and an escort would somehow deter me.

My escort was a five-foot tall guy with a wispy mustache and squeaky plastic shoes. His nametag said Mr. Teters. He struck me as the kind of teacher who gets spitballs shot at his head for eight hours a day. He didn't say 'Hello' or anything else, just walked with me in silence. He pointed me down a hallway toward their storage room, past the 'Snack Attack' collection boxes I now realized were everywhere, and let me go. Apparently, my danger to VHS had been assessed and deemed low, or it was dangerously close to my escort's break.

Just before the storage room I noticed the nurse's office. The door was open and a couple of kids hung around surely trying to get a medical reason to blow off social studies or whatever the hell Mr. Teters taught. Under the nurse's office sign the name placard said 'Ms. Bentley'.

I guess I had stood in front of the door for longer than I thought because I was interrupted by a pretty thirty-something woman with short black hair just barely touching her shoulders and an attractive, but a bit weathered, face. Pretty kind of overstated it–she looked like ten years ago she was a knockout and since then life had gotten in the way.

"Can I help you?" She didn't smile. Behind her a fat kid held his stomach and groaned on the couch.

"Jimmy, stop it. Your mother's coming in and you'll get

to go home." Jimmy immediately stopped and suppressed a smile.

"Are you Ms. Bentley?"

"Yeah..."

"My name is Duffy Dombrowski. I'm a counselor at Jewish Unified Services."

"Yeah?"

"Do you have a second to talk?"

She looked at fatso Jimmy, who had ceased moaning.

"Sure, come in to my office."

She ushered me into a small office with a battleship grey desk. There were posters on the wall about brushing your teeth, underage drinking, and abstinence from sex.

"What can I help you with?"

"I'm your ex-husband Sparky's counselor and..."

"He wasn't ever my husband, and I don't have anything to do with him any more."

"Yeah and—"

"Is that why you're here? I didn't sign up to be part of his treatment. You can't just come out and talk to people without permission. Do you have a release? Are you familiar with HIPPA regs?"

I had forgotten she belonged in the human services sisterhood.

"I know, this is technically wrong. It isn't an official visit. I'm actually here picking up a used computer."

"What?"

"You see, I wanted to let you know Sparky is doing really, really well. He's going to meetings; he's taking getting better very seriously."

"Well, I'm glad for him, but we are very much through." She shook her head and looked away from me.

"Look, this isn't any of my business, but not being able to see his little girl is really messing with Sparky. He's trying..."

"That's it, this conversation is over." She stood up. "You are one of the most unprofessional human services people I've ever run into. You don't just go up to people you don't know, not ask their side of the story, and plead your case. I'm sorry. I've got to go back to work." She walked around the desk and past me.

"Just think about it. I'm betting he never had a counselor advocate for him like this. Let that mean something, Ms. Bentley."

She didn't say anything. She went out and checked on fatso Jimmy, who was amusing himself by making fart noises into the back of his hand.

14

I grabbed the old Mac computer with the handle on the back and headed down the hallway. We had a Windows system at the clinic, which rendered this donation pretty useless, but that's how human services donations worked.

When I got to the lobby, I took a look at the school's trophy case. I loved looking at the dated trophies, faded leather footballs and basketballs, and the cut away nets from championship games. VHS played in the Suburban League, made up of all white country-boys and rich kids. They never ever went up against McDonough or any of the other urban schools. It was part of why their parents moved out here in the first place.

I looked at the football stuff from their big Suburban League championship year in '99. The Mountain Crows went 10-1 and lost the Class B state championship in overtime on what the plaque suggested was a bad call. The memorabilia saluted the players and the heroes of the great '99 time. On the Suburban league trophy they had the coach and the captains names engraved: Coach Skip Steenburg, Captains Mike Pendergast, Bill Meyerson, Chip Newstrom, and Karl Greene.

Yep, Karl Greene.

"Can I help you, sir?" A guy in a VHS golf shirt, with a whistle around his neck, said.

"Nah, I was just going down memory lane with the Mountain Crows."

"You can't hang around. You have an orange pass, not red."

"I don't follow?"

"The orange ones are temps. You need a red one to hang around all day."

"Oh, sorry," I said, though I wasn't sure about what. "Hey, can I ask you something?"

"Sure."

"The captains of the football team, do you remember them?"

"Of course. Two of them are still in the area. Pendergast works for the state and is the offensive coordinator on the football team and Meyerson is an accountant with some big firm."

"What about Newstrom and Greene? You remember them?"

"Sure, great kids. Besides being football captains they were class officers. Newstrom was president and Greene was his VP. After graduation they enlisted. I think they got in Special Forces in the military, but we've kind of lost track of them in the last few years. I wouldn't be surprised if they're both big time heroes now," the coach said with a smile.

"Yeah? Really? You don't say?" was all I could say.

My interaction with Coach Whoever slowed down after that and I realized he was staring at me as I looked into the trophy case. Life just isn't fair when you got the wrong colored tag, so I figured it was time to go.

I got back to the clinic with the computer everyone immediately deemed useless. Just the same it had been worth it to me to get out of the office. Trina watered her plants and I hung around just long enough to see her water the plant hanging from the ceiling. It was my favorite, not because I care about plants, but because she had to stretch to reach it. Trina's black clingy T-shirt rode up, as she stretched to reach the pot, to show a very flat stomach and an adorable belly button. An inny–which was good. Outies kind of gross me out.

"Duff? Hello? Why don't you take a picture?" Trina said. Her tone had mock anger to it, but her eyes smiled as she said it. I smiled, too.

"Need any help?"

"Not the kind you're offering?" A pretty good line considering our history.

I also got a twinge of guilt. I wasn't quite sure where admiring Trina's navel fit in on the engagement-commitment continuum. I was pretty sure I wouldn't be asking clarification from my fiancé on the matter.

"Hey, check this out. I went out to Vorhees High, and did you know Karl captained the championship football team?"

"Is that why he wears a football helmet all the time?"

"Not only that, he was vice president of the class and generally an all around big man on campus."

"Damn. How does that guy become Karl?"

"I'm guessing the Army didn't help."

"That sucks. You never really hear much about the mentally screwed up guys. It's almost worse than getting hurt physically."

"Yeah, I think I'd rather get hurt physically," I said.

"Hey–by the way you seem better today–even better than just yesterday. Did you go to the doctor?"

"Better? Better than what?"

"You're not staring off in to space, you're not wobbling, and you haven't repeated yourself in this whole conversation," she said without smiling.

"I wasn't doing that shit, was I? Really?"

She just looked at me and shook her head.

My head still throbbed every now and then, but in the last couple of days it did seem a lot less painful. Today was the one day of the week we had our consulting psychiatrist in. Dr. Laura Meade was this season's model. I say that because we switched shrinks every couple of months for a couple of reasons. One was our pay sucked, so they usually picked up extra hours in our clinic until they could find extra hours someplace that paid them more money. The second reason, they got to do very little therapy, because they had to manage all the psychiatric medications the clients got prescribed. Mostly clients came in for fifteen minutes, got a new prescription, or got the old one adjusted, and moved on. It wasn't much fun for the shrink.

I have to admit that though I've had my problems with some of the whack jobs who have been assigned to us in the psychiatric department, I liked Laura. She had just completed her psychiatric residency and couldn't have been even thirty yet–she looked closer to twenty-five. She did triathlons for fun, so she had an athletic build that was still attractive, probably because she did them for fun and not competition. She wore her long straight dirty blond hair gathered in a ponytail and leaned toward cargo pants, T-shirts, and running shoes for a wardrobe. Never a hint of make up, but she had something incredibly feminine about her–strong and feminine.

She'd been around for a couple of months, but because of her schedule I barely had said hello to her. Today, I wanted to catch her with a few questions.

"Excuse me, Doc?" I said as she came out of the ladies room.

"Hi Duff. Do me a favor–don't call me that," she said.

"Why? You're a doctor, right?"

"Yeah, but the term 'Doc' kind of has a certain feel to it. Like some sort of special authoritative fraternity. I don't want to be thought of in those terms."

"Okay, I think I got it." It seemed like a fair request.

"What can I help you with?"

"I have a couple of questions about one of the guys on my caseload. You haven't seen him yet. His name is Karl."

"It will be tough for me to comment on him then." I

noticed I could see the veins in her arms and when she put her hands on her hips the biceps flexed. Not like a weightlifter's, but like an endurance athlete's.

"Well, Karl came back from the war and he's got some major paranoia. He's all into conspiracy theories and he's got some pretty strange behavior."

"Like what?"

"He wears a football helmet and rubber gloves because he thinks people are out to get him."

"Is anyone out to get him?"

"Well, he keeps getting beat up around town, probably because of his bizarre behavior."

"Sounds like people are out to get him. Maybe a football helmet makes sense," she said.

I hadn't anticipated that kind of comment from a shrink.

"Anyway, by chance I found out that in high school, before his Army stint, Karl was a high-achieving kid from the suburbs. An athlete, a scholar; your basic big man on campus. My question is, how does a guy get to where Karl is now when only a few years ago he did so well."

"I can only answer in generalities, but there are a few possible explanations." She paused and looked up at the ceiling while she thought.

"He might be schizophrenic and its onset came on in the last few years, but he should've shown some danger signs in high school. It might be trauma from the war he dealt with by breaking from reality or, if he's a drug user, the drugs could've caused a chemically induced psychosis. It could also be a little bit of all three."

"*Hmmm*...so he could've been normal and then something happened along the way."

"Something clearly happened along the way. We just don't know what. The question is, did something happen organically, meaning was there something in his brain chemistry pre-set for him to have psychiatric episodes, or did

94

an environment filled with trauma touch it off? That trauma can also include heavy drug use."

She looked at her watch.

"Duff, I have to get to my next med review. Nice talking to you." She extended her hand and gave me a firm, quite androgynous handshake.

It got me thinking. Could there be a crazy time-bomb in any of us waiting for the right fuse to set it off? Or were the cards dealt in this existential game of Texas Hold 'Em what held our fate? Did 'Ol Karl just land on the wrong Monopoly square and now he's destined to sport Redskins headgear and be equipped for washing the world's dishes. I had an awful lot to think about.

When I had that much to think about, it was best for me to do something mindless. Since my files ran out of date back to Nixon's term, I decided to write in some of them. Trina was doing something with the petty cash box when I went to grab some files.

"Hey, Duff."

"Hey, Trina"

"Did you hear?"

"Hear what?"

"Homeland Security just arrested six members of Al Qaeda in Chicago."

"Holy shit. What happened?"

"About to dump some bio poison into the reservoir."

No kidding, holy shit.

15

"It's if they all live in the same house," Rocco said.

"It doesn't have to be in the same house," Jerry Number One said.

"Hold it–you're saying if a bunch of women live together they have the same periods?" TC said.

"They don't have to be in the same house; it could be in the same office," Jerry Number One said.

"What about the Ladies Auxiliary of the Knights of Columbus? Could they all have the same period?" Jerry Number Two said. He wore a T-shirt that said 'AA is for quitters.'

"It has to be in the same house. Period!" Rocco said.

"I think the Knightettes are long past their periods," TC said.

"The change?" Jerry Number One said.

"I don't got any change. I left it for AJ," TC said.

"No. I'm talking about the hot flashes, the irritableness, and the puffiness," Jerry Number One said.

"I don't think they get puffy. I think that's part of it; they don't puff up any more," TC said.

"Maybe they just get a little puffy," Jerry Number two said.

"The Ladies' Auxiliary is more than a little puffy, especially Marcia, the lady who makes the sausage and peppers at field day," Rocco said.

"You know if we were all women we'd probably have the same period," Jerry Number One said.

The group just stared at him.

I created a happy diversion for Rocco.

"Hey, Duffy what's new?" he said.

"I'm puffy and irritable from my period. You guys got it too?" I said.

"I got your period right here!" Rocco said.

"See…" Jerry Number One said.

"That's it. No more talk on this subject. It's over, period, end of sentence," Rocco said.

"I've heard during menopause there's some confusion and indecision," Jerry Number Two said.

Fortunately for Rocco and his puffiness the news came on.

"Today, in Chicago, four Pakistani nationals were arrested. They had six 100-gallon drums of an unspecified biological poison in their possession. It is believed the men intended to poison the Chicago water supply…"

The group sat quietly, with their attention on the corner television. The bio-terrorism expert was now on the split screen with the anchor.

"…this type of bio terrorism is particularly heinous in that even small amounts would rapidly poison thousands of citizens. It is believed the drums were transported into the country through Niagara Falls, Canada, hidden with a truckload of drums of industrial cleaner. This once again points out how vulnerable we are, as a people, to the terrorist organizations of the world…"

"What the hell was in that shit?" Rocco said to no one in particular.

"Nothin' good," TC said.

"Unless they've come up with something new it's probably stuff like Ebola, botulism, or maybe some sort of liquefied Anthrax," Jerry Number Two said. "The problem with those things is they don't keep and I'm not sure how effective they would be liquefied and dispersed into the drinking water."

97

"It's effective enough to scare the living shit out of everyone," Jerry Number One said.

"Maybe that's enough," Jerry Number Two said.

"Whatyamean Jer?" I said.

"Well, what do the terrorists really want to accomplish? Sure, if they could, they would annihilate us from the earth, but, despite all the bogeyman stuff, it's not as easy as it sounds," Jerry Number Two said. "So, what's the next best thing?"

"Scaring the living shit out of us?" I said.

"Exactly. John Q. Public now has to worry about getting on airplanes, drinking water, going to the mall. It's not annihilation, but it does fuck things up in every day life."

"I got a client who believes it's all bullshit started by our own government to keep our minds off all the other shit," I said.

"Whoa? What kind of nonsense is that?" Rocco said.

"The government would pour shit in the drinking water? That's a little nutty Duff," TC said.

"Well, Duff's client isn't the only one who believes this kind of stuff," Jerry Number Two said.

"Here we go. Let's hear it professor," Rocco said.

"We just heard about a nasty-scary-bogeyman-type terrorist plot and we're all talking about it, and we're all a little uneasy," Jerry Number Two said.

"Yeah, so?" Jerry Number one said.

"What aren't we talking about today?" Jerry Number Two said.

"Huh?" TC said.

"Exactly!" Jerry Number Two said.

"What the fuck are you talking about?" Rocco said.

"Let's see, we're not talking about the trillions the Senate approved for the defense department today, or the six American soldiers who died in Korea yesterday, or that the Supreme Court upheld some more of the Patriot Act," Jerry paused for effect. "Why? Because we're all scared to death about a terrorist act that didn't quite happen at the hands of some scary people of Arab origin," he said.

"The Arabs are scary," TC said.

"Sometimes, but they're not the only people doing scary things. In World War Two, we had the Japanese, then the Koreans, then Vietnamese. Why? They look different than us. It makes it easy to dehumanize them," Jerry said.

"But Jerry, they got six Arabs with poison in drums. Isn't that the truth?" I said.

"Does it raise any questions they got caught right before they did anything? These guys were smart enough to get this shit in the country, yet they're stupid enough to get caught right before they execute their plan?" Jerry Number Two said.

"Good thing Homeland Security caught them," Jerry Number One said.

"Maybe," Jerry Number Two said. "Or, it was all set up so we could argue about this and not the other stuff that happened today, or yesterday, or what will happen tomorrow," Jerry said.

"This is some nutty bullshit," Rocco said.

"You might be right, Rocco. But how come we keep having these near misses of terrorism every 60 to 90 days right around the time there's growing dissatisfaction with our military involvement, our defense budget, or something similar?" Jerry Number Two said.

"Are you saying the government could be actually doing this?" I said.

"I'm saying there's evidence to support that. It's not all the evidence supports, but it is one explanation," Jerry Number Two said.

Rudy came in through the front door. His underarm stains formed concentric circles down his dark blue shirt. I wondered if you could empirically measure his age by counting the circles like you could on a tree stump. It was far too disgusting to ponder. The group exchanged 'Hellos' with Rudy, and AJ slid a Hennessey in front of him.

"Your whack job buddy gets out tomorrow night," Rudy said.

"How's he's doing?" I said.

"Well, he insists on wearing his Redskins helmet and he wants most of the monitors turned off so they don't emit mind erasing gamma rays or something. All in all, he sounds better to me."

"Yeah, sounds like Karl is back to himself. Is anyone coming to pick him up?"

"I don't know. Who were you thinking, Sonny Jorgenson, Billy Kilmer or Doug Williams, or one of the other retired 'Skins?"

"I'll get him. One thing about Karl is he's never boring."

"Sure, it's probably because you're a double agent. Anyway, they're going to discharge him tomorrow night, so they can bill Medicaid for another half a day." Rudy slurped his Hennessey, which kind of neutralized the upscale image of the cognac. I gotta believe the folks back at the Cognac distillery would wince if they knew Rudy was drinking their product in public.

"Hey, I almost forgot. How's the party plans going?"

"The pool's almost in; I got a caterer and some sort of string quartet. It's costing me a month's pay."

"All this to get Maria back?"

"Yeah. Sad isn't it? I had my shot and I blew it for this goddamn job. No offense, kid, but hangin' out here with you and the brain trust isn't exactly how I want to spend my golden years." He slurped again.

I raised my glass to salute Rudy and his plan. I hoped for his sake it worked out.

Meanwhile, the Foursome was still transfixed by CNN. There was Dr. Theodore Martin, the talking-head guy, going on about the psycho-emotional effects of a foiled terrorist act on a community. He said it tended to make people frightened and a little uneasy.

No shit.

After that the Foursome segued into a discussion about going over Niagara Falls in a drum.

"They use a drum because you can sit in it like a little tiny boat and because its floatacious," TC said.

"Whatyamean you can sit in it?" Jerry Number One said.

"You know, the big bass drum, the one that has the band's name on it. Dennis Wilson's said 'The Beach Boys' on his," TC said.

AJ started whistling 'My Little Douche Cup' on cue.

"You jackass. They use industrial drums," Rocco said.

"The kind of music isn't important," TC said.

Jerry Number Two started singing 'Little Douche Cup' under his breath.

"You're just an idiot," Rocco said. "I'm goin' home to paint another coat on 'The Deuce'," he said.

TC started humming with the other three.

They kept awful time.

16

The next day at work figured to be a beaut. Without nearly enough caffeine I had to have a session with Suda-Fred, my long-time client, who got himself addicted to over the counter cold medication. Fred wasn't doing so great in terms of his ability to stay off the little red devils. On this particular morning I had to call his sobriety into question.

"Hey, Duff, whatsgoinon? Everything good? Good. HowabouttheYanks? Phew, isithotinhere?" Suda-Fred said.

"Uh, Fred…"

"Oh shit, hereitcomes. I'm busted, right? Damn, shit, piss." Fred patted his wet forehead and started to drum his fingers.

"Fred–"

"Sorry, Duff 'bout the language. Shit, piss. I've been tryin', really Duff, really. Shit, piss."

"Fred–"

"Duff, I just get the snots and then I can't breathe and that's what the shit is for. I gotta breathe, Duff. You unnerstand, right?" Fred's eyes were wide.

"How many did you take?" I asked. I tried to be soothing.

"Eleven…no, no…I ain't lyin' no more. It was more like 22." Fred shook.

And so it went.

Right after Fred, there was Martha, whose last name happens to be Stewart. Martha struggles with food issues and sex issues–meaning she can't get enough of either. On this day, we worked through the grieving process of her having to give up 'Hog Wings' at Stan's Sports Bar.

"I've never heard of 'Hog Wings'," I said.

"They taste just like chicken wings but they're pork," Martha said.

"When pigs fly!" I said and laughed a little bit.

Martha just stared at me.

"Oh, this is funny to you? I loved those things." Martha was wounded. I spent the rest of the session trying to be genuine, which is actually kind of tough when you're suppressing a laugh.

Sparky was in after that, and he had a big smile on his face. He had just hit seven months clean and sober. Even though he didn't always connect with people at AA, they made a cake for him and toasted–er, saluted his achievement at the last meeting.

"It felt good, Duff." He allowed himself a bit of a smile. "Like the first time I've been on the right track and doing something positive."

I didn't want to bring up the daughter thing and shit on his day. I didn't have to.

"If only…" Sparky put his hand up to his eyes and squinted hard. A couple of fat tears ran down his face.

"If only I could make things right with Kristy." He bent over and let more of a cry out.

Once again, I didn't have much to say in terms of anything worthwhile. I sat there while the guy cried. That's me, Mr. Therapeutic. It gave me a sick feeling to watch a guy, who life was giving a raw deal to. This whole counseling thing often seemed like bullshit, but on days like today it felt worse.

Afterwards, I grabbed a cup of coffee and headed back to the cubicle. Doing paperwork after dealing with Sparky just didn't seem right and I just sat there and pondered my bulletin board. I don't know how long I had been looking into space when Trina broke me out of it.

"Hey, genius," she said.

"Yeah?"

"Claudia's planning a full review of your charts this week. You might want to get started soon." She did that thing with her eyebrows, raising them up and making a face. It was a face that let me know she knew the potential trouble I was in.

"What else is new?"

"That's it, good attitude. Go ahead and get your ass fired." She headed back to her desk.

I took a less than half-assed stab at the paperwork and got through Fred's and Martha's. I did some old chart stuff on the Abermans, Sheila, and Eli. I picked up Sparky's and looked at it for a little while, then realized it was quitting time.

I decided to give the gym another shot. It had been almost a week, my head hadn't been throbbing a lot, and I wasn't hearing a bunch of shit about being wobbling or repeating myself. To be honest with you, if I'm tired or under-caffeinated I tend to be kind of stupid.

I wrapped my hands in front of the mirror when I felt someone watching me. Smitty was in the doorway to his office, chewing gum and staring at me. He didn't say anything, but he didn't break his stare. When I started to warm up, he took a couple of steps closer and watched me as he stood there with his arms folded.

I just shook things out, throwing jabs, and an occasional left and began to circle the ring. Jab, jab, left, slip, move to my right. Jab, jab, jab, stutter, step, move to my left, flurry with a series of uppercuts to the body, spin to my right. It was how I loosened up every single day and it did a couple of things. It got me loose, but it also ingrained in me automatic patterns that, hopefully, my nervous system would respond to when split-second things happened in the ring. It wasn't unlike what I did when I trained in karate and we'd do katas for hours and hours. It programmed the nervous system to do things without the delay of consciousness.

Guys drifted into the gym little by little. Angel, the 116-pound guy with a dozen fights, and seven or eight wins, was there. Fat Joe, a guy who didn't ever get in the ring, but who hit the bags, grunted and scowled, was there, not doing much. I think Fat Joe liked telling people he went to the boxing gym. Larry, the middleweight, came in, probably high, and started right in on the speed bag. He did three or four rounds there and then left.

Tashaun, the 200 pounder, came in and wrapped his hands. I was on the heavy bag and checking him out at the same time. He shadow-boxed and I caught him glancing over at me once in awhile, but he pretended not to. Unconscious and semiconscious stuff is going on constantly in a gym, especially when someone comes in who's a potential sparring partner. Eyes dart around, evaluations are silently made, weaknesses are explored, and a mental game no one ever admits to begins from the moment a fighter crosses the threshold. No one talks about it, no one wants to get caught doing it, and no one ever, ever admits to it. When the coach suggests two guys work in the gym both guys will act like they didn't even know the other guy was there and they'll shrug like the sparring partner is an inanimate object.

Smitty came out of his office, looked at me again. I knew he was evaluating me and he knew I knew, but neither of us spoke. It was my first day back in this gym and he probably didn't know anything about Ravenwood, so it was about the time he would let a guy get back in the ring. That is, if he felt the guy was okay.

"Tashaun and Duff. You want to work?" I'd been waiting for the call.

Both Tay and I gave muted affirmative shrugs and got our gear on. Smitty helped each of us with the gloves, and he took a long look into my eyes without saying anything. I held his look for a while before it creeped me out a bit. I turned away and started to dance a bit in effort to look like I was loosening up, but it was mostly to break his stare.

The bell rang. Smitty stood on the ring apron, which was a bit unusual for him. He called out instructions to both of us at different times. Sometimes he'd bark one word 'guard', which meant get your hands up. Other times, 'recoil', which meant bring your hands back after throwing. 'Work and get out' when we tied up and 'Hook off that jab' were his standards.

Tashaun was a pro, with six fights and a four and two record. He had won the state amateur championship, but he got sloppy with his training habits and had kind of under performed. He caught me with a hook that landed a bit high on my headgear. I felt it, and it had some steam on it, but it didn't land flush and it didn't do any damage.

Honestly, I felt a little relieved to take one and not have it do anything weird to my head. I feinted Tay to the body, jabbed to the head, and caught him with the cross that followed it. My timing felt good. The bell rang. Mostly uneventful give and take sparring round, but it left me loose and a little excited.

The second went the same, and Tay tired. I feinted, coming in with a stutter step, and he went slightly back on his heels. I caught him with a combination. A nice move and it showed the differences in our experience. The whole thing probably occurred in less than two seconds, but it had about five components to it. I maneuvered Tay into the center of the ring; I jabbed, I stutter stepped like I was going to jab again, then I stepped in with three punches. It wasn't an accident; it was the game within a game that goes on all the time in boxing.

Tay landed a thudding right and I partially blocked it, but part of it caught me in the face straight on. I felt the throb, but it wasn't bad and something I probably wouldn't even have noticed if I wasn't looking for it. That round ended and the next one went pretty much the same, only with less action. The rule of thumb in the boxing jungle is in a sparring session like this one where there's no important fight coming up, you don't take it to your partner when they're tired. You can step it up a bit and give enough action so the guy knows he needs to work on his stamina, but you don't punish him with it. Again, not said, probably not even in some guys' consciousness, but it's one of those rules of the gym.

"Time" Smitty called. "All right boys, that's enough. Tay you probably ought to get in here more often and get out on the road if you want to fight." Tay breathed heavy and he nodded knowingly without saying much. He knew he was a little out of shape.

"Not bad, Duff," Smitty looked at me. "Still, not turning over the hook," a criticism Smitty had said to me every time I sparred here for a decade and a half. "How'd you feel tonight?" Smitty's way of checking in about my head.

"Good... Good, Smit." I still breathed heavy. "I wanted to get off with the jab more, but Tay's movement kept me from it." That was the answer that my head felt fine. Smitty held his eyes on me a little longer, evaluating me. After a second, he nodded and helped us both off with our gloves. He headed over to Angel with the mitts and I headed to the medical center to give Karl a lift home.

17

I felt satisfied with how things went, more tired than I usually am after three rounds of work, and my head throbbed a bit, but it wasn't a big deal. It was well worth the feeling I had from getting in the ring. It's hard to explain to someone who has never done it. It feels like a cleansing–like you just did something important. I'm sure it has something to do with exertion, which you get from all exercise. It also probably has something to do with the relief you feel from not getting hurt and having it over. Although those two together don't add up to the entirety of it. I think it has something to do with facing your demons. Facing what scares you the most and keeping on even when you don't have to. I know a very small percentage of the population is willing to do what we fighters do in the ring. To me anyway, that gives a person some rank. It's not the only way an individual gets rank, but it sure is one way. People who face what they're afraid of, I believe, are people of the strongest character.

Speaking of characters, it was headed toward seven o'clock and time to give Karl a ride. I swung by the hospital and wound the El Dorado through the serpentine path to the parking garage. Parking garages weren't made for Cadillacs built in the middle of the seventies, so negotiating some of the turns wasn't much of a party. I got the $6.00 ticket for the privilege of picking up my friend recovering from an assault, and felt like another assault had just taken place, though this one was to my bank account.

Inside the medical center I followed the arrows around to the area known as 'Discharges.' In the room were about twenty people, most in wheelchairs, and most with one or two family members. Most of the non-patients had kind of a relieved look on their faces as their loved ones were deemed well enough to go home. Karl got wheeled into a corner by himself. He didn't look relieved at all. He nervously twitched and looked around like something bad was about to happen.

"Hey, Karl, how are you? Must be good to be going home."

"Duffy, what are you doing here?" He looked up at me.

"I came to give you a lift."

"Why?"

"I don't know. I heard you were being discharged and I figured you could use a ride."

"They just called the Mission."

"Huh? The Mission? I thought you had your own place?"

"Nope."

"But I had an address for you in the Westview Apartments."

"That was a lie."

"You didn't want to admit to being in the mission?"

"Yeah, but not because I was embarrassed like you think. I'm too vulnerable in there."

"The Mission can be a bit of nightmare, but you got benefits. Why not let DSS get you an apartment?"

"Sure, get me on another government tracking system. That's just what they'd want."

"So are you going to the Mission?"

"To get out of here and then I'll go out for a walk and split."

"And wind up in the park and get your ass kicked again?"

"It's not the park that's getting my ass kicked. It's what I know." He looked out the window and then around the room. "Shit, they could be right here. I'm such a fool!"

Karl dropped his head into his hands and started crying.

109

He cried so hard he shook. It was pathetic.

"You want to stay with me and Al?" I heard come out of my mouth.

Karl sniffled away some tears and looked up at me with a squint.

"What?"

"Stay at my place. It's not the Trump Tower, it's a trailer, but if you can stand basset hound flatulence, it ain't half bad."

Karl looked down, back up at me, and then down again.

"Why do you want me at your place?" He said it without the paranoid tone. It was more of a tone of disbelief.

"I don't know. You wanna come or not?"

He snickered and smiled on one side of his face. He wiped his eyes with the back of his hand.

"The dog lives right inside with you?"

"Yeah."

"I'm in," Karl said.

I had ño idea what had gotten in to me.

Karl signed a bunch of papers and I signed some more. I'm sure I had just released me and my heirs from every possible right under the sun and agreed to reimburse everyone in North America for all their expenses for the next fifty years. I had gotten over worrying about such things.

I wheeled Karl out to the curb and told him I'd pull the car around for him. He didn't object, mentioned something about still being a little weak in the legs. The problem was working my way around the labyrinth of a parking lot and finding where I had been. I walked up to the second level and couldn't find the El Dorado. Although I swore I'd parked it on the second level, the place was confusing enough that I thought I just might've been on the third level.

I headed to the stairwell and saw a soda machine. I went to get a Diet Pepsi, but there was some sort of Army guy standing in front of the thing, apparently unable to decide between a Pepsi and a Mountain Dew. I guess after a few years of leaving the thinking up to someone else that sort of thing can happen.

I got to the third level of the garage. It didn't look familiar at all though that didn't really surprise me much, because I didn't pay attention to anything when I parked except for what level I was on. Two more guys in Army get-ups passed me. I figured somebody in the reserves must've got hurt doing weekend maneuvers or whatever it is they do.

I walked around level three for a few minutes and decided that wasn't right. So I headed back down the stairs. The three Army guys were gathered around the soda machine talking, but they got quiet when I came down the stairs. Now all three of them stared at the soda machine, which seemed a bit odd.

"Hey fellas, there's no chance you guys saw an old orange El Dorado on any of these levels?" One of the guys grunted and none of them looked at me. I stood there kind of waiting for an answer. Finally, I just turned and went through the doorway to the second level.

As I stepped out of the door's threshold, a car came screaming around the tight turn of the garage, coming so close to me I had to jump back. As I jumped back I felt a sharp whack to the back of my head, like I banged my head against something. Everything went a little wobbly and when I turned, things were a bit murky. The pain was sharp and a weird wobbly feeling came over me. I looked up. The three guys in fatigues stood in front of me. The one in the middle, the biggest guy of the three, threw a punch right square into the side of my head.

I went down and everything went black.

18

"I think he's coming around," a soupy voice said.

"Duffy–Duffy. He's blinking like he hears me," I recognized Trina's voice.

"Easy, kid, easy." That was Rudy.

I wasn't in a ring. I was in a hospital bed and my head really fuckin' hurt. I had one of those rubber ID bracelets on that said 'D. Dombrowski', with a long number next to it. There was tape on the back of my head and I wore one of those silly dresses they give you when you're in the hospital. I had taken a shot to the head, but the last I remember, I was working with Tayshaun and he wasn't in any kind of shape.

"Phew…kid you had us scared," Rudy said.

I looked at him and thought about speaking, but I still felt detached.

"Don't worry kid, they got you on some shit to make you comfortable. It's why you feel weird," Rudy said.

Trina was crying. She still looked good, but she was crying.

"It's all my fault for getting him involved." A voice came from somewhere behind Rudy, but lower. Rudy half-turned around. There was Karl in his Redskins helmet still sitting in a wheelchair.

"Did they get you?" came out of my mouth. It came out slushy.

"Not this time, my friend. They got you instead. From the way it looks, I don't think they counted on you waking up at all."

"That's enough, Karl," Rudy said.

A male nurse, or at least an official looking male who wasn't a doctor, came in and asked everyone to leave except Rudy. Trina kissed me, sniffled, and scurried away.

"I ain't got nowhere to go. I'm staying," Karl said.

"Is he family?" the male nurse guy said.

I looked quickly at Karl, who had a panicked expression on his face.

"Yeah, he can stay," I said.

I heard someone else crying, and looked toward the doorway to my room. It was Rene.

"I'm okay. I'm okay...take it easy," I said and smiled. My head really, really hurt.

She just stared at me and got really pale. The room got uncomfortably quiet.

Rene looked me up and down and then looked at Rudy and Karl.

"Can I be alone with Duffy for a minute?" she said without expression. Rudy nodded and he and Karl walked out.

"I'm okay, I'm okay. It's not–"

"Duff, the timing of this sucks but I have to tell you something. I can't live like this. I won't." She sniffled.

I just looked at her.

"I'm moving on. I can't marry you. I just can't."

I tried to say something, but nothing came out.

"I'm sorry I had to say it to you like this, but I'm moving. I have to go in the morning. I'm sorry." She stopped crying. She wasn't looking at me, but she wasn't crying either.

"Good bye, Duff," She said and left. Just like that.

Rudy came back into the room.

"What was that all about?"

I just shook my head. I was having problems thinking. Things didn't quite feel real.

"Look, Kid, I have to talk to you a bit," Rudy said. He touched my arm and my focus sort of returned.

"Yeah, go ahead."

"You got a concussion and it's nothing to fool around with this time."

"Yeah, yeah..."

Rudy looked down for a full a few seconds.

"That's not all Duff, they found damage."

"What do you mean 'damage'?"

"There were at least two other recent traumas to the head. There's a chance you might be in some trouble. Head injuries are nothing to mess with."

"Trouble?"

"In addition to headaches you might have problems with memory, short term and long term. There could be depression, post traumatic stress, your behavior could become unpredictable...but now as I think of it, I'm not sure how that would be any different than it usually is."

"Those are all 'coulds'."

"They're likely," Rudy said. He was sweating.

"For how long?"

Rudy didn't say anything.

"C'mon, Rudy—how long?"

"It might not even happen..."

"Or..."

"It might be chronic..."

"Chronic—plain language, Rudy!"

"You might be fucked up forever," Rudy said.

19

They let me out of the hospital the next morning with a pretty good headache and even better broken heart. The other thing that ached pretty good was the fact I got whacked over the head by a couple of G.I. Joe types and I had no idea why. I started to give Rudy's scary message about being forever fucked up some credence because I started to think everything had to do with Karl, just like he said it did. That, in itself, scared me. I began to fear I wasn't too far away from getting my own Redskins helmet. Of course, if I was as screwy as Karl, I would've been wearing one and when the guys whacked me on the head it wouldn't have harmed me. Karl was crazy, but just because you're paranoid doesn't mean people aren't out to get you.

My new roommate, Karl, and I got to the Moody Blue. He got to see firsthand what it's like getting assaulted by an 85-pound basset hound. When we opened the door, Al went double nuts at the prospect of his company increasing by 100%.

He jumped at me and pushed me back and then went after Karl.

Karl dove on the floor on his back and lay perfectly still. Al went over and began to sniff Karl's crotch and ass. Karl just stared at the ceiling.

"Karl, buddy, what the hell are you doing?" Al's nose did double duty over my new roommate's privates.

"Two things, Duff." Karl kept his eyes focused straight up at the ceiling while he spoke. "First I got into a submissive position to let him know I wasn't threatening his territory and

115

I just wanted to offer my genitals so he could get to know me."

"Excuse me?" Before I could get an explanation, Karl was up on all fours sticking his nose dangerously close to Al's ass.

"Now, he's returning the favor and offering me his scent."

"Trust me, he's very generous with his scent."

Karl made exaggerated sniffing sounds around Al's business end. Al maintained a very concentrated and stoic look. Then, he turned and rolled over on his back. Karl sniffed him from head to toe.

This had become an olfactory runaway train and nothing I could do to stop it.

"This is his way of saying we can be friends," Karl said.

"I guess I'm more of a 'Hey, go fetch my slippers' kind of guy."

"Typical species-centric attitude. Like all creatures are here to serve humans."

"Don't worry about Al's servitude. He's never gotten my slippers once, mostly because I don't own slippers. Trust me on this one–Al hasn't embraced the whole master-servant deal."

"You go brother–sticking it to the man!" Karl said. In my home for ten minutes, and already trying to lead an uprising.

I got a beer, cracked it open, and it dawned on me I was drinking a beer in front of one of my addicted clients. I thought about it some more and figured he was living in my house–it was up to him to live by rules. I could get fired for him living here, so drinking a beer in front of him wouldn't really add anything of consequence.

"Karl, this whole 'sticking it to the man' thing…do you ever let up on it? I mean is everything a matter of the world out to get you?" I sipped the Schlitz.

"Look, man, I appreciate you hooking me up in your crib, but it doesn't necessarily mean I'm opening up everything in my life to you. Suffice to say, I've got enough evidence of the man fuckin' with me and everyone else."

"But what about all this prediction stuff? I mean you say these general things and then shit happens. You got information no one else has?"

"Maybe I do and maybe I don't. When you've been through what I've been through, more of it becomes transparent. Then, you can't help but see it."

"Someday can you maybe fill me in?"

"I don't know, Duff." Karl turned away and stared at the wall. Al slurped the whole left side of his face. Karl focused his attention on Al and away from his history with the man.

"Hey Karl, these guys who jacked me in the back of the head–that has something to do with all this right?"

"Did they take any money from you? Do you owe some servicemen money? Did you screw some Army guy's wife?"

"No."

"Then what do you think it was all about?"

"…and you're not going to tell me the details…"

"If I did it wouldn't make us any safer."

Then, things got a little odd.

First my vision blurred a little like I wasn't there, but there at the same time. I got a clammy cold feeling and felt a little sick to my stomach. At the same time my heart started to race and it became hard to breathe. My field of vision locked on Karl playing with Al, but something came over me. I felt like something awful could happen, but I had no idea what. It felt real, but I knew it wasn't. My body overrode any logic and it knew something bad was going to happen. My chest hurt and I couldn't catch up with my breathing. I felt cold, but I felt sweat on my forehead and running down my face. I could taste something bad at the back of my throat.

"Duffy!" I felt a hand on my forehead. "Stop. It's me.

117

Karl. You're all right. It's just a flashback."

I felt something help me sit down on the couch and I felt my breathing rev up again.

"Duffy, focus in on your breathing and nothing else. Don't fight the thoughts or the emotions, let them do their thing. Just breathe."

"What the fuck is happening?"

"Don't fight it. It's a flashback."

"What the fuck?"

"Breathe it out."

I listened to Karl. With nothing better to do, I breathed. The feeling of out-of-controlness got a little better. I stopped hyperventilating and my vision began to clear. Karl sat next to me, holding my hand, and Al was staring at me.

"Welcome back."

"What was that?"

"That's one of the hallmarks of PTSD. You just had a flashback. It's kind of a waking nightmare. Have you been getting nightmares?"

"On and off."

"Yeah, I thought so. These things really suck."

"I'll say."

<u>20</u>

It's weird, but after a few nightmares and now these fucking awake things, I didn't trust sleep. I felt dead tired and I hurt, but I didn't want to close my eyes and let the demons mess with me. Lack of sleep wasn't going to help my stress management, but I didn't know what else to do. Except drink more. I told my clients drinking didn't help, that it actually added more stress to the body, so when the effects faded off you got left with a body and a mind in worse shape than when it started. I still drank despite that knowledge. I got a good idea why the alcoholics I've been counseling for years ignored a lot of what I had to say.

Ironically, all the times I've gone out on bogus disability leave had come back to haunt me. The fact is, I couldn't afford to take any sick time off. There was some quirk in the disability law that allowed employers to fire employees if they've reached a certain amount of days away from the job for whatever reason. Over the years I've cooked up fake diagnoses, so I could train or spar. Fibromyalgia, irritable bowel syndrome, post traumatic stress and some others all did the trick. The key was to get a doc to write you a condition really hard to prove with objective symptoms. I knew it was bullshit, and I'm sure Claudia knew it was bullshit, but there was really nothing she could do.

Now, I could use some genuine disability time and I didn't have any, so I had to show up at the clinic. Disability law was something I didn't quite understand. I knew Claudia did, so I knew I had to get to work.

"Duffy, what the hell are you doing here? You should be

home and in bed," Trina said when I walked through the door.

"Good morning to you too."

"I'm serious. You're in no condition to be here."

"I got to. Otherwise the Michelin woman will have cause."

"No way."

"Yeah, she's let me know I've run out of disabilities."

"Oh my God. Be careful."

"Yeah."

She looked at me in the way that told me she was assessing me. She also had a way of looking at me that set off a little bit of a spark. I had headed toward the cubicle when she called for me.

"Duff, I heard about Rene." She bit her lip and scrunched her forehead. "I don't know what to say except that I'm sorry."

"I'm not sure what to say either." I felt my chest tighten, and just wanted to get to my desk. "Thanks though, Trina."

She stood and looked at me while I walked away.

On my desk sat a package from the Veterans Administration. There was also a note from Claudia to come see her as soon as I got in. I'm sure she wanted to give me a hug and express her concern for my well being. Whatever it was, it was going to have to wait because I was dying to read about my buddy Karl, and his military experience.

I wanted to know Karl's back story and maybe get a better handle on the helmet, rubber gloves, and his hate for the New World Order. The package came with a form letter about confidentiality and the general phone number to call for veteran medical records.

The first page of the file contained a discharge summary, which is kind of an executive summary of everything in the chart. It's kind of like CliffsNotes for the lazy counselor.

This is how it read:

DISCHARGE SUMMARY
VETERANS ADMINISTRATION HOSPITAL
ALBANY, NEW YORK

Karl Greene
Date of Evaluation: 1/8/08
Case No.: 1667-9289-11A
Date of Report: 1/10/08
Unit 7
Admission Date: 1/2/08

PURPOSE OF EVALUATION

This is the first psychiatric admission for this 28-year-old, single, white male, who was referred through the office of Veteran Affairs following what was described by his commanding officer as 'Behavior consistent with PTSD'. Greene, a sergeant in the US Army Special Forces division was admitted to the VA following a brief stabilization admission in Germany.

Sergeant Greene was receiving psychiatric services at this hospital until 1/7/08 when he assaulted a mental health worker, breaking the worker's nose, and causing facial bruises and lacerations. Greene refused to attend group therapy and objected when the mental health worker grabbed his elbow to escort him. Staff report that Greene claimed the mental health therapy aid was part of conspiratorial activities against him. Greene rendered the mental health worker unconscious with a martial arts style blow. It should be noted Greene did express remorse at assaulting the mental health worker and did seek out assistance in reviving the unconscious worker.

121

BACKGROUND INFORMATION

Sergeant Greene had been an active-duty sergeant in Special Forces for the last four years. He enlisted during the Iraq conflict, verbalizing he wanted to be part of the nation's war against terror. Greene was cleared of any mental illness history and did not show any symptomatology consistent with mental illness at the time of enlistment until a series of trauma-related events occurred within battle.

The event that appears to have precipitated his current admission involved a raid on a suspected insurgent headquarters within the city of Baghdad. On December 25, 2007, Greene and 3 members of his team entered the house believed to hold the insurgent leaders. Sergeant Greene was the first soldier through the door. He immediately took on fire from two of the insurgents. Greene was not wounded and was able to neutralize his attackers with gunfire.

As Greene and the three members of his team proceeded through the house, they were surprised by another Iraqi who emerged from a closet. Two of Greene's team members were shot, one fatally, before Greene fired upon the assailant. As Greene continued to fire on the Iraqi, he heard the shrieking of several children. When Greene stopped firing and looked into the closet where the Iraqi had emerged he found two young children, a brother and a sister, ages 5 and 3, dead from his gunfire.

Sergeant Greene had been cleared of any wrong doing in this situation, but the next morning following the incident he was found wandering outside the camp with his firearm. His fellow soldiers were concerned about his behavior and were concerned he might be suicidal. His commanding officer requested psychological services and Sergeant Greene was immediately sent to Germany for observation.

MENTAL STATUS EXAM

Sergeant Greene presents as an angry, distrustful individual who did not appear willing to open up, though he wanted to be compliant within the rules of the military. He reported he wasn't sleeping well but '...he never really did...' When asked if the circumstances that got him referred to psychiatric help bothered him he responded '...wouldn't you be bothered by something like that?'

Initially, Greene appeared oriented to time and place, but while in psychiatric care his stability deteriorated. It may be the case that this is related to his post traumatic condition and as time went by the events of the incident exacerbated Greene's condition as he repeatedly found it difficult to rationalize the events in regard to battle circumstances.

Several medications were tried in an effort to stabilize Greene, but they did not appear to be effective. It may be the case that his state worsened after medication, though it is impossible to discern if that is a cause and effect related to the medication or just the natural progression of his deteriorating state.

SUMMARY AND RECOMMENDATIONS

Sergeant Greene came to the military with no history of mental illness. At the time of this summary he shows symptoms consistent with Post Traumatic Stress Syndrome. It is quite possible he also has developed schizophrenia with paranoia and some of his behavior suggests substance abuse. It is recommended that Sergeant Greene receive ongoing care for mental illness and substance abuse and that he remain on a regimen of medication to control his reaction to stress.

Theodore Martin, MD
Staff Psychiatrist

Simply put, at least as best as I could understand it, Karl lost it after he accidentally killed a couple of Iraqi kids. If you were going to lose it over something, that would certainly do it. That made some sense, but it didn't really explain the Redskins gear, the rubber gloves, and his theory on the massive plot to fatten all of us with partially hydrogenated oil. On second thought, maybe living with killing a couple of innocent kids did explain that.

I flipped through the rest of the chart, which consisted of his medical history, a section on military mumbo jumbo and the day-to-day case notes. I skipped to the case notes to see if Karl was confronting everyone at the VA who used non-dairy creamer.

Karl was in the funny farm unit for over four weeks, so there should be at least a page a day of notes. Hopefully the VA counselors were a little more diligent of their paper work than yours truly and I'd be able to tell what Karl's stay was like.

I flipped through the daily progress notes and noticed something wasn't right. The section was too small. The first few days were documented thoroughly then one note went on to a second page and stopped abruptly. Then a brand new page started with two weeks of abbreviated notes. It looked like someone ripped out the original documentation and replaced them with new notes. They did a shitty job because it would've been pretty obvious to anyone who had ever written in a chart. It was even obvious to a counselor who hated paperwork.

I was about to get a second opinion from Monique when

a shadow blocked the ceiling fluorescent light hanging over me.

"Duffy I left you a note to come see me as soon as you got in," Claudia said.

"I was just coming in."

I followed Claudia to her office.

I'd been down this road before and it wasn't a good road to go down. Getting in trouble at work was something I had gotten used to. Watching The Michelin Woman gloat as she read me her riot act wasn't.

"This is a warning of pending termination," Claudia said glaring at me.

"C'mon Claudia the charts have been worse," I said.

"Oh, I know. That's why this isn't a termination…yet." She half smiled. "It has come to my attention that you have violated a client's confidentiality."

I couldn't imagine how she heard about Karl. The Michelin Woman was a nosy bastard and she would've had her ways, but I decided to keep my mouth shut.

"I received a call from Paula Bentley, the ex-partner of your client, Mr. Spain. She says you came to her place of work to advocate that she allow her ex to have visitation with their daughter."

"I didn't go to her place of employment. I went to pick up that computer and I bumped into her."

"It doesn't matter. It is grossly inappropriate."

"Even so, that's the first time I've ever been caught–I mean–ever done something like that. I've never been warned. You can't fire me for that."

"No, but if you're charts aren't up to date I can combine these two offenses and have just cause to fire you."

"That's a bullshit technicality and you know it."

She smiled and closed her eyes.

"Please watch your language in my office."

Under my breath I muttered "Fat fuckin' bitch."

"Did you say something?"

"No."

From there, she outlined her plans to can me. She would further investigate my breach of confidentiality and then review my charts. If she was able to confirm that in both cases I was negligent and inappropriate I'd be out on my ass. I've been close to getting canned before, but on those occasions there were always ways out.

I wasn't so sure this time.

21

I finished the day by taking a look through my files. I was in deep shit. Claudia had said she'd review the files and investigate my breach in a matter of days. I didn't see any way possible of somehow tying up both ends and saving my ass. I knew this day would come. I just didn't know it would come this week.

My friend, the throb, joined me and Elvis for the ride home. Elvis did *Are You Lonesome Tonight* and he stuttered through the soliloquy in the middle of the song. The way my head felt I could understand the trouble the king had. My stomach did that car-sick feeling, which I knew wasn't related to being in the car. It had more to do with getting hit on the noggin.

I pulled up to the Moody Blue, headed toward the door, and immediately got the sense something was wrong. I couldn't put my finger on it and wondered if my new emotional state was playing tricks on me. The one Rudy told me would involve weird unpredictable mood swings. I realized it was much simpler.

There was no barking. Every night Al would start going nuts as soon as he heard the El Dorado pull up. Tonight, silence.

I ran up the steps and bolted through the door, fearing the worst.

My fears quadrupled when I rattled the knob and still got no reaction from Al. I opened the door and saw what had happened.

Karl sat naked in the center of the floor across from Al.

Al had no collar on so I guess, technically, he was also naked. In between them a candle burned. Karl sat cross-legged staring at it. Al wasn't staring at it, he had his eyes closed, and he snored.

"What the fuck?"

"Please, we are centering," Karl said without moving.

Having a naked man, in front of you in the middle of your living room, next to your dog, is a bit disconcerting.

"Join us in centering if you like."

I shook my head and decided to center myself in my tried and true way, and got a Schlitz. I sat on my couch in front of the circle of the bizarre, pondering if it would be okay to turn on my television.

"KUBALA! KUBALA! KUBALA!"

Al opened his eyes and furrowed his brow.

"GONDOFI! OH! GONDOFI! OH!"

I chugged the Schlitz and got another.

"OH! OH! OH!"

Karl slapped the floor three times. Al sat up.

Karl looked at me with a big smile.

"Hello, Duffy. Al and I were centering." He had a peaceful grin on his face, which for some strange reason intensified his nakedness.

"Karl, could you throw on a pair of cargo pants and a T-shirt?"

"I am comfortable in my nakedness."

"That makes one of us."

Al went to the window to check the sparrows. Apparently, even with his centering, Al remained suspicious of his enemies. I wasn't nearly as centered as my roommates. Drinking Schlitz twice as fast as usual wasn't speeding my own centeredness. To be honest I was still a bit uneasy about the last panic attack/nightmare. I thought if I stacked my consciousness deck with a few extra Schlitz I might just skip the nocturnal special features I'd been getting.

I flipped on the TV to MSNBC to watch the evening news. Their lead story talked about the price of oil going up. Karl came back in the room and I was grateful to see he'd thrown on some sweat pants and was pulling a T-shirt on over his head. His shirt said, 'If you're not furious you're not paying attention'. I guess I wasn't paying close enough attention.

"Oil's going up again. Well, they're at it again," Karl shook his head.

"Karl, what does that mean?"

"Ha–"

"Don't give me that 'Ha' bullshit. What does it mean?"

"What are you getting all ticked off about Duffy?"

"You keep muttering about shit and then you make some sort of half assed prediction that gets sort of fulfilled. Then you act like Nostre-fucking-damus."

"The truth hurts."

"No. Fucking bullshit hurts!" My head started to throb. I noticed my breathing had accelerated.

"You're having a reaction right now Duffy. Slow your breathing."

"I'm not having a fucking reac–" My chest got really tight and my head felt like a screwdriver went through it. Al came running around the corner and sat in front of me.

"Rub Al's ears."

"What?" Everything felt tight. The stupidity of Karl's comment jarred me.

"Rub his ears and don't think of anything else."

I did. I don't know why. The pain in my chest remained, the weird feeling, like someone hit the fast forward button on my thoughts was there, and I felt like I imagined asthmatics felt. I don't know anything about this shit, but I knew I hated it.

Karl continued to speak softly, in a monotone.

"Feel the softness of the texture. Sense how it relaxes

129

him. Feel the ears. Feel the ears."

I did and I kept doing it. It got better than focusing on my chest caving in on me. I kept doing it. Al lifted a paw and rested it on my leg. He sort of purred.

Little by little my breathing eased. I sweated and I felt, all of a sudden, exhausted. My vision widened and I felt like I just had done wind sprints up a hill. My chest pounded, but slowed. I had no idea if 20 seconds had just passed or a couple of hours. I had no idea what these fucking things were, or what brought them on, but I began to understand how people who got them never left their house or got out of bed.

I started crying uncontrollably.

"What the fuck is happening to me?"

"Now you know why I take drugs. I think you clinical types call them panic attacks."

"It didn't feel like anything fucking clinical to me."

"It never does when it's happening to you."

I sat up and watched the TV. I didn't want to talk. I didn't want to think. I drank the rest of the Schlitz. The three of us sat in silence while MSNBC went on about oil prices, Afghanistan, and the Middle East. I was barely focusing when, after about twenty minutes, Karl couldn't restrain himself from commenting.

"The average idiot who thinks they know about these things likes to say 'It's all about oil.' That isn't even the tip of the iceberg, man." He shook his head.

"When did you start seeing everything as a conspiracy? I mean, damn."

"I see things that way because I've got a lot of experience getting conspired on."

"You know, Karl, I went out to your old high school. I didn't realize you were such a big man on campus back in the day."

"Yeah, before the world got in the way."

"Football star, class officer...Mr. BMOC. Have you kept

up with the classmates?"

"Nah, phony bastards. I've got no use for them."

"What about Newstrom? Wasn't he in the Corps with you?"

"Was, then he went private. He was part of it."

"Part of it. What are you talking about?"

"The shit went down. I found he planned on going private the whole time."

"What do you mean private?"

"He's a mercenary, except now they call them 'private security'. Shit, we got more private troops in Iraq then we do U.S. military. They make three times the pay and have no rules or discipline."

"And he had something to do with screwing you over?"

Karl looked at me and nodded. He got quiet and I couldn't tell for sure if he was sad or really angry. I didn't want to put the guy through the anguish of his memories, but I also had a pretty good size knot on my head letting me know I was intimately a part of his mess.

"Karl, I read your VA file today. I can't imagine the shit you went through. It's easy to see how that could fuck a guy up."

Karl stayed quiet. I started to wonder if I should've said anything about his file.

"So you know about the kids."

"Yeah."

"You think that's why I'm nuts?"

"Well, no, but I can understand the impact–"

"Now you're talking like a social worker again."

Karl stood up.

"Look, shooting a couple of innocent kids fucked me up, no doubt, but what happened after that sealed it."

"What happened?"

"Nah, Duffy, no way, not yet. Don't get me wrong, I appreciate everything you've done for me, but to be honest,

131

I've been screwed before by people who did nice things. No, not yet."

I noticed Karl's hands trembled.

"Do you think whatever the shit is had something to do with the Army guys who got me at the medical center?"

"Without a doubt."

"And you're not going to tell me what this is about?"

Karl looked away and paced back and forth. He chewed away at the tip of his thumb. Al started to follow him as he paced, making the turns, albeit not as easily as his two-legged buddy.

"I found out about shit that would get a lot of people in trouble. It's important to certain people, very big deal people. I'm seen as a lunatic so no one ever takes what I say seriously. When people start taking me seriously…"

"What Karl?"

He didn't answer. He stopped pacing and turned his back to me. I could hear him starting to cry.

"Karl, goddamn it–what happens if people start taking you seriously?"

"They'll kill me."

22

My head ached both from being whacked and from listening to Karl's logic. I decided to administer my own pain medication and head to AJ's. Karl asked to come along. Before I could come up with an excuse why he shouldn't I said, "Sure."

Karl insisted Al come. He made the point I was being species discriminatory and it wasn't right. My head throbbed and it was about to get worse.

When the three of us came through AJ's front door, Rocco was making a point.

"I'm tellin' ya–he served shoulder to shoulder with Lee Marvin in the Marines," Rocco said.

"Captain Kangaroo, C'mon!" TC said.

"Well, he did have the rank of captain," Jerry Number One said.

"What about Mr. Cream Cheese. Was he in the Corps?" TC said.

"Who the hell is Mr. Cream Cheese?" Rocco said.

"The captain's best friend," TC said.

"Green Jeans," Jerry Number Two said.

"What are you gonna wear them with?" Jerry Number one said. "I mean other than on St Patrick's Day."

"That was Captain Kangaroo's best friend," Jerry Number Two.

"You sound like a commercial for Levis–'let your green jeans be your best friend'." TC said.

"I'm serious. Bob Keeshaw was a battle-honored Marine," Rocco said.

"What about Mr. Moose?" Jerry Number Two said.

"He was governor of Minnesota a long time ago," TC said.

"I thought he was a puppet," Jerry Number One said.

"They all are beholden to special interests," Jerry Number Two said.

"What the hell kind of special interests do Mooses have?" Rocco said.

"Moose," Jerry Number Two said.

"Yeah?" Rocco said.

"It's 'Moose' not 'Mooses'," Jerry Number Two said.

"It could be Meese, couldn't it?" Jerry Number One said.

"He was corrupt as hell," TC said.

Karl stood and watched as though he was at a tennis game.

"And they say I'm nuts..." Karl said.

I took my seat next to Kelley, who silently watched the Classic Sports Instant Classic of last week's Arena Football game. I lifted Al up to his stool, on my right, and Karl sat next to him.

"You always bring your clients out drinking?" Kelley said without turning around.

"Special circumstances," I mumbled.

Al stood up on the bar and walked down to say hello to Kelley. Kelley rubbed the top of his head, reached into his pocket, and slipped Al a snausage.

"Everybody, this is my friend Karl," I said during the first three-second lull in the discussion. The boys all shouted a hello.

AJ slid a Schlitz in front of me. Karl ordered one for himself.

"Cheeseburger for Shorty?" AJ said.

"Sure," I said

Al understood 'cheeseburger' and swagged his tail.

Karl got up to use the bathroom. When he closed the

134

door, Kelley turned to me.

"Is that really a good idea? I mean how hard did you get hit on the head?"

"He ain't got any place to go," I said. Kelley just shook his head.

AJ came out with Al's burger and slid it in front of him. He'd remembered the sardines this time, so Al didn't bark at him.

"Did you hear about lover boy over here?" AJ said, tilting his head toward Kelley. "Dating a forest ranger."

That was all AJ said. If it wasn't Kelley, there would've been a volley of lines about how she likes his wood or his stump or something equally inane.

People didn't kid with Kelley.

I looked at him and raised my eyebrows.

"She's with the state, as an environmental cop. I've been seeing her for a few months," he said.

"Good for you." I didn't bust his balls or say anything else.

I looked down the end of the bar and saw Karl and Rocco locked in deep conversation. I'm sure Rocco had wanted to know about the bandages and the scars. I could only imagine the direction that conversation took.

AJ slid a fresh Schlitz in front of me and I turned toward the TV. MSNBC showed a graphic about the defense budget and a shot of protesters outside the Pentagon. They held signs about blood money and corruption.

"Oh they won't like that," Karl said so everyone could hear. "Oh boy, the powers-that-be will get the ball rolling now."

"What the hell are you talking about?" Rocco said.

"Wait and see, my friend. Wait and see," Karl said.

"Wait and see what?" TC said.

"Let me see if I can remember. We're probably due for some sort of college campus tragedy," Karl said.

Everyone stared at Karl and then they looked at me.

I just shrugged.

"What the hell are you talking about Karl?" Rocco said.

"It's just that it's time for another *domestic terrorist* event, don't you think?" The sarcasm was thick.

"You say it like you think it's bullshit," Jerry Number One said.

"Depends how you define bullshit," Karl said.

"Hold it pal. You're saying someone knows this shit is gonna happen?" Rocco said. Rocco wasn't happy.

"Oh, someone knows. Someone definitely knows," Karl said

"Who knows?" TC said.

"Well, it ain't Mr. Moose," Karl said.

The brain trust was beginning not to enjoy Karl's company.

"Don't be a wise guy, pal." Rocco had pivoted in his seat. "What the hell are you trying to say?"

"I'm sayin' watch your coincidence. Or at least, acknowledge they're there, man. Open your eyes!"

Kelley tapped me on the shoulder and raised his eyebrows. He whispered, "Not sure I've ever seen the Foursome stomp a guy to death."

"Keep focusing on Captain Kangaroo and Mr. Cream Cheese and you'll never see anything else…"

This was getting bad. It was the first time I got to see the shit that got Karl's ass kicked, up close and personal. If he ran through this routine on a nightly basis it wasn't hard to see his assaults as part of a New World Order conspiracy. He was just getting his ass kicked for being an asshole and pissing everybody off.

"Duffy, this is some friend you got here," TC said.

"Yeah, some friend," Rocco said.

Now, Karl pissed me off. AJ's is my oasis, my last bastion of idiocy, where I go to get away from the rest of the world. If Karl fucked it up for me I'd kill him. Time to split.

I threw down the rest of a three-quarters-full Schlitz, woke up Al, and grabbed Karl by the elbow.

"Say good night to all of your new friends."

The guys offered muted 'good nights' saving their most enthusiastic ones for Al, who didn't annoy anyone, except for a hint of basset flatulence that always came post-AJ's grease burger.

"But I didn't finish my brew," Karl said.

"Oh, you're finished, Karl. Trust me, you're finished here tonight." He came along with Al and me, a bit hesitantly, but he came along.

Inside the El Dorado, I was all over him.

"Look, Karl." I could feel the anger in my voice. It made my head throb as I started the car and slipped it into drive. "Those guys are my friends and if you want to piss people off all over town that's one thing, but I don't need you ruining my nights!"

"Oh, I'm supposed to ignore the truth!"

"How about ignore being an asshole!" I heard myself yell a little too loudly. I heard Al shuffle in the back seat. We drove down Central Ave. heading toward the park.

"C'mon Duffy open your eyes. It's not hard to see what's been going on. They've been doing it for years."

"What the hell are you even talking about!" I yelled even louder.

"Open your eyes!"

"If you know shit is going to happen, then say what it is! Otherwise shut the fuck up!"

"You and your friends in denial can't handle the truth!" Karl yelled back at me.

"That's it!" I made a sharp turn to the side of the road and slammed on the brakes. I could feel Al slide into the back of my seat.

I reached over and grabbed Karl by the collar and pulled

him toward me.

"Tell me what's going on! My fuckin' head is throbbing because a bunch of G.I. Joes whacked it. Before I met you, I never knew a single soldier. Now, if I'm close enough to you to get knocked out, then I'm close enough to know what you know."

I got so angry my neck twitched and my head pulsed like there was some sort of pump inside it. I held Karl off the car seat, starring him in the eye. He looked terrified by my sudden anger and we stayed like that for a moment or so. It felt a lot longer.

Karl started to cry, first just a little, then he really broke down to sobs. He snorted and almost wailed and it got impossible to be angry with him. I let go of his shirt. He crawled into a fetal ball and pressed himself against the door like he wanted to disappear.

"Shit, I'm sorry man." It was pathetic to see a man breakdown like this. It hurt to know I caused it, at least was the cause for making him revisit the demons inside of him.

Al whimpered in the back seat.

Karl shivered now like he was freezing. He was all cried out, but he wasn't back in his right mind. Through his labored breathing he said something. I thought I heard him say "Newsman."

"What's that Karl? Newsman? The media?"

"No, Newstrom." He struggled to annunciate.

"News storm? What the hell is that?"

Karl sat up. Without looking at me, he wiped his tears and snot with the back of his hand.

"Newstrom knows the whole story," Karl said.

"The guy from high school?"

"Yeah, you talked about him the other day."

"What about him?"

"We were best buddies and then he went over."

"Over?"

"We lived like Marines—you know—*Semper Fi* and all that bullshit. Always true, my ass." Karl started getting back to his right mind, such that it was.

"What are you talking about?"

"He sold out. He left the Corps and joined one of those private security outfits. Mercenaries are what they are. Five times a soldier's pay and none of the rules. The only problem is when there's no war, there's a lot less work." He wasn't looking at me; he looked straight ahead.

"What does it have to with all the conspiracy stuff?"

"Newstrom once told me the privates would always have work for us. That it wasn't just going to be Afghanistan or Iraq. That they were always going to have work for us."

"That's a long way from conspiracy shit, isn't it?"

"Newstrom became an expert of all sorts of weird Black Operations shit. He knew how to handle POWs; he knew how to get people to believe what he wanted them to believe and, well, he was something else, too."

"What?"

"He was the best at killing."

I took a big exhale. I tried to follow what Karl said and tried to stop my head from throbbing.

"Karl, I still don't get it."

"After I got fucked up, Newstrom came for me. He thought I would join up with his private security deal, an outfit called Blackgard. I didn't want anything to do with it. He thought it was because I thought the work wouldn't have been steady enough."

"Yeah?"

"Newstrom said one of the VPs told him something, with much more detail, about their plans for insuring they'd stay profitable."

"And?"

"Do I have to spell it out for you?"

"Karl, what the hell are you talking about?"

"Duffy what happens every time there's an instance of domestic terrorism, or for that matter, domestic tragedy?"

"I don't know. The news covers it to death, people mourn, and everyone talks about it until the next thing. That's all you have talked about since I've met you."

"Did you know earlier this week the Senate approved another 100 billion dollars in defense funding?"

"No."

"Exactly."

"You're saying somehow somebody or some group is engineering these things you're predicting for their own profit?"

"That's what I'm saying."

"You got any proof?"

Karl stopped and took a heavy breath. He looked out the window, down at his hands. He took another deep breath and then looked at me.

"Newstrom came to Germany to visit me. He had some documents he wasn't supposed to have and he showed them to me. It outlined all the shit that's been happening."

"The fire, the People's Church, the poison?"

"Yeah. It was all spelled out in detail. They had pages and pages for how the shit was going to be carried out, the strategy behind it, and how to identify the people who would do it"

"You mean this Blackgard is doing all this domestic terrorist shit?"

"They might as well be. They find people and groups who are whacked out and close to doing this kind of shit, and they get them going."

"What does that mean?"

"It's the Black Operations stuff. Newstrom can take a group and amp them up so they're ready to take it to the next level. The result…well, we've seen the results."

"And no one pins Newstrom or Blackgard."

"Yep."

"And Newstrom showed you this document? Did you get a copy?"

"No. That's why I can't give you specifics. Newstrom has to identify the groups to carry the shit out. I got a sense of what's coming, but I can't say exactly when or where."

I took a deep breath and tried to sort this shit out.

"Duffy, I wanted no part of it and backed out. The guys who run Blackgard caught Newstrom with the documents and confronted him. He told them I saw them. Newstrom signed on for life with them, so the secret's safe with him. They were pissed at him, but he was too valuable to lose."

"And you?"

"I was still being treated for PTSD. Right around that time the doctor, good 'ol Dr. Theodore Martin, put me on medication."

"I know that name from somewhere."

"He's the guy on TV breaking down traumatic events and their psychological impact–what a crock."

"What happened when you got on medication?"

"Since then I've been fucked up…crazy, scared, doing drugs, paranoid. Duffy…I was never nuts before. I mean the kid thing fucked me up, but I was sane. They did something to me after I knew about the plan."

"So you think the VA conspired with Newstrom?"

"Well probably not systemically. Newstrom has wide connections. He probably only had to make a call to a doctor, who started prescribing shit he knew would scramble my brain. The funny thing is the doctor who came on board to prescribe me the shit, is now the guy you see on TV talking about the emotional effects of terrorism after each of these events occur."

"The shrink commentator?"

"Yeah. Can you believe it?"

My head spun so fast and throbbed so hard I had no idea

141

what to believe. The pieces fit together a bit more, but Karl was still nuts–even by his own admission. He was a smart guy. I guess crazy and smart will add up to pretty good stories. I didn't know what to think.

I did have one question though. "So what happens next?"

"You remember Virginia Tech?" Karl said looking straight ahead.

"Yeah."

"You remember Columbine?"

"Yeah."

Karl took a deep breath. "You ain't seen nothing."

23

The blood kept coming and coming. I stood over the cop, watching him die. He was in and out of consciousness and when I tried to put my hand on the wound, my hand got lost in the blood. At first I thought my hand disappeared, but then I felt this horrible pull. I was being pulled through the cop's bloody wound, first my arm, then my shoulder. There was a horrible growl like the wound was alive, and it sucked me in. My head was covered and everything I saw was crimson. I couldn't breathe, because I was choking on the cop's wound from the inside out. It was swallowing me and choking me at the same time. I screamed, but nothing came out because I was smothered in blood. Suddenly, I felt wetness, different than the blood and a scratchiness, followed again by more wetness and then a loud piercing shout.

My eyes opened and I looked right into the dark eyes of whatever beast had grabbed me. It licked me again and I realized the beast was Al.

Another fucking nightmare. I was covered in sweat and breathing hard. I looked around. Slowly, the inside of the Moody Blue came into focus. I was home, I was okay, and little by little reality replaced the dream state.

"Welcome back," Karl said from the threshold of my bedroom.

"You could hear me?"

"Blood curdling screams are tough to miss."

"How long did I do it?" I sat up and wiped the sweat from my forehead.

"Half an hour with intensity, but on and off most of the

143

night."

"You were up all night?"

"I'm not big on sleep."

Al flopped off the bed and went over to Karl, who scratched underneath Al's chin. It made Al's rear leg spasm and he loved it.

"I'm sorry for getting a little rough with you last night. I'm a little fucked up lately," I said.

"No sweat. I had it coming."

I threw in Elvis's comeback 8-track to give my mind something other than the nightmare to think about. It was cued up to *Guitar Man*.

I grabbed a cup of coffee and tried to sing along. The words went too fast for me, especially when I was under-caffeinated. I couldn't get my lips around the phrase '...so I slept in the hobo jungle...' without blowing the line.

"I wondered what Elvis would've been like if they hadn't got to him," Karl said, half to himself.

Under-caffeinated or not I couldn't let this statement just hang out there.

"Karl, I don't take statements about Elvis lightly. You want to give me a run-down on the meaning of that last statement?" I sipped my coffee.

"It's pretty obvious isn't?"

"No, Karl, it isn't obvious at all." I got a tad annoyed.

"When Elvis started out, what kind of music did he do?" Karl used his Socratic tone of voice.

"Well they called it R & B or race music. Basically he did Black music."

"He wiggled."

"Right, he expressed himself sexually in a way only black performers did. He opened up the world to a different culture."

"Yeah, I guess you could say it like that." I wasn't sure where Karl was going.

144

"So now black kids and white kids sang and danced to the same stuff. Then what happened?"

"I don't know; he went into the Army, I guess."

"He got *drafted.* In a peacetime draft, the government takes the first guy to integrate the culture with popular music and put him away for two years."

"*Hmm*...I never thought of it in those terms."

"And if you're a student of Elvisology you know what happened to the King over in Germany, don't you?"

"I don't know–a lot of things happened to him..."

"Elvis gets introduced to amphetamines. The Army gave them out to guys who had guard duty at night. Elvis got introduced to drugs by the government," Karl raised his eyebrows.

"Yeah, but back then didn't everybody in the Army get uppers?"

"Not everyone, Duff. And what, Mr. Addictions counselor, do amphetamines do to you?"

"Keep you awake, give you energy, give you confidence, and–"

"Stop right there. What happened just before Elvis got sent to Germany?"

"His mother died."

"And Elvis's mom was everything to him, right?"

"Yeah."

"So is it such a stretch to know in advance Elvis would really, really like a drug that would make him feel confident during a part of his life filled with existential insecurity?" Karl's eyebrows went up again.

I didn't say anything. I just thought.

"Then he comes back and he does movies where, through his music, he embraces different cultures. The Mexicans. The Native Americans, the Polynesians."

"C'mon Karl even I thought the movies were silly."

"Of course, you did. They wanted you to. Elvis knew

they wanted him cleaned up and non-threatening, but he found ways to champion the little man's causes. But you had to be paying attention."

"You said something about 'they got him'."

"Even in the '70s Elvis brought different cultures together with his music. He sang the music of the Irish, the Italians, and still did R & B and traditional Southern Gospel. To the end, he brought the masses together."

"Why would it be threatening?"

"C'mon Duff. If everyone stops hating and starts singing and dancing together, then how will the powers-that-be turn us on one another? If the poor and disenfranchised culture gets celebrated, then a boundary is broken down. The powers need boundaries."

"But Karl—how did they *get* Elvis?"

"First of all, they got him hooked and knew they had something on him. They also knew he was under control, because with the drugs his expression got limited. And after he was used up and died, they covered his tracks by discrediting him."

"I don't follow."

"Duff, I'm sure you're tuned into the media and our culture. What do they say about Elvis? He got fat, drugged up, stupid, into weird sex—remember the Albert Goldman book? Today, kids think of Elvis the caricature, not the heroic culture-defining man from the poor integrated background."

"So you're saying they discredited Elvis because he brought people together?"

"He brought the wrong people together. How did the greatest entertainer of the last century become a caricature of himself?"

"Uh…"

"Because if the masses don't take Elvis seriously, then they don't watch and listen. They follow along. That's the way they like it." Karl raised his eyebrows as if to say 'you understand?'. I think I was starting to.

Maybe Karl wasn't crazy. Maybe I hadn't been paying close enough attention to what had been going on around me. Maybe things weren't as they appeared. If they could make Elvis out to be a nut and make him something to mock, what couldn't they do?

"Duffy, can I ask you something?"

"Sure."

"Are you crazy enough to want to do something about all this shit–I mean the shit Newstrom has in mind?"

Karl looked at me and his face lost all expression. He had stopped scratching Al and stood still.

"We should call the FBI or the police or something."

"They'll laugh," Karl said.

"Karl, if a bunch of innocent people are about to get murdered I think we have to do something. The hard part is you only seem to know things in general terms. The fact that something is going to happen somewhere doesn't really put us in a position to do anything."

Karl looked at the ground and shook his head. He was quiet for a long time.

"I can get the specifics. Would that make a difference?" He didn't look at me.

"Well, yeah, I guess it would."

Karl lifted his head and looked me straight in the eye.

"Duffy, since those kids died, I ain't been right, I know that. I also know I went from being a hero to being a crazy person everyone laughs at. They did that to me, they fucked me, and they're fucking with a lot of people."

"Karl–"

"If we're going after them, I'm going to want to finish it and know I've finished it. I don't want them getting away with anything and knowing they're getting away with it."

"I think I understand," I said.

"You want to do this?"

"Yeah, I think I do."

"And you're sure you're ready to hear what I can tell you?"

"Yeah, Karl I am. What I really want to know is how they are able to pull this shit off with other people."

"Some of its easy–I mean setting a fire isn't hard. What gets more tricky is when they have to manipulate people."

"Huh?"

"This guy Rukhaber. No doubt he was CIA or Secret Service or something. He probably fucked up and they got to him like they got to me–except he took to the programming."

"Programming? What the fuck are you talking about?"

"You said you saw my file right? How about all the drugs they had me on? And what happened to me after they started giving them to me?"

"You got worse."

"Exactly–I fought them. Maybe Rukhaber had a different reaction, maybe he gave in. Who knows, maybe he was nuts. The important point is they set it up for him to flourish, then they went in and blew him up."

This made my hair hurt. I couldn't tell if Karl was nuts or a genius, or whether I was the one who was getting nuttier.

"So you're talking about mind control?" I said.

"Yeah, but not like Star Trek stuff. The military is good at it and Newstrom was their very best. When they combine it with the right pharmacology they can be very, very good at it."

"How would they set up a Columbine-type thing?"

"Easy. Find the right group of disenfranchised kids, get them to take drugs–nothing hard to do there–give them the right suggestions and access to guns and sit back."

"Is that what happened at Columbine?"

"It could have. You got a better explanation?"

"Holy shit, Karl. Is this really possible?" I shook my head.

"Now you know why I don't tell everyone the details."

"Maybe Karl, I just don't know. If it is happening, how come no one is doing anything to stop it?"

"Anyone who believes it is considered crazy," Karl said.

"Yeah, I guess you're right," I said.

It became quiet between the two of us for a couple of moments.

"Duffy, you mind if I ask you something?"

"No, go ahead."

"You think I'm crazy and you're worried you might be getting crazy if you follow what I'm saying aren't you?"

"Maybe a little."

"You still want to get involved?"

"Yeah."

"Why in hell do you want to do this with me?"

I thought about it for a minute. I wasn't sure of the answer, but I had an idea.

Elvis sang *If I Can Dream*, a song about visualizing a better world where all types of people walk hand in hand. He reached the crescendo.

"A few reasons," I said.

"You want to share them with me?" Karl sat still and looked right at me.

I thought about it for a second before I said anything. I wasn't sure if I could get the words around what I felt, but I gave it a shot.

"I think it's something like this, Karl: One, I don't like people fucking with other people who can't defend themselves. Two, I don't like the fact somebody fucked with you."

I hesitated.

"Is there something else, Duff?" Karl said.

"I don't like the fact three guys suckered me in the back of the head."

<u>24</u>

I may have gotten hit in the head too many times, but I had never spent a lot of time following my head anyways. Still, deciding to listen and believe Karl Greene told the truth was something else. I wasn't so confident about my own sanity, and now I had teamed up with a guy who liked to wear a football helmet as his main sartorial statement.

Nuts or not, if we were going to foil world-changing terrorist events, I was going to make damn sure I did my homework. Despite how silly even thinking it sounded, I believed it. If you believe something hard enough it becomes true–at least to you.

It was time to talk to Kelley. He'd chew me out and tell me I was nuts, but he'd listen and tell me what he thought. We met during his lunch break at AJ's, which would mean me taking a long lunch at the clinic, but I figured I could call it a consultation with a community member. The Michelin Woman had her door closed, so I got out without reliving her version of the Spanish Inquisition.

Only Jerry Number Two was in AJ's at this early hour. He sat at the bar with his laptop, sipping a Cosmo.

"Hey Jerr, you look lonesome," I said.

"Nah, spending some quality online time with my D&D friends," Jerry said without taking his eyes off the screen.

"D&D?"

"Dungeons and Dragons. You know, role playing."

I didn't really ever get what that was all about, but when your main hobby is getting punched in the face repeatedly you don't spend a lot of time making fun of other people's pastimes.

AJ stacked boxes. He stopped to slide me a Schlitz, without saying anything by way of greeting.

Kelley came in on cue and in uniform. He got a Diet Coke and ordered a burger.

"I don't got a ton of time, Duff," he said. "How's your noggin'?"

"It's mostly all right."

"So what are we here about?"

"You're going to think I'm nuts."

"Too late. Let's hear it." He sipped his diet coke and ran his hand through his flattop.

"All right, you know Karl, my client from the clinic?"

"Yeah–he was in the other night."

"I told you how he's been making predictions about tragic events and terrorism."

"Yeah."

"It turns out its not just crazy paranoia stuff. He got a little fucked up in Iraq because he accidentally shot and killed a couple of little kids."

"That'll do it. What does that have to do with him being able to predict his or anybody else's future?"

"Well, his best buddy, a guy he enlisted with, finished out his tour and joined a private security force over there." I looked at Kelley to see if he listened and if he had any reaction. He listened, without reaction, so I kept on.

"When Karl got fucked up, he tried to convince Karl to come join the private security firm and he told him there would always be work. Somehow Karl asked a bunch of questions and his buddy said he was guaranteed a lot of work for years to come whether there were any wars or not."

"Duffy, is there a point to this?" Kelley took a bite out of his burger and frowned. AJ's burgers often did that to people.

"According to Karl, he saw documentation about a plan for events inside the United States that would keep people supporting the wars and the defense funding."

"A plan?"

"Yeah, a plan in which they would engineer and set up tragic terrorist-linked events."

"Who would?"

"This private security firm. They're called Blackgard."

"And you know this because the guy in the Redskins helmet said so."

"He wasn't always nuts; he knows what he's talking about," I said, just raising my voice a tad.

"Duff, this is Bigfoot stuff, it's Area 51, the Chupacabra. It's bullshit. Man, you really took a shot in the head."

"C'mon Kell, I'm not nuts–"

"Look Duff, you asked me, I told you. I think Karl's nuts and I think you're right behind him." He got up, wiped his mouth with the paper napkin, and left half a burger in front of him. "Sorry, but I got to get back to work." He put his hat on and headed out.

I felt ridiculous. AJ gave me another beer. I had started paying attention to ESPN when Jerry said something without looking up from his laptop.

"Northwoods," he said.

"What's that Jerr?"

"Northwoods, the name of a project the CIA proposed around the time of the Cuban missile crisis."

"And?"

"They proposed staging a fake invasion of the continental U.S. to make it look like the Cubans did it." Jerry finally looked away from the computer at me.

"Why would they do that?"

"So the American people would endorse the military bombing the shit out of Cuba."

"Why didn't they do it?"

"I don't know." Jerry looked away from me. "The point is they considered it."

152

"Jerry do you think it could happen–I mean, fun conspiracy stuff aside–is it really possible?"

Jerry took a hit off his Cosmo and smiled a little bit.

"In 70 B.C., a Roman named Crassus wanted to be in charge and take power from Spartacus. So he paid mercenaries to pose as Spartacus' troops and had them invade Rome. Spartacus showed up not knowing what the hell was going on, but before he could explain to anyone that they had been duped, Crassus had rallied the Roman troops and defeated the same mercenaries he, himself, hired." Jerry folded his hands in his lap and seemed very proud of his point.

"So you're saying he set up a situation where he could scare the citizens and then he could be a hero," I said.

"Exactly!"

"Don't take this the wrong way Jerr, but strategies from 70 B.C. really don't help my confidence level on this."

"Well, then, how about a nice Hitler story? Did you know Hitler had his soldiers dress in Polish uniforms and attack a radio station in Germany, no doubt to insure solid media coverage, and then used that attack as justification to invade Poland. From there you got the beginnings of World War II." Jerry raised his eyebrows and did the Groucho Marx thing.

I just stared at Jerry, not saying anything.

"Ahh…but young Duffy is thinking, not here, not in good 'ol God Bless America." Jerry smiled.

"Well…"

"Far be it for me to ruin a young man's view of his homeland…"

"Go ahead," I said.

"A hundred years ago, William Randolph Hearst wanted the U.S. to invade Cuba. He sent a team of photographers there to take shots of the Cuba-Spain war. Except it wasn't really going on. Hearst had the photographers stage the pics, so it looked like war was raging and published them in his newspapers so people would get riled up."

"*Hmm...*"

"Then the U.S.S. Maine, in Cuba as a show of force, blew up. The ship's own captain said it had nothing to do with any war; it just blew up because of a fire on the ship. That part never made it to the papers and the U.S. got drawn into the conflict because Spain blew up our ship. The only problem–they didn't." Jerry smiled.

My head started to hurt.

"Need something more modern? How about FDR and Japan? The US suffered in a terrible depression and FDR wanted to go to war with Hitler, but the people railed against it. When Japan signed on with Germany and Italy, FDR had what he wanted. He set up oil embargoes to Japan and placed the Navy in Hawaii to keep Japan from going to Indonesia. Without any oil, Japan had to make a move."

"Huh?"

"Never mind. FDR knew to get the people worked up sufficiently the attack from Japan had to look barbaric. The reports said the Japanese were silent and made no radio transmissions while they headed toward Pearl Harbor, but it turns out it wasn't true. Our Admirals weren't informed about the Japanese advances and got left there as sitting ducks. The *New York Times* published that the attack was known in advance in their December 8, 1941 edition–the very next day. People just chose to ignore it." Jerry grouchoed his brows again.

"Jerry–"

Jerry rolled on.

"In 'Nam we upped our involvement based on our ships getting torpedoed in the Gulf of Tonkin. The problem was our ships didn't get torpedoed. The sonar guy on the ship read his information wrong. LBJ knew that and still went on TV that night and dramatically presented what he knew was bullshit so his defense contractor buddies could get the war they wanted." Again Jerry Grouchoed.

"Uh…" I looked at my watch and knew I'd be in trouble at work.

"Need something even more modern?"

I couldn't stop him, so I just let him run with it.

"In the early nineties, the first Bush saw Iraq had started to glut the market with too much oil, which drops the price. Well, 'Ol Herbert Walker is an oil man and he didn't want to see that happen to him or his OPEC buddies. So we got involved in Kuwait."

"How did he do it?"

"He actually sent word to Hussein we would not intervene if he invaded Kuwait. He then hired a PR firm to set up scenarios for the U.S. people to swallow."

"Huh?"

"Try to keep up, Duff. Don't you remember the story and the vast coverage about the Iraqi troops storming the hospital and looting the incubators and killing all the little precious infants? They even had a Kuwaiti nurse in tears on camera." Jerry looked at me.

"Yeah, I remember. That was hideous," I said.

"Hideously effective. It never happened. The nurse was an actress, but the whole act played on the American psyche and we were ready to bomb the shit out of them. First, we all but invite him to invade Kuwait, then we set up a gut-wrenching PR stage act and presto! You got Desert Storm, which, by the way, didn't remove Saddam from power, but it did get the Iraqi oil off the market and did get the prices back up where George Herbert Walker and his OPEC friends wanted them," Jerry said with the biggest Groucho of all.

My hair hurt. I became a bit overwhelmed and a lot confused.

"I guess, in short, Duff, I'm saying you and your buddy might not be nuts. Or, at least, this conspiracy thing might not be why you're both nuts."

"Jerry, this is heavy shit. Karl says this guy he went to school with showed him a memo outlining a bunch of this Northwoods shit involving a private firm. Is it even possible?"

"It seems kind of weird some guy at soldier-level would be hip to what's going on, but these companies get so cocky it's possible they've gotten flip with their internal security. Or, maybe he's close with someone who is in the know and who leaked him info. That would seem more likely."

"Could you find out anything that might shed some light on this shit?"

"You never can tell. What's the name of the private security firm?"

"Blackgard."

"Hang on; let me see what comes up when I look them up." Jerry started hitting keys, making faces, nodding. He smiled.

"What's so funny?"

"Blackgard is in the top five of the website Compwatch.com."

"What's that?"

"It's a watchdog group about companies that benefit from defense contracting. They're huge. They do private security, which is pretty much mercenary stuff, but they also are into field food service, logistics, and ancillary healthcare."

"So there's no question they benefit from a big defense budget."

"Yeah, but Duff, you could say the same thing about three quarters of the Fortune 500."

"Are they big enough and powerful enough to even pull off what Karl is saying?"

Jerry typed a few things into his laptop, smiled, and spun it around so I could look at the screen.

"Jerry, what the hell am I looking at?" he showed me

some sort of financial statement and it made my eyes glaze over.

"The bottom line with all the zeroes."

"18.3 million dollars. That *is* a shitload of money."

"Duff, look a little closer."

"What? Oh shit. That's 18.3 *billion* dollars."

"The answer to your question is 'yes'. They can pretty much do anything they want to do."

"But Jerry...how? Is it all the shit that Karl is crazy about: mind control, drugs, post hypnotic suggestion? That's comic book stuff, isn't it? Is it even possible?"

"It's pretty common knowledge the military did experiments with LSD on soldiers without their knowledge to see what they could use it for. They didn't treat a bunch of black men with syphilis because they wanted to see how their bodies reacted to it, and thousands of guys who got exposed to Agent Orange are all fucked up and the VA says the stuff was harmless."

"So that would be a 'yes' it is possible,"

Jerry just raised his eyebrows and smiled.

<u>25</u>

Trina was watering my favorite plant when I came in the door. God, how I loved that plant.

"Where have you been?" Trina said.

"I had a lunch meeting with a community member."

"How is Kelley?"

"He's good. He's got a girlfriend, some sort of forester or nature cop, or something."

"Hard to picture him being lovey-dovey."

"Well, they can probably work police procedural stuff into their foreplay or something."

"Hand cuffs, up against the wall frisks, and whatnot—ooooh," Trina winked.

"*Hmmm…,*" was all I could think of saying. She held my look for a little while and then went back to her botany. I wasn't sure if she looked at me with pity because of Rene or was sending available signals now that I was out of the matrimonial game. Frankly, I wasn't confident about any of my thoughts.

My voice mail light flashed. When I checked it, it was a call from the Veterans Administration. Always a little on the anal-retentive side, I guessed they were calling to confirm the receipt of Karl's chart. I called the number the male voice left.

"Lieutenant Koniuto," the voiced said by way of telephone greeting.

"Yeah, this is Duffy Dombrowski returning your call. I'm a counselor at Jewish Unified Services."

"One moment please, Duffy." I heard through the phone the sound of him getting up, closing a door, and returning.

"Yes, Duffy, how are you?" He seemed a little too chipper for a military type.

"I'm good."

"Good, good, good. Look I'm calling just to check on Karl Greene's aftercare since he came to you guys."

"Well, Karl…hang on just a second and let me double check I have a release to talk with you."

"That's not necessary. I got one on this end."

"I still have to have one." Even though I didn't follow the rules, it didn't mean I didn't know them. I flipped through the chart to find the release. There wasn't one there. In fact, not surprisingly, Karl hadn't signed any releases.

"Sorry, Lieutenant, I can't talk to you."

"Sure you can, it's no biggie," he said, again a little too cheerfully.

"No, I really can't. I can call you back if–" He hung up.

Releases are routine stuff in human services. Everyone knows about them and knows the score. It shouldn't have been any surprise to this military guy.

I could hear Monique humming along with whatever was jamming on her iPod.

"Hey 'Nique," I said just loud enough for her to hear.

She didn't answer, but rolled her eyes up as if to say *what*, and pulled out an ear bud.

"Do you know this guy at the VA?" I showed her the 'While you were out' memo.

"Nope." She handed it back to me.

"He just called and asked about Karl and tried to convince me it was okay to talk without a release."

Monique pursed her lips and raised her eyebrows. She asked to see the note again.

"Duff, why would a Lieutenant, or for that matter, any conventional Army guy call on a social work matter? They have a civilian counseling crew there."

"Yeah, I didn't think of that."

159

Monique went through her Rolodex.

"What are you looking for?" Monique kept looking without answering. She pulled out a card and looked at it.

"What's up 'Nique?"

"This isn't a VA number."

"Huh?"

"In fact, I'm pretty sure it's a cell phone number."

"Maybe the guy used his cell."

"When was the last time a civil servant used their own dime to call anyone or for that matter, when have you heard about a federal agency giving out cell phones?"

"Never."

"Uh-huh," Monique said.

Before I could get too worked up about the identity of my fake VA man, Trina buzzed me and let me know Sparky had arrived for his 3:30. I didn't remember him having an appointment today, but I chalked that up to shots to the head.

I went out to greet the Sparkman. He sat with his elbows resting on his thighs, holding both sides of his head.

"Spark?"

He looked up, sniffled, and wiped his eyes.

I motioned him to come back to the counseling room, and he sniffled his way back. I didn't acknowledge his tears or ignore them. Spark was the kind of guy you just didn't do that to.

"She won't even return my calls," said Sparky, looking at the wall. "And you know, legally she doesn't have to."

"Uh…"

"Meanwhile, my daughter grows up day by day without knowing who I am."

"Don't let it make you drink." I had to say something.

Sparky nodded and was polite about my ineffectiveness to give him anything inspirational or helpful. We moved on and filled up the rest of the hour with stuff that wasn't terribly emotional. I felt he needed a break. I also felt like I had to be honest with him about my job.

"Sparky, there's something I have to tell you," I felt my head throb a little bit.

He just raised his eyebrows and looked at me.

"There's a good chance I might not be working here in a week or so."

"Huh?"

"I've got myself in a little trouble that I might not be able to get out of. I don't do real good at paperwork and I might get fired because of it." I didn't see any point in mentioning his ex's role in my problems.

"Paperwork? Who gives a shit about paperwork?"

"It's important, trust me." I hesitated. "I'm going to try to not let it happen, Sparky, but I don't know if I can pull it off."

Sparky just looked confused.

"Paperwork seems like a stupid reason to fire a counselor," he said.

"I just didn't want you showing up here and me not be here without any explanation."

"When would this go down?"

"If I don't get this shit done–a week from Monday at the latest." I felt shitty.

He nodded and didn't say anything. It wouldn't be like a guy like Sparky to say something about it.

That just made me feel worse.

26

I pulled up to the Blue, my head throbbing. I felt a little nauseous and jittery, but tried to tell myself not to worry about it because I'd get over it. It didn't make a really convincing argument.

Elvis neared the end of *It Hurts Me*, the '68 Special version, not the studio one. I stayed to listen to him finish it before getting out of the car. When I opened the door I immediately heard Al making a sick moan. Even though he was inside, it came through loud and clear.

I raced into the trailer. Al stopped his moaning for a second when I came through the door. He sat in front of a slumped Karl, who was in a T-shirt and shorts and soaked in sweat. His head slumped down on his chest and he acted like he had passed out.

"Karl, Karl, Are you all right!" I yelled while grabbing his chin and forcing him to look at me.

"Nestrrr..." Something unintelligible came out of his mouth.

"Karl, say it again."

"Newstr..."

"New what?"

"Newstrr..."

He began to cry, but it was slowed by whatever else he had taken.

"Karl, what did you take?"

"Lotta shit..." he slurred.

"Karl–why did you do this to yourself?"

"Him..."

"Who?"

"News...told me to."

"Newstrom? The guy from the Army?"

Karl nodded and began to cry again. I looked at Al who had furrowed his brow.

"He came here?"

"Phone..."

"Are you in danger?"

Karl nodded, tears streaming down.

I didn't want to take any chances, so I rushed Karl to the emergency room. I knew Karl hated the hospital, but he probably wouldn't like dying much either. They took him someplace as soon as I brought him in. I had to sit in the little waiting room with the vinyl chairs. I found myself praying for the first time in as long as I could remember.

Two hours later a doctor with freckles and shaggy red hair, who looked about 14 years old, called my name from a clipboard. Dr. Picard introduced himself in a hurried way and I could tell he concentrated on being empathic, but really didn't have the energy for it. He told me Karl had taken an overdose of Valium and some anti-depressants and they would make him pretty sick, but they wouldn't cause him any permanent harm. He went on to tell me Karl would have to stay in the mental health unit and be evaluated before he could be released. At a minimum they would have to wait until the drugs had cleared his system. I got asked to wait until they admitted him to that unit before I could talk to him and then it would only be for a few minutes. I made myself as comfortable as possible on the orange vinyl.

Two hours and twenty minutes later a young and attractive, but exhausted looking nurse called my name. She wore bright yellow Crocs and had her straight brown hair pulled back into a hastily thrown-together bun. Her name badge said 'Shea' and she certainly looked Irish.

"You can talk to Karl, but please only for a few

minutes," she looked me right in the eye. "We want him to sleep soon."

I nodded and went around the curtains to talk to my buddy. He sat in a wheelchair. Other than looking pale and sleepy, he looked all right.

"He called me, Duffy," Karl said slowly, without slurring. "He told me to kill myself like I wanted to in Germany, because it would be easier than what he intended to put me through."

"Karl–"

"I tried, Duff. He got to me enough that I tried to do it." Karl started to weep and brought a hand up to his eyes. "I can't believe what this man can do. I tried to kill myself because he said to." He went back to crying.

My neck started to twitch and my head throbbed. I looked down at my hands. They were fists.

"He had me try to kill myself!" Karl said again through the tears.

"Karl, stop it. He may have tried, but you didn't take enough to carry it out. And you know how to do it. You didn't want to." I knew it was a weak argument.

"He told me about his plans, too."

"What plans?"

"He laughed and bragged about getting away with whatever he wanted to. That no one even knew enough to want to stop him. That everyone knew I was a nut job."

"Did he tell you his plans, Karl?"

"There will be a college-type massacre Saturday."

"What!"

"Yeah, he said to keep my eye on the sports page for college football Saturday."

"What the hell does that mean?"

"He said something about 'Shaking down the thunder' for real."

"He used those words…'Shaking down the thunder'?"

"Yeah, I have no idea what that means."

"I do," It sent a shiver through me. "That's part of the Notre Dame Fight song."

"Notre Dame?"

"Yeah, they open with Michigan this Saturday."

<u>27</u>

"Notre Dame? *The* Notre Dame?" Kelley said.

I'd stopped off at AJ's after leaving Karl to get some rest on the happy unit.

"Yeah. It makes sense. National TV, the most famous program, a prestigious University," I said.

Kelley stared at me.

"What?"

"How's your head?" Kelley let the condensation run down the side of his Coors Light.

"Oh, fuck you, Kel!"

"Do you have any idea how ridiculous this sounds? It makes the Foursome sound sane and rational."

I sipped my Schlitz and got more and more angry. I don't know if anyone ever looked at you like they really believed you're crazy or not, but it's not fun.

"Check it out, Duff. Let me ask the brain trust what they think."

I just sat there and shook my head. I finished off the Schlitz and AJ slid another in front of me.

"Uh, excuse me fellas." The Foursome stopped their conversation. In all the time I've been coming to AJ's, I don't think Kelley had ever started a conversation with the Foursome.

"What's up Kel?" Rocco said.

"You know Duffy's friend, Karl?" The Foursome nodded, almost in unison. "He's told Duffy a sniper is going to shoot up the Notre Dame-Michigan game. Says it's going to be another Virginia Tech," Kelley said.

"Notre Dame has got Asian students," TC said.

"I thought they were the Fighting Irish," Jerry Number One said.

"Not in the math department," Jerry Number Two said.

"Uh, fellas–do you think our buddy Duffy ought to take it seriously?"

"Hell no," Jerry Number One said. "No offense, Duff, but your buddy is a little out there."

"You said so yourself. Shit, he told me, himself, he's a paranoical schizomaniac," Rocco said. "Probably just a delusion."

"He's the one who meditates in the nude with Al, isn't he?" TC said.

"Duffy, your head okay?" Jerry Number One said.

I didn't say anything. I just sat and drank my beer. The only one who wasn't laughing at me was Jerry Number Two.

"So Duff…when are you leaving for South Bend? Maybe Knute Rockne will speak to you from the grave and clue you in," Jerry Number One said.

"Or, the Gipper or better yet, Ronald Reagan as the Gipper," Rocco said.

"Is he the hunchback guy?" TC said.

I had heard enough. I felt my blood pulse through my neck and my head throbbed. I swallowed half of the Schlitz and slammed the bottle down on the bar with enough force it shattered and glass went all over the place. All the guys stopped laughing and got quiet, real quiet.

"Fuck you guys!" I headed for the door.

My head went spinning. People I trusted told me I was crazy. A doctor friend told me to keep an eye on myself because he thought I'd get a little loopy. Trina even told me to get some help.

The only guy who seemed to share my sentiments wore a Redskins helmet and meditated in the nude with my basset hound.

After work the next day, I picked up Al and we headed back to the Medical Center to see if Karl was ready to be discharged. Elvis sang *Help Me* from '74 and I dueted for the entire ride. Usually when someone ODed, the hospitals would discharge them to a psychiatric appointment, but I called them and was able to convince them that because Karl was my client they could send him home in my care.

We stopped at the reception desk to find out where to pick Karl up this time. To my chagrin, the same receptionist sat there. Before I could brace myself Al did his stink-seeking missile routine and went right between the legs of the gravitationally-challenged woman behind the massive phone system.

"There's my buddy!" she said while trying to lift Al's head from her nether regions. "You're such a good boy!"

The good boy sneezed.

The fat lady yelped.

"Uh, I'm here to pick up Karl Greene," I said because I could think of nothing else.

The receptionist looked at her monitor, which took two hands and Al's nose torpedoed to its prize.

Al sneezed again.

The fat lady yelped.

"He's on the fifth floor and you'll have to meet with his social worker before he's discharged," she said with less enthusiasm then before.

I pulled Al out from between her legs. He did the tornado thing to get the slobber from out of his jowls. Apparently, he had worked up a bunch from his spelunking adventure. Loogies flew all over the place and Al sneezed again.

Another socially awkward interaction.

Up on the fifth floor I had to meet with another receptionist who thanked me and said 'please' and 'thank you' and all that kind of stuff while at the same time managing to give me the feeling she held me in contempt. Al barked at her like he wanted to tell her to loosen up and she frowned at him.

"Dogs aren't allowed on the unit."

"He's a therapy dog."

"We don't allow therapy dogs on the mental health unit."

"Well, we won't be here long."

"I will call security and they can watch him."

"We really won't be here long," I watched her call security.

A twenty-something guy dressed like a cop, who looked liked he just woke up, came and took Al by the leash. Al didn't care for that.

"*Grrr*," Al said.

"Is he, like, you know, dangerous?" The hospital rent-a-cop said.

"Not usually," I said. "Al, take it easy buddy. It's okay."

The security guard walked–actually, more like dragged–Al down the corridor. Al kept looking over his shoulder while the security cop talked on his radio.

A social worker, who looked like she got out of social work school that morning, came out with Karl and a clipboard.

"Good Morning. I'm Cynthia O'Hara-Rodriquez," she said and offered her hand. She was pretty, but looked like she tried hard not to be. She had short hair made to look unkempt, a faded green t-shit, and way too baggy cargo pants.

"Good morning. Hey, Karl, how are you?" I said. Karl made eye contact with me and nodded. He looked with it, but depressed.

"Karl is showing signs of dysthmia. He's really going to need your support and he will have to take it easy for awhile," the social worker said. "Can you provide a supportive, calm, and nurturing environment?"

Karl made a face.

"Of course, I can," I said.

"I have discharge plans I'd like to go over with both of you." She pulled out what looked to be a four-page form. Karl rolled his eyes.

"The first opportunity statement is–"

"Excuse me?"

"What?" she said.

"Opportunity statement?"

"Yes?"

"What the hell is that?"

"It's like, you know, a problem."

"Why don't you call it that?"

"Mr. Dombrowski I–"

There came an *ahroooo* echoing down the long hospital hallway. Outrunning the Doppler-effected sound came Al, running at full speed, ears flapping and tail wagging.

"Al–my man!" Karl came alive. Al had what looked to be a walkie-talkie in his mouth. He must've paused to spit it out before yelling his battle cry. He charged Karl, jumped up, and lapped him across the face. Then he started barking. He wouldn't stop barking. The walkie-talkie skittered across the linoleum.

"Mr. Dombrowski, could you–" Al jumped on her lap and crumpled her beautiful discharge plan as he tried to climb up her to give her a smooch. She pulled away, dropped the papers and said something like "Ewwww...."

The big security guard came down the hallway a little disheveled.

"I'm sorry Miss Rodriquez-O'Hara. I turned around and he got loose," he said.

"It's MS. and its O'Hara-Rodriquez."

"Huh?" The security cop said.

Al ignored this interaction and started chewing and slobbering on the discharge papers.

170

"He's destroyed the discharge plan! You know how long that took me?"

Karl got down on all fours, giggling and playing with his buddy. Al started to get excited and hop around and bark. I really enjoyed myself, but decided to quit while I was ahead.

"Look, Miss Rodriquez-O'Hare, if I promise to be nurturing would it be okay for us to go now?"

"Please go," she said while trying to get the slobber off her glasses with a tissue.

We did.

28

Karl said he felt okay, just like he had a pretty good hangover. I asked him what had gotten into him that made him OD.

"Newstrom can push the right buttons, man." Karl stopped, looked down, and shook his head. "He started on some shit about it would be easier for me to do myself in than to have him come for me and terrorize me. For whatever reason, I bought it."

"The guy is that powerful?"

"Yeah, Duff, believe it or not he is." We both sat in silence until it felt awkward. I decided to move ahead.

"You sure he said 'Shake Down the Thunder'?" I tried to get a handle on Karl's latest prediction and its level of craziness. Al wasn't concerned; he slept with a complete lack of curiosity about anything Karl had to say.

"Yep. No question."

"And you think this guy is nuts enough and powerful enough to set off a college-type massacre?"

"You've already seen what he can do."

"We've seen what you've *said* he's done."

"I know," Karl folded his arms.

"Karl, there's one thing I don't get. I still don't get how this guy, Newstrom, gets other people to do this shit for him. I mean, he's not the one pulling the trigger in any of this stuff."

"Look Duff, Newstrom was special forces. He trained in all sorts of psychological shit. He explained it to me once. He doesn't create monsters, he just feeds them."

"What the hell does that mean?"

"It means he scouts people, situations, environments, whatever. Then he gets a feel for it, takes the pulse, and fertilizes whatever he wants to grow."

"How?"

"Think about it Duff. You think it's hard to find people who hate the government, the system or the situation they're in? You just find the people, bring them along, finance their craziness, and give them what they need. Newstrom used to call it gassing them up."

"What the hell does that mean?"

"He's a motivator. He's like Bill Parcels or Joe Torre or some Fortune 500 exec. He knows how to get people to do what he wants."

"That's it? He gives them a rah-rah speech and they're ready to kill?"

Karl frowned and scrunched up his forehead.

"Let me ask you this Duff. You think it would be hard to find a kid stressed out with pressure on a college campus?"

"No."

"How about a violent kid?"

"No"

"A kid with some mental illness, who maybe likes what drugs do to him?"

"Easy."

"How about a kid who listens to a charismatic leader, who gasses him up?"

I didn't say anything. It made too much sense and I started to wonder if I was as nuts as people said.

"Newstrom is expert at finding the right people, assessing the situation, and giving them the tools. It's like the cops say—he finds motive, helps the opportunity along and then he does what he's best at."

"What?"

"He creates capability."

173

"I guess I kind of see it."

"You saw me on the floor filled with enough drugs to stop a rhino didn't you? That was Newstrom's work."

"So you think we should take an 800-mile trip to Notre Dame to somehow see what Newstrom is up to?"

"We can always go to the game."

The next morning we loaded up the El Dorado with a cooler full of snacks and Schlitz, and headed west. Karl asked Al if he wanted the front or the back. Al responded by jumping in the front seat and crawling over the arm rest to the back. I double-checked I had all the Elvis 8-tracks I needed because it was going to be about a 12-hour ride.

Between Karl's New World order bullshit and Al's flatulence, it was going to be a hell of a trip.

"All right, Karl, how do you want to do this? We can listen to the Elvis catalog in chronological order, frontwards or backwards. We can start with the movies, do all the live concerts, or go alphabetically," I said.

I took Al's snoring as an abstention.

"I'm really more of a Zeppelin guy," Karl said. "So, I guess it's your choice Duff."

"Zeppelin?"

"Yeah, Guns and Roses, Clapton and some folk stuff. Don't get me wrong…I respect the King, especially after, you know, that stuff we went over."

We traveled only about 45 minutes out of Crawford when Karl asked if I minded getting off the Thruway. He reasoned surveillance would be easier on the major highway and we ought to break up our road trip by using some smaller country route. Never mind it would add hours to an already long trip.

Somewhere between Amsterdam and Utica we saw a crowd of people with signs and placards. They were outside a gate and a couple of police cars with their lights on were

174

parked nearby.

"Pull over," Karl said without shifting his stare from the window.

"Karl, we got a long trip ahead of us."

"Pull over. This is the people fighting back."

Against what I knew to be my better judgment, I pulled over. Thirty or so people with signs marched in front of the gates. As I got closer I saw a banner they had spread out and hung on the fence surrounding whatever it was they protested. It said PETA, and the group had broken into a chant.

Al had woken up and made some weird noises in the back seat. He did that whistling thing through his nose he does when he wants something. It's almost like crying, but maybe not as bad. I went to get him out of the backseat and he marched in place nervously. He looked like he really wanted to get out of the car.

The three of us walked toward the protestors, trying to make out what they said. A couple of them had signs saying 'Close Down Puppy Mills' and 'Animal Freedom' and things like along those lines.

Finally, we could hear them chanting,

"No more puppy mills! No more puppy mills!"

A lady, wearing army fatigues and Birkenstocks, handed Karl and me fliers. Al had lowered his head and neck and pulled me with all of his force toward the main gate. He went out of control, making a really strange sound that seemed to be half anger, half sadness.

"Look, there's one of the survivors!" A guy with a ponytail and glasses yelled at Al. A bunch of these crunchy protestor types gathered around Al and started petting and stroking him and talking to him. Al had his front paws on the fence and was doing his best to see in.

"He probably remembers," the ponytail guy said.

"No doubt—it isn't something you forget," the lady who

handed us the flier said. I had no idea what they were talking about. Karl had worked his way into the crowd and was now holding a sign. He pumped a fist in the air and yelled something sounding like "Kill the man."

Al wouldn't calm down and the group of protestors didn't help. I pulled really hard and started heading back to the car. I didn't know what the hell was going on, but Al didn't like it. When we got about fifty feet from the fence Al chilled out a little, but he continued looking over his shoulder and whimpering a bit. Karl came running up behind me with his new friend, the ponytail guy.

"Duff, you gotta hear what this brother has to say." It was like being in a bad TV movie about the '60s.

"This is a puppy mill, where they breed dogs under deplorable conditions. We are set on shutting them down. Your dog might have come from here," ponytail guy said.

"What?" I said.

"He's a basset—one of the breeds they breed here. Where did you buy this dog?"

"I didn't. He belonged to a friend who has since died. I have no idea where he came from."

"The way he acted at the fence looked to me like he was familiar with the place. These places are horrible, horrible places. They over-breed the bitches and the place is unsanitary. If you like dogs, you would join our cause."

"Yeah, Duff, let's help out," Karl said

"Is it illegal?"

"Technically no, but there's no question it is immoral," ponytail guy said. "This particular place wraps itself in the flag and hides behind bullshit patriotism."

"What?"

"It's some sort of ultra right-wing organization and they use this place as their clubhouse," ponytail said.

"C'mon Duff, we gotta join in," Karl said.

"I don't know, Karl. Can't we solve one of the world's

problems at a time? We've got someplace to get to. Remember?"

"Yeah, I know, man but we're coming back to stop this shit," Karl said. He had Al by the leash now. Al did that marching in place thing he did when he was nervous.

The crowd suddenly got louder as a big red pickup truck approached. The truck was one of those extra heavy duty ones with the extra back tires. It had a flag design all over its fenders, a sign on the passenger door that said: 'Give The Soldiers A Snack Attack–Give Can Goods!' I realized this was one of the places collecting all the goddamn canned goods that were all over the place.

The crowd chanted louder and the three crew-cut guys in the truck laughed. The protesters reluctantly parted and the guys went through the heavily armored gate. On the other side of the gate, two scrawny shaved-head types, with big black Doc Martens boots on and a load of tattoos, did their best to look quietly menacing at the protestors.

In all the confusion I felt my head do the throb thing. It was worse than it had been the last few days. I got sick to my stomach, but I took a breath and stabilized it.

"Duff, you all right?"

"Yeah, I just got this weird feeling like something about this was familiar and then I got the head thing."

"Was it from getting Al?"

"No. I've never been here before," I said. Karl turned his attention to Al who did the whimpering thing and marched in place.

"You remember huh, Al?" Karl said. He got down on his knees massaging Al's ears. "Breathe my brother, breathe."

My head kept throbbing, but we had to get on the road.

29

We drove straight through the rest of New York. Thankfully, Karl curled up with Al in the back seat and they slept all the way to Erie. Elvis's early '60s, post-Army period got me through to Cleveland. Critics dismiss this period of Elvis's music, but I thought it was one of his greatest. On numbers like *Such a Night*, originally done by Johnnie Ray, *Are You Lonesome Tonight*, originally done by Al Jolson and *It's Now or Never*, Elvis's interpretation of Mario Lanza's, *O Solo Mio*; it was like listening to a music history class. Elvis was great as a crooner, which to me didn't take anything away from his ability to rock.

After the early sixties, I switched gears and listened to his complete Gospel work, which got me all the way to Toledo. Gospel music is an interesting study in Americana because there isn't one type of Gospel music. Elvis did Black Gospel, he did white rural Gospel, and he did traditional white upper class Protestant gospel. That's a huge swath of music and Elvis did them all better than anyone. The fact he brought all of those types of gospel music together is just more testament to how much of a uniter Elvis was. No wonder the government wanted him discredited.

It scared me that I now thought like Karl.

Toledo to Indiana we listened to the seventies period. Although everyone assumes this is when the King went into the tank, I disagree. The live album from Memphis is my favorite, followed by the afternoon show at Madison Square Garden and the studio album, his last, *Moody Blue*. When we made the turn off the Indiana toll road to US 31, Elvis kicked in to *Moody Blue*. That's when we got the first glimpse of the Golden Dome.

"Man, check it out," Karl said when we made the turn down Notre Dame Avenue.

"This is some special place. TV doesn't do it justice," I said.

Al had his head out the window and his ears flapped in his face. The Golden Dome, straight ahead and in the sunlight, it gleamed almost like it was supernatural. The way the N.D. football team had played in the last couple of years, gave plenty of evidence the structure was not supernatural or, at least, God's mom had focused on other things.

We parked in a student lot and headed into the campus. It was the Friday afternoon before the Michigan football game, so the place was buzzing. Music blared out of the dorm rooms and lots of older guys, wearing green tartan pants and Notre Dame sweaters, walked around. The meat grilling made the whole place smell like a huge tailgating party.

"Uh, Karl?" We walked down what I learned they called the South Quad, and had just passed a dorm with gargoyles on it, called Alumni Hall.

"Yeah, Duff?"

"Now that we've traveled nearly a thousand miles to thwart Newstrom. How the hell do we find him and whoever he's 'programmed' to do this massacre?"

"I have no idea."

"That's great."

"Let's follow the crowd and keep our eyes out for Newstom and anything that looks funny." As he finished, a dozen Notre Dame Students with just their underwear on, their bodies painted green and their heads spray- painted gold, ran past us.

"I gotcha, Karl."

We walked past the Knute Rockne memorial gym, cut across the lawn in front of Morrissey Hall, and came down around a lake. In the distance, we could hear a marching band. It was hard not to get into the spirit that seemed to fill this place. I had to remind myself we came here to stop a sniper from killing a bunch of college kids.

Al definitely got into things, especially the number of pretty college girls in tight sweaters and short skirts who bent over to tickle under his chin. Al wasn't the only one. We kept walking and found another lake. Between the two lakes there was this beautiful stone grotto where thousands of candles lit the twilight. I guess people really wanted to beat Michigan.

"Hey Duff, let's say a prayer," Karl said.

"I didn't picture you a religious guy. Certainly not Catholic."

"Something about this place makes me feel like saying a prayer."

It was beautiful. There were about fifty people, some lighting candles, some praying, and some sitting. Karl walked ahead and lit a candle. I knelt and said a prayer. Al lay quietly next to me. I noticed a small figurine of St. Francis of Assisi off to the right and figured it made Al feel good.

I stood up and met Karl as we walked toward the marching band.

"Hey, Karl. If this place has a French name how come they're called the 'Fighting Irish'," I said.

"Your first name is the name of one of the original Irish clans and you don't know?" Karl said.

"Hey, I'm half Polish."

"The Fighting Irish came from stickin' it to the man back in the twenties. This place was Jackie Robinson to the Catholics."

"Huh?"

"In the twenties, Catholics were oppressed, man. Notre Dame is so popular because they won football games against big state schools filled with Protestants."

"What does that have to do with being Irish?"

"Back then, Catholics were oppressed, but the Irish were even more so. It was an insult to call all Catholics 'Irish'. So, when Notre Dame kicked the shit out of a school like, say, Michigan, the papers would say 'The Fighting Irish Win' but they meant it to be derisive. Like saying the 'Grambling Niggers Win'. Because the school was proud of being Catholic, they adopted the derisive term. Kind of saying 'That's right we're Catholic and we just kicked your ass'."

"Really?"

"Yeah, oppressed groups often adopt derisive terms and wear them defiantly and proudly. African-Americans will call each other 'Nigger', Gay people adopt the word 'Queer', Italians call each other 'Dago'. It's a way of taking the power out of the term."

"No shit. So this place stands for something besides rich Catholic kids and a good football team?"

"Yeah. Back in the thirties, the Klu Klux Klan marched on South Bend. The school president forbade the students to do anything. The kids defied him, met the Klan, and drove them out of the city," Karl said.

"Kind of makes you proud to be Irish and Catholic," I said.

"Fuckin' A-right."

We both took a second to look back at the candles lighting up the Grotto.

"Let's go stop this. This place stands for something special," I said.

We walked, but just below a trot. We saw the crowd ahead of us and the tubas in the back row of the marching band. There were thousands of people following the band, singing along and pumping their fists. The sun had set and it was chaotic and very difficult to watch and see anything except a sea of people.

We caught up with the band and walked along the middle of the pack. Karl broke away and jumped up on statue of Moses holding one finger in the air next to the library.

"Duffy! Duffy!" I heard him scream through the band's rendition of something called 'On Down the Line!'.

I ran to the statue.

"He's here, I just saw him." He pointed into a sea of people dressed in green and blue and gold. "He's wearing a green 'Irish' shirt." Karl climbed down off the statue.

"That helps," I said.

Karl didn't listen. Instead he sprinted all out in the direction he'd pointed. Al and I followed along with no idea what Karl planned. The band and the mass of people had marched around the basketball arena called the Joyce Center and headed inside for the pep rally. Karl ran to the entrance and stood on a sawhorse, used as a barricade. He looked back and forth, trying to spot Newstom.

The band marched right into the arena. A quick glance told me it was filled with crazed Irish fans waiting for the pep rally to begin. I tried to follow behind the band, but a security guard asked for a ticket and wouldn't let me through.

"You need a ticket for a pep rally?"

"Yes sir," he said. Al disagreed and ran right between the big guys legs. You could hear him barking over 'Cheer, Cheer for Old Notre Dame'. Without a word I took off after him while the cop seemed confused by the sight of a short legged Irish fan. Karl jumped off the barricade and ran with me, as we searched for Al in the crowd.

Coach Weis stood at the microphone and the crowd went nuts. We ran up on the top level by the bleachers where the students stood. I saw Al whip around a corner and cut through one of the tunnel-like entrances to the concourse. Al barked like crazy and I could see him, though he was about 20 yards ahead of us. Suddenly Al took a sharp right turn into one of the arena's men's rooms.

Karl and I caught up with Al, who stood in front of a long row of urinals barking at nothing. I looked up and down.

With the exception of a guy in the last stall, there was no one in there. I could see the guy standing, like he had just finished taking a crap and he had pulled up his jeans.

A knapsack dropped to the floor of the stall with a loud metal clang.

Karl and I looked at each other. Karl nodded at me and I moved quietly over to the stall. I took a deep breath and threw all my weight into the stall door.

The door banged off the wall violently, grazing something and slammed into the tile. A short squatty Asian guy wearing black jeans, army boots, and a camouflage jacket stood there fastening his jeans. I rushed him and pushed him up against the wall over the toilet. I had taken him by surprise with his hands down.

I was in close with him, but I put as much as I could into a hook to his body. My fist slammed into something firm, but I had too much adrenaline going through me and I doubled the hook up to his head. He went down awkwardly between the toilet and the stall wall. I jumped down hard with my knee on the guy's chest and again hit something firm. I didn't pay attention and threw a right hand across the Asian kid's face.

The Notre Dame fight song blasted across the bathroom tile in a weird distorted way. I barely heard the shouting behind me. Then I felt a couple sets of arms pull me off the kid.

"Stop or I'll shoot!" the guy standing above me said. I was on my back now, with a cop's knee in my chest, his partner's service revolver pointed at my head.

"Check his bag, check his bag–he's got ammunition!"

The one cop kicked the bag over to the guy holding the gun. With one hand holding the gun on me, he zipped open the knapsack. Cans of Spam, chicken spread, and Vienna sausages soup spilled out.

"It's canned food for the soldiers' night at the pep rally, asshole," the cop kneeling on my chest said.

<u>30</u>

Jail really kind of sucks.

Jail on the weekend of a gigantic college football game sucks more.

First, I was stuck in a holding cell with a dozen guys, half of them dressed in green, the others in blue and gold, or as I came to learn from one especially adamant Michigan fan, maize and blue. His commitment impressed me. The fact he barfed regurgitated beer and some sort of pork product right after making his point impressed me less.

On Friday night these drunk Notre Dame and Michigan fans almost seemed as though they were having a good time. It was as if getting arrested at a pep rally and fighting with opposing fans made one the ultimate athletic supporter. By Saturday, when they awoke hung over, not at the game, and facing felony charges, they all seemed far less jovial.

I got charged with assault. When they ran my name through whatever computers they run things through, they noticed I was licensed as a professional fighter. Somehow that upped the ante of my charges to something-something assault with a deadly weapon. Apparently, if you've fought competitively, and then hit someone with your hands, then you used a weapon. If they charging me with assault with a deadly weapon, they had obviously not looked at my record as a pro fighter. Of course, there probably aren't charges known as assault with a light jab and weak cross.

Fortunately, Karl didn't get charged and he had custody of Al. I had no idea where they were, but I knew Al was in good hands. Al might be wearing a Notre Dame helmet and rubber gloves on his paws, but he was probably safe. That was about the only thing I was reasonably sure of, and the fact jail sucked.

At one point I got ushered into a small court room, which by the way looked nothing like the court room Sam Waterson worked on in every episode of *Law and Order*. This one had a lot of battleship grey paint, cheap wood paneling, and it smelled like the stuff they spray on puke in grade school.

They arraigned me and set bail at $10,000, which didn't exactly put me in Martha Stewart status, but it might as well have because I had fourteen bucks in my pocket. Compared to Karl, that made me Donald Trump.

I had one of those little boxes of Cheerios for breakfast, with milk that tasted pretty close to spoiled. Lunch was a bologna sandwich with one slice of bologna and bad brown mustard. Dinner was supposed to be spaghetti with meat sauce, but it tasted more like lumpy ketchup over egg noodles.

Now, thirty-six hours in jail didn't exactly make me Nelson Mandela or some hardened guy from *Goodfellas*, but I could see why violence happened in penitentiaries. The jail consisted of ten cells on the first floor, that I was on, and I don't know how many on the other floor. Three cells down, one black guy sang bad rap songs about 20 hours a day. Next to him was a middle-aged man, who cried a lot, and right next to me was a fat Michigan hooligan with bad gas. I had delusions of making a shank out of my commissary plastic fork and making myself king of the cell block. It's amazing what you'll do when you're sleep deprived.

At 10:30 Sunday night a middle aged, balding guard with leathery skin and a look of utter existential indifference came to my cell and turned the key.

"Dombrowski, you got bail. Stop at the desk and complete the paper work," he said.

"Huh? Who made bail?"

"Stop at the desk," he said. I got the impression this guy liked an economy of words.

I filled out a form and signed the bottom without really taking the time to read it. I got a copy of it and several pages of directions. I headed through the door that brought me back into the public area. I was a free man. Standing in front of me was Dr. Rudy.

"Hey Rudy! What are you doing here?" I couldn't help smiling ear to ear.

"Oh, I'm a Big Notre Dame fan. C'mon asshole, let's go; we got a flight to catch." He turned without looking at me or saying anything else.

"Where's Karl and Al?"

"Your brothers-in-arms? Your militia? Or should I say the other avengers?"

"Hey Rudy—"

"Hey Rudy, my ass. They left yesterday morning after that nut-job called me. They're driving your El Dorado back to Crawford. They're probably there by now."

"Wow. So you came all the way out here to make sure I was okay and get me out of jail?"

Rudy didn't say anything, just shook his head. He drove north toward Chicago and O'Hare Airport. He handed me a ticket when we returned the rental car, and we sat in silence at the gate waiting for the flight to Albany. It was after take-off, actually after the captain had turned off the seat belts lamp, that he said something.

"Kid, you gotta listen to me." He wiped the sweat off his forehead with one of those undersized cocktail napkins. "Remember when I told you you might have some damage…"

"Rudy, I don't think—"

"You're showing the signs of a guy who has some impairment." 'Impairment' sounded clinical and told me he was trying to make a point. "Kid, you're showing the exact signs of someone who has been damaged."

"What are you talking about?"

"The main thing is you're taking what Karl says as gospel. For crissakes, he's *your* patient. You know he's paranoid-schizophrenic and you drive a thousand miles and beat some math student with a knapsack full of canned goods because Karl says he's trying to bring down the free world! C'mon!"

"It's not like you think."

"Oh, fuck you, Duff. The guy wears a football helmet and rubber gloves, believes the government is fattening our food and thinks doctors are tracking them on their car's GPS systems."

"It's not—"

"Part of what you got messed up in your head tells you it makes sense. Look, I've known you for years, and probably know you as good as anyone. I'm telling you that you're in trouble and you've got to get it together."

"Rudy—"

"I mean, stay at home, walk that fat fuckin' dog, and watch Elvis movies. I don't give a shit what you do, but don't be chasing bad guys with Karl because you're going to get hurt, or I probably should say hurt worse."

I decided to keep my mouth shut the rest of the ride home.

<u>31</u>

I could hear a loud pound...no, it was more like a pumping sound. The flow of blood, my heart racing, and a loud marching band. The band was playing something faster and louder and it was out of control. As the tempo shot through the roof so did my heartbeat.

It was the Notre Dame Marching Band and they were going faster and faster, but it was also inside my head at the same time. The force sped up my heart and my thoughts raced. There were thousands of crazed people in green running and singing, but they were doing it with rage and they just kept on.

The band and the throng following it all turned into the Asian kid, whose eyes burned red with fire. Without any warning, they all began to bleed–spurting blood from their eyes, screaming, bleeding, and screaming. The band kept playing louder and faster while the blood kept pouring.

Something wet and scratchy came across my eyes. I woke up, panting, covered in sweat. Al was right in front of me.

"I figured they'd come back after this weekend." My vision broadened. Karl stood right behind Al. I shook my head, just like an actor would in the movies when they come out of a nightmare. It looks stupid in the movies and it didn't help me in any way.

"When did you guys get back?"

"Just in time to catch you screaming in your sleep."

"What the hell happened at Notre Dame after they arrested me?"

"Well, for starters, Michigan kicked their ass, but Al and I had a good time at the tailgaters."

"Karl!"

"That's okay, we found Newstrom there. Or should I say he found us."

"Karl–it's been a hell of a weekend; don't speak in riddles now." I got out of bed and headed to the kitchen to make the coffee. Al sat on the back of the chair doing surveillance on the sparrows.

"I'll fill you in on Newstrom in a minute. I gotta tell you about the puppy mill. That's a whole mess of injustice going on there." Karl started to get animated. Though Newstrom's schemes seemingly had to do with war, billions of dollars and the killing of innocent people, I knew enough not to interrupt Karl's train of thought.

"Go ahead, Karl."

"Me and Al broke into the place on the way back from N.D. They probably have 40 hounds in there, under deplorable conditions. Tied up, dog shit everywhere, many of them over-fed and it's all set up to produce puppies for profit." Karl got so excited he had to wipe the spit from his lips with the back of his hand.

"Karl, look, I'm all about the dogs, but we have to be realistic. This *is* a business for some people–like it or not."

"Man, Duff, you had to see the place. The dogs had their names stitched on their collars. I felt like I got to know them personally, even after just a few minutes with them." Karl's eyes got real wide.

"Take it easy. Karl, take it easy," I hoped he would chill out a little.

"There was a beautiful basset girl named Sadie; she just looked at me with those big eyes, and I felt sick. There was a guy right next to her in a cage named Arthur, and he really wanted out."

"Karl…" He wasn't even close to stopping.

189

"There was also Louie. Man, what a character he was. There was Lola Love, and you know what? She couldn't bark because her vocal chords looked screwed up, like someone had kicked her." Karl shook his head and gritted his teeth.

"Karl, look, just..."

"Then there were these two best friends in one cage. One was a tri-color and the other was more white. They were Blake and Sherlock."

"Karl, focus," I said.

"There was one named Maui, another one named Sally, and there was even one named Guffy, and they were really happy and wanted to play even though they were in cages."

"Karl, please..." He was a runaway train.

"There was even this strange Maltese/Pom mix; a tiny little thing named Tedward. That's not the worst of it." Karl got real quiet.

"Huh?"

"Al's mom is there."

"What the fuck are you talking about?"

"He ran right to her cage–skipped about 35 others and went ballistic when he saw her–crying, howling, trying to get in the cage."

"Karl, I don't–"

"She's pregnant again, Duff. Those bastards just get the females pregnant twice a year, have them give birth, sell the puppies, and eventually discard the mothers. That's how this shit works." Karl paced back and forth.

"How the hell can you tell if it's Al's mom. Karl you're getting way out there."

"Her cage had 'Gladys' written above it. It had a list of the fathers. The way I figured it 'Vernon' must've been Al's father."

"C'mon!"

"Call whoever you got Al from and ask him to look at the papers and it will say. As sick as this place is, they have

190

to file AKC papers to get the dogs registered. Otherwise their price drops."

Al was originally owned by the Nation of Islam. He had been trained as a bomb sniffing dog and a man-trailer, but they gave him away because he kept pissing and farting all over the place. A client of mine named Walanda had adopted him and when she went to jail for 60 days, I took Al. Walanda got murdered in jail and Al and I became life partners.

A buddy of mine named Jamal, who I knew from the gym, knew the whole story. He was in the Nation back then, didn't box any more, and worked at McDonough High. I rang him up on his cell phone.

"This is Jamal."

"Jamal, it's Duff."

"The great white hope. I seen you made the papers for your football game antics. Man, Duff, you gotta stop gettin' hit on the head, my man." Jamal had tendency to say what was on his mind.

"Yeah, yeah. Look I got an Al question."

"Man, Duff, he's a dog. You're always calling me with Al questions."

"You remember where you guys got him?"

"You guys'? Duff, I left the Nation years ago."

"Sorry J, You know what I mean."

"They got him just west of here. I forgot the town's name. It was just outside of Syracuse."

"Johnsville?"

"That's it. Some funk-ass country folk had a whole hound dog production line. Kind of fucked up, to be honest with you. They almost wouldn't sell him to us 'cause we were of color, as you liberal whiteys like to say."

"Look Jamal, this is going to sound like a really crazy question."

"Duff…those are the only kind you got."

"Do you know, or do you have papers, that tell you about Al's parents?"

"You won't believe it, but I do. Typical cracker-ass lineage for a hound dog. They must've thought they were all sorts of clever."

"What was it?"

"Well my short-legged friend was originally named after the hero to all you white folk–or at least the ones with some soul."

"What the hell are you talking about?"

"'Ol' Al was born E-L-V-I-S. And you know the Nation had that changed before they got out of that big ol' gate at that farm."

I didn't say anything. I couldn't.

"Duff, you there?"

"Yeah, yeah. So let me guess. Al's parents were Gladys and Vernon?"

"There you go."

I thanked Jamal and sat down hard on the couch. Maybe I was going crazy.

"I was right wasn't I?" Karl got out of his chair again and started pacing. "We got to stop those bastards."

I began to think he was right. Now, I knew I was going crazy.

"Karl–"

"I also found out the guy who owns the place is Luther Campbell," Karl said.

"So?"

"Luther Campbell is a right-wing nut. He's Rush Limbaugh on crack. His followers are para-military 'Give-America-back-to-Americans' types. Here's an article on him from some ultra-conservative newsletter." He handed me a cheaply produced newsletter featuring Campbell on the cover, in front of a flag, posing with his hunting rifle.

"So you got a Republican raising hounds. I'm not sure

he's broken any laws Karl."

"Duff, you gotta open your eyes, man."

"Karl, can we get back on our original conversation?"

"All right, all right. Let me tell you about Newstrom." Karl stopped his pacing, almost for what seemed like dramatic effect.

"Go ahead," I exhaled. It was all getting a little hard to follow, but I figured I might as well hear all of it.

"He's coming for us. He told me. He's coming to Crawford. He said we're making too much noise and there's too much at stake. He's coming to eliminate us."

"Hold it–you talked to him?"

"Yeah."

"The same guy that a few days ago had so much of an effect on you, you almost killed yourself?"

"Yeah."

"How the hell do you explain that?"

"He switched gears; there were people around. I don't know; it's the way he is. He's unpredictable, he has no emotion. He knows the suicide didn't work, so he moved on."

"What has he moved on to?"

"He's coming for us. He's coming to Crawford."

"For what?"

"To eliminate us while carrying out his other plans."

"What plans?"

"The massacre didn't happen at Notre Dame. He's bringing it here and wants to take care of us with it," Karl raised his eyebrows.

"Look, Karl, I got arrested in Indiana. Everyone thinks I'm Looney Tunes and I'm exhausted from traveling. I think it might be time for me to give up my battle with the NWO."

"Sure, I don't blame you," Karl said it flatly and he wouldn't look me in the eye. He did blame me.

I couldn't just sit there feeling like a shit, so I went to the kitchen. I poured myself a cup of coffee and sat back on the couch while Karl looked out the window with Al. It was sad, but things had gotten out of hand. I was going to take Rudy's advice. The phone rang.

"Dombrowski?" The voice hushed, almost whispering.

"Yeah."

"Karl is being eliminated because he creates too much attention. It's up to you whether we eliminate you or not. We don't have to, we don't want to, but if you're along for the ride, we will."

"Who is this? Who the hell is this!"

"Separate yourself now." The voice disconnected.

I hung up the phone and sat there. Karl turned toward me.

"It was him wasn't it?"

"Yeah."

"He's going to kill me," It was not a question.

I didn't say anything.

"And he's going to kill you if you stay with me."

I didn't say anything.

"Duff, I never told you I wasn't crazy, but this shit is real. You know it and you feel it." He looked right at me.

I didn't say anything.

32

I didn't want to call in sick for Friday, but I figured Trina would cover me. I didn't want to push my luck, so I called in and told her I wouldn't be in today, maybe not for a few days, because my head was bothering me. She warned me calling in wasn't going to help my situation, but it didn't matter. There was just no way I could go in there today.

I dropped by Ray's to see if I could catch up with Kelley. It wasn't his official haircut day, but he didn't pick up at his apartment or his cell, so by the process of elimination, I went to the barbershop. He usually gets there around 9:15, but I didn't want to chance missing him so I got there at 8:55. Right by the front door they had their own 'Snack Attack' can collection box.

"Duff, what're you doin' out? I thought they had you in the hospital; you know like locked up, you know what I'm fuckin' sayin'," Junior said by way of greeting.

"Yeah, Duff, I didn't think, once they said you had, you know, psychotrayic stuff, that they had to like wrap you up in sheets and give you some of the Protrack or somethin','" Jackpot said.

"What are you guys talking about?" I said. The guys at Ray's didn't make a ton of sense, but they were going out of their way this morning to be weird.

"Holy shit. He hasn't seen the paper, you know what I'm fuckin' sayin'," Junior said.

Jackpot went to the counter, by the mirror behind his chair, and fiddled around with the newspaper. He pulled out a section and walked over and handed it to me.

"You're famous, Duff, but not the kind of notoriousness you were looking for," Jackpot said.

I read the lead story of the Local section of the Union-Times.

Local Boxer Arrested At Notre Dame: Released Into Psychiatric Care

Crawford journeyman pro boxer and social worker at Jewish Unified Services, Duff Dombrowski, was arrested on the campus of the University of Notre Dame during the pep rally before the Notre Dame-Michigan game. Dombrowski, whose boxing career can best be described as mediocre, assaulted a Notre Dame student in a Joyce Center restroom during the pep rally.

Dombrowski claimed the student was part of a plot to start a massacre during the pep rally, similar to the incident at Virginia Tech in 2007. The college sophomore, Wan Lu, had a knapsack filled with canned goods for the soldier drive that was going on campus-wide. Dombrowski said he had heard the rattle of cans and believed they were explosive devices or assault weapons.

He was released into the medical care of Dr. Rudy Villone, a Crawford internist, who stated he would place the fighter under inpatient psychiatric care. The police at Notre Dame, along with the district attorney in South Bend, agreed to the arrangement after the student said he did not want to press charges. The student suffered bumps and bruises, but was not hurt seriously.

"What the hell…," I said.

"I hear that campus is beautiful, Duff. All that tradition and whatnot, you know what I'm fuckin' sayin'," Junior said.

"This is this morning's paper, right?" I said.

Both of the guys nodded. It was quiet and a little uncomfortable in a place that didn't have many lapses of silence. Neither of the guys had anyone's hair to cut yet, so it made the silence that much more awkward.

196

"Duff, you want a cut? I guess maybe you ought to, seeing as you'll be going some place to, you know, psycho-recover. The fuckin' barbers in those joints suck, you know what I'm fuckin' sayin'," Junior said.

I sat down, just staring at the paper. My chest started to pound and my head throbbed. I started having problems breathing. My hands started to shake and I could see only the floor in front of me, but it was blurry. It felt like something was sitting on my chest and the walls seemed to be pushing in on me.

"Duff, Duff!" Something shook me hard by both shoulders. "Duff, Duff!" Something cracked me in the face. Instinctively, I countered with a left cross. There was a loud thud followed by someone yelling.

"He fuckin' punched me, you know what I'm fuckin' sayin'." Came through my senses.

Abruptly, there was a figure, a person, in front of me. It, he, whatever, had his hands lightly on my shoulders and he spoke to me in a quiet voice.

"Duffy, it's Kelley. You're having a panic reaction. You're safe. Breathe and sit back,"

I don't know why, but I followed the directions. My chest heaved, but it slowly began heaving less. The throb throbbed, but it did it lighter. The room started to come in to view. Kelley slowly came into view. Little by little the room came into focus. Junior and Jackpot were standing behind their chairs, with their eyes wide. Junior was rubbing his jaw.

"What the hell happened?" I was exhausted.

"You had some sort of panic reaction," Kelley said. "We've gotten some training on spotting them. You should apologize to Junior."

"For what?"

"How 'bout for fuckin' hittin' me with a left cross, you know what I'm fuckin' sayin'," Junior said.

"No, I did? No." I looked at Junior. "Man, Junior, I'm

197

sorry, man. I had no idea."

The three guys in the room stared at me. Their faces showed a combination of fear and confusion.

"Duff, don't take this the wrong way, man, but you're losing your fuckin' marbles, you know what I'm fuckin' sayin.'" Junior rubbed his jaw.

"Kell, the guy who's been after Karl is coming and he's coming for both of us this time. The next thing is a high school massacre and they're going to make it happen at McDonough. I saw the guy. I–" Kelly held up a hand.

Kelley didn't say anything. He frowned just a little bit at first, looked down, and then out Junior's front window. He stood up, remaining quiet, and so did Junior and Jackpot. They looked anywhere but at me The shop was quieter than I ever remember it being.

"Kell–"

"Duff, we've known each other forever. You know I tell you the truth, maybe even too much." He paused and looked down. He looked up at me. "You're fucked up. You're not in your right head and it's not just a little bit any more. You've been arrested, you're having attacks, and the stuff you're talking about is delusional."

I could tell he didn't want to say what he just did.

I sat there and looked at Kelley, then Junior, then Jackpot and then back to Kelley. I don't know the word for what I felt because embarrassed wasn't enough.

33

I didn't know what to do. I didn't feel crazy, but isn't that part of being crazy–you didn't know it? Karl seemed to be aware of being nuts. Did it make him a higher functioning fruitcake than I had become? Scary.

I walked through town trying to sort it all out. I guess that's what we mental health guys do. We wander through city streets talking to ourselves, trying to make sense. Crazy or not, it was time to organize my head. Oddly enough, when it came time to do that in the past, I sought out Jerry Number Two. Jerry was smart, knew a lot of what other people didn't, and had access to the world through his computers. Jerry also loved Dungeons and Dragons, Star Trek, and other things, but hey, nobody's perfect.

Jerry lived in the college section of town, in a basement apartment. He prefers the damp basement because it helps his horticultural hobby flourish. That is, his pot plants grew really well and no one could spot them. Jerry never seemed to mind an unannounced visit.

"Duff...what brings you here in the middle of the afternoon?" Jerry's doorbell played *Keep On Truckin'* by The Dead.

"You got a few minutes to help me understand something?"

"Sure, Duff. I was doing some online gaming, but I'll just commit suicide. It will take just a minute."

I didn't ask.

I took a seat in a big round rattan chair, struggling to get comfortable. Jerry came back with some dark, odd-looking tea, and sat in front of me on a floor pillow with his legs crossed.

"All right, Duff. Shoot."

"Jerry, I know everyone thinks I'm crazy, so you don't have to pretend otherwise. I want to lay some shit out to you and I want you to tell me what you think."

Jerry nodded.

"First of all, let me run down what I know; Number One: Karl, who by the way is nuts, believes that defense contractors, specifically private security firms, are benefiting from a large national defense budget."

"So far no one will argue," Jerry said.

"Two: Karl claims he, after he had a horrible time accidentally killing some children, was recruited by an old high school buddy to be part of a private security firm."

"Ditto. Sounds very possible."

"Three: Karl claims his buddy, in an effort to sell the job, showed him some highly classified documentation this firm or somebody had for a plan to influence…bring about…create the right atmosphere…I don't know how to say it. To perpetuate terrorist acts within the United States so the public would be both distracted and remain scared enough to stay positive about funding a huge defense budget."

Jerry sipped his tea, looking deep in thought.

"Alright, Duff let's break this down with what we know and what we don't know." He sipped his tea, wiped a dribble of it on his chin." Fact: there is at least 25 billion–that's with a 'B'–in U.S. funds unaccounted for in Iraq and Afghanistan. There's no doubt many, many people have gotten rich in the last 10 years."

"Twenty-five billion? That's hard to conceptualize."

"Yeah, which works to their advantage."

"Yeah."

"All right. Do the security firms have a history of nefarious conduct to guarantee they continue to get the bucks? No question. There's documentation of pay-offs, people disappearing–you name it. The problem is they operate outside any laws so there's only speculation on how far they'd go." Jerry sipped and thought.

"Is domestic terrorism out of the question?"

"Do you realize how many people get rich on multiple billions? I think it's entirely possible."

"Is there any precedent for this happening? Anything we can prove?"

"Like we talked about at the bar, there's plenty of evidence. There's certainly plenty of evidence of people in power screwing those who aren't in power, for money. There's no question. I told you before that our own government now admits it considered bombing ourselves and making it look like Castro did it, so there would be support for invading Cuba. That got out. Can you imagine what we don't know?" Jerry slurped some tea.

"Here's the thing I don't get. How do they get people to do the terrorism for them? Karl says they find people ripe for it and they take it from there. Is it even possible."

Jerry raised his eyebrows and thought for a moment.

"Duff, we have to assume they have unlimited financial resources, which means they have unlimited resources, period. There are those who claim brainwashing techniques exist and are effective on the right–especially troubled–people. There are also drugs that make people more suggestible, but I think it might be even easier than we think."

"How so?"

"Duff, you work with troubled people. You know there are no shortage of pissed off, angry people who've been kicked around for their whole lives. Is it really inconceivable with the right prompting, and maybe some pharmacological influence, a charismatic figure could get them to pull a trigger, set off a bomb or poison the forces that have treated them so badly?"

"So let me get this straight. This guy, Newstrom, finds people ready to explode, or who have the potential, and the make up to do it, and he pushes them over the edge. But it can't work on everybody he tries can it?"

"I doubt it and it probably explains why the events occur at unpredictable intervals."

"So, Jerry, I might be nuts, but not necessarily. I mean, there's a chance this shit could be true."

"Well, Duff there's a chance, but you also have to look at some other things."

"I don't understand."

"You've been subject to severe stress, some of it for years. You've had clearly diagnosable head trauma–multiple trauma, and you've been experiencing dissociative episodes–panic reactions whatever."

"So?"

"You might be right on with this shit or…"

"Or what?'"

"You might be fuckin' nuts."

<u>34</u>

"He's been here," Karl said. I had just walked in the door. Al wasn't even barking. His eyes just went back and forth from me to Karl.

"How do you know?" I felt a throb go to the front of my forehead.

Karl handed me a single page of paper. There was a single paragraph typed on it.

I tried to help you out after your trouble. If you had come along, you could've been better by now and had enough money in your pocket to be set for life. Instead you made your choices. The thing is, there's always going to be the military whether it's needed, sort of needed, or not needed at all. There's just too much money in it, and if it's just going to be, you should've come on board. It's too late for all that now, buddy. I'm here and it's over. You made too much noise and continue to make too much noise. You've been discredited, but now I'm afraid with your new social work friend, people may start to listen. We're working on Dombrowski and he's already being seen as an idiot. Anyway, the mission will *be carried on. You used to speak of suicide and how you'd like to have at least that kind of control. You may want to give that some thought again because we're here and we're coming for you. It's up to you how you go out. In the mean time, we need to get to school– If you know what I mean.*

N.

"He wants you to kill yourself again? Is that what this all means?"

"He was around when I got suicidal. I used to say I'd

rather go out on my own doing than have them get me. I still feel that way," Karl said.

"So he's in town to carry out the next part of his plan, isn't he?"

"Yeah."

"Which is a Columbine-type thing?"

"That's what he wants us to believe."

"How do we know when? Where? Who?"

"We don't." Karl looked down. Al looked up, smacking his tail on the floor. It wasn't a happy wag, more like a nervous one.

"What do you want to do?" My head throbbed at a pretty steady rate now.

Karl paused. I wondered if he thought of killing himself. I had a little dose lately about what your mind can do to you. I was at the point where such decisions didn't seem illogical.

"Duff, I'd rather die fighting these bastards than give in." Karl looked up, right in my eyes.

"You sure?"

"As sure as I've ever been at anything."

I nodded and looked down at Al, formerly Elvis.

"You don't have to be a part of it, Duff. There's a good chance we'll die. They're better at this than we are, have more resources, and they have the advantage of knowing all the details."

"Yeah, there's that."

It got quiet for a few seconds, except for Al's tail action.

"Well, what else is there, Duff?"

I smiled and laughed, mostly to my self.

"Karl, I don't like being sucker-punched and having someone get away with it."

"Me either," Karl said.

I called Jamal, who still worked as a hall monitor and assistant football coach, and asked him if I could come visit him at school and bring my buddy Karl. He said it would be no problem and to come around lunchtime when we could talk.

We skipped the main office, even though there were signs imploring us to stop and badge up before we went any further. I figured as an alumnus I had special rights. I didn't, of course, but I kind of went through life believing I had special rights.

"You really think Newstrom would come here and not back to his alma mater?" I asked Karl as we turned down a corridor toward the cafeteria.

"Strange as it sounds. I gotta believe he's still rah-rah on all the football crap and class presidency shit," Karl said.

"I don't get it Karl. Was he straight up back in the day or crooked and looking for greedy angles even then?"

"Duff, he was truly the all-American boy, pure as the driven snow."

"What happened?"

"War, killing people, people trying to kill you, and the corruption of the military can get in you and become you."

"Yeah, I guess."

"Truly the All-American boy in that sense, too."

We came up on the noise and chaos of a high school at lunch. I caught a whiff of the cafeteria smell, and my high school years came back to me through my nostrils. I tried to decipher the aroma. The best I could come up with: fried frozen food and the horrible gravy that seemed to be there every day, in one form or another. Here it wasn't hard to believe Karl's theory about evil food conspiracies.

The cafeteria doubled as an auditorium. Kids ran around yelling to each other, some wore ear phones connected to iPods, while others hunched over laptops staring at their computer screens rather than doing any human interaction.

"Can I treat you to a Salisbury steak with Maybeline's famous yellow gravy?" a voice said to us from behind. It was

Jamal.

"Please, just the mention of it gives me the shits. 'Ol Maybeline still in charge of the kitchen?"

"Yep and still fuckin' up everything she can."

"You know, Jamal, I thought old black southern women were supposed to be able to cook."

"Ah shit, Duff, and I can tap with Sammy Fuckin' Davis Jr. You white people kill me."

"Hey, this is my buddy, Karl." Up until now Karl had been standing, turned three quarters away from us, surveying the cafeteria. He turned to shake Jamal's hand.

"What's up, man" Jamal said. "Hey, you played for VHS awhile didn't you?"

"Yeah, halfback," Karl said.

"I remember you. You had some hop."

"For the Suburban League."

"Yeah, I'm glad you said it," Jamal said.

Karl went back to looking around the room.

"Yo Duff, I love you like a brother from another mother, but you mind telling me what coming here is all about?"

"Ah, well, we're kind of looking for someone or, more accurately, some thing."

"You wanna explain?"

"Uh, do I have to?"

"Hey, man, you call me to come visit the school, you bring your friend here, who's been doin' some sort of surveillance thing, and I'm not supposed to know. I think not, my friend." Jamal raised his eyebrows in the impossible way that gave him one of the most expressive faces I've ever seen.

"Okay, everyone else in town thinks I'm nuts, why shouldn't you. We're looking for kids, maybe kids who are a little fucked up. Depressed, disenfranchised, angry, maybe even violent kids who might, you know, be angry with the world."

"You just about describe all of adolescence, Duff."

206

Jamal starred at me. "What the hell are you really talking about?"

"We're looking for kids who might want to go Columbine."

Jamal put his hands on his hips and starred at me. I looked back at him and kept his eyes as long as I could.

"Duff, what the f–"

"Them," Karl said, softer than his usual voice. "Them, what's their story?" He pointed with a nod of the head. In that direction was a group of kids dressed in black, with the requisite black boots, dyed black hair and dark tattoos.

"C'mon, fellas. Those are the resident Goths. They're the wannabe angry teens trying to make a statement by being different–all of them being exactly the same different at the same time," Jamal said.

"Duff, I got a feeling." Karl turned toward Jamal. "You remember Chipper Newstrom. He was the quarterback on my VHS team?"

"Yeah, sure. He could play a little ball. It's weird you bring him up because I–"

"He was here wasn't he?" Karl broke in.

"Yeah. I saw him in the parking lot before class. How did you know?"

Karl looked up at me. So did Jamal.

"Holy shit." It was all I could think of saying.

35

We followed the kids in black after school. Eight of them and they smoked cigarettes behind the bowling alley, five blocks from McDonough. We sat in the El Dorado, two blocks away, watching the area they'd disappeared into through the woods and broken-down cement half-wall that used to be part of a garage years ago. After 45 minutes, three of them came out, and looked like they were headed home. They laughed and walked like any other kids, except they all dressed in black and all had the same tattoos on their forearms. The one in the middle had another tattoo on the back of his neck.

"Karl, how long are we going to sit here?" I said after another 45 minutes of watching kids through the trees and bushes.

"I don't know, but it feels like we've got to do something," he said.

"So far the most nefarious thing we got them doing is smoking cigarettes. You want to call Richie and Potsy and tell their moms?"

"Either Newstrom has intervened already or he's still working on them. This thing could be going down tomorrow."

"Or never," I said, starting to feel pretty stupid.

Fifteen more minutes went by without us talking. It was getting darker. I didn't see the use of waiting around much longer.

"Karl, I can't just sit here, it makes me nuts. I'm going to visit our friends in black."

"Duff, I don't think that's a good idea. They could be dangerous."

"Yeah, well, sitting around in a car listening to the two of us breathe is dangerous for my mental health." I opened the door and headed to the brushy area behind the bowling alley.

I heard Karl's door open and close, a few seconds behind me, and his running footsteps as he caught up with me.

"What are we going to do when we get there?"

"They're scrawny kids. What are they going to do? Pop a zit on us or something? We're adults and they'll be scared of us because they'll think they're about to get in trouble."

We got to the edge of the bowling alley. I looked at Karl. He raised his eyebrows as if to say 'What the hell?' I nodded as a signal to go.

We walked around the corner, stepped over an overgrown hedge, and looked into a cleared circle with empty beer cans, cigarettes, milk crates, a tire, and an old bike frame. There were no kids there. It looked like every kid's spot for bush drinking I had ever seen.

Karl walked ahead of me looking around.

"They went out this way." Karl pointed to a hole in the fence that went to the back of the bowling alley. He bent over and picked something up.

"Duff, you better see this."

I walked over and looked at Karl's find.

"Those are shell casings to a high powered assault weapon. They're similar to the ones I used. Newstrom would have access to them. He's been training them and he's equipped them."

"How do we know it's not kids screwing around and this is their clubhouse type of thing? Maybe there is nothing more serious than target practice going on."

"BB gun, slingshots, CO_2 pistols are one thing, Duff. These are high-powered assault weapons. Where would

McDonough kids get them?"

I didn't have a plausible explanation for any of it and I knew it. It felt like something awful was about to happen and I didn't have a clue what to do about it. I decided to call Jamal and tell him what we had found.

"Duff, I'm at practice. Can't this wait?" he said after picking up his cell phone. I told him I didn't believe it could wait and asked him for some of the kid's names. He told me the ringleader, if you could call him a leader, was Andy Katzman, and his two best friends were Michael Corona and Eddie Stain. He didn't know their exact addresses, but said they lived north of Jefferson Hill on the west side of the city.

"Hey, Duff, what makes you so sure they're going to do something?"

"Sometimes you get a feeling, Jamal."

"How have your instincts been serving you lately?"

I didn't have a good answer and hung up. Next I called Kelley and begged him to come see what Karl and I had found by the bowling alley. He wasn't pleased, but agreed to meet us there in a half an hour. In the meantime Karl and I went the six blocks over to the public library to look up the kids' addresses. We found three addresses for kids with the names Jamal gave us in the West Jefferson neighborhood.

We got back to the bowling alley and saw Kelley had beaten us there. His cruiser, parked like any other car in the lot, idling like he was taking a break.

"You got something to show me?" Kelley sounded just a tad more impatience than usual.

"Follow us," I said. The three of us walked back to the area behind the bowling alley.

"We found some shell casings to some serious assault weaponry. This isn't kid stuff," Karl said.

We got to the back of the bowling alley, each of us swinging our legs over the half-wall. In silence, the three of us walked to the center area where Karl and I had been about half an hour ago.

"They're not here. They were here just a minute ago. Somebody must've come and scooped them up to cover their tracks," I said.

Kelley just looked at me for a minute. Then he put his head down and kind of gently kicked the gravel. He looked up at me again.

"He's not crazy, Officer," Karl said. "I saw them myself. They were from a military issue."

Kelley kind of squinted at Karl; then he looked at me, and he put his head down again. He sniffed a little bit, looked up at me again, and then exhaled hard. It looked like he tried to say something, but he couldn't find the right words. Then he started to walk away.

"C'mon, Kell, I'm not nuts, I swear to God I'm not nuts."

He kept walking and didn't slow up.

36

Back at the Blue it was time to make a plan. Everyone who knew me at all thought I was crazy. I knew Karl was crazy and Karl called himself crazy. I don't know if we made the foundation of a real strong think-tank. Fortunately, we had a Black Muslim basset hound to help us–though his arch enemies appeared to be the sparrows.

"Karl, if we're going to go through with this, we have to at least get some handle on what Newstrom and his high school buddies are going to do and when." I paced back and forth in front of the couch where Karl sat with Al's head on his lap.

"Yeah, that's kind of the tough part," Karl said.

"Let's break down what we know. Let me think out loud and you fill in the gaps."

Karl sat up with his elbows on his knees. Al let out a heavy exhale and spun around on the couch three times.

"Go Duff," Karl said.

"Alright, what's Newstrom's goal? Money, right?"

"It's only part money. The rest is power and control."

"Okay, what are his resources? He must have the backing of someone or some group."

"His resources are almost endless. He's literally got billions of dollars at his disposal."

"What are our resources?" The room got quiet as we looked at each other and Al. "Okay, let's not focus on our resources too much." I chewed the end of my thumb because that's what guys in movies did when they thought deep thoughts. I was no Brad Pitt.

"We have the knowledge of what's going on–no one but Newstrom seems to know or care," Karl said.

"Which is why he cares about us. We know what he's up to, but everyone thinks we're nuts. Why does he even bother with us?"

"We're loose ends. He's military, he hates loose ends," Karl said.

"So why not just kill us, make us disappear and be done with us?"

"He might do that, but think about it Duff. You're reasonably well known and I'm your client. If we both turn up dead for no good reason, there will be questions asked. It's not efficient." Karl petted Al's head while he talked.

"So you think his goal is to eliminate us while he has his gang of misfit kids go Columbine on McDonough."

"That seems to be what he said. He would prefer it if I just killed myself. Then he might not have to do the other stuff here."

"Do you think he believes you'd do it?"

Karl looked down at Al, thinking.

"There was a time I would've, and it was when he knew me. He could still believe I would," Karl said.

"Could we fake your suicide and get him off our backs and maybe save ourselves and McDonough?"

"How do you fake a suicide? We'd need help and everyone who could help thinks we're nuts."

"Yeah." I stopped pacing and looked Karl in the eye. Al opened his eyes for a second and furrowed his brow. Then he closed them and rolled over on his back.

"So if Newstrom's goal is to take us out and do a Columbine at McDonough, what can we do?" I said. The room got quiet while we both thought.

"Duff?" Karl almost whispered.

"Yeah?"

"We can get him another way." Karl stood up.

213

I looked at him and waited.

"Look, he's used to getting what he wants. Shit, he's good at getting people to do what he wants. He's committed and he does what he sets his mind to. His goal is to get us out of the picture and get his Columbine. It's all about efficiency."

"Yeah, so?"

"Sometimes you got to go with the flow." Karl smiled.

"What the hell are you talking about?"

"We set ourselves up."

"Huh?"

"We make killing us and the school thing easy."

I stared at him wondering how nuts he really was.

"Look, Duff, we send him a message that we're going to be there to foil his plans and he'll have to kill us to make it happen. Give him what he wants on a silver platter." Karl started pacing in the living room, too. It made for a tight space. "That way he'll come for us and we'll be there knowing he's coming."

"So we somehow get a message to him saying we're going to stop him and he'll react and come for us. We tell him we're going to protect McDonough or something like that and he'll know exactly how to plan everything."

Karl broke into a smile.

"Can we get the message to him?"

"Yeah, I can get it to him easy enough with a call or two. He'll be waiting. It won't be hard." Karl was excited about his revelation.

"Karl, so we'll flush him out by making it easy to kill us and do his school project at the same time?"

"Yes!"

"You mean make ourselves sitting ducks?"

"Exactly," Karl almost shouted.

<u>37</u>

The kid with the bad skin pulled out a rifle and shot me in the center of the forehead. Blood ran down my face and into my eyes. My chest hurt. The second kid, the shorter one, pulled out his own gun and shot me in the chest. Blood poured out of me, but I still stood.

Jamal is saying to me I'm nuts and nothing is really happening, it is really all inside me. As he speaks to me he is shot in the head and though half of his skull is exposed, he continues to talk to me like nothing's happened. Blood continues to come out of my head and get in my eyes to the point where it is getting very hard to see.

Jamal keeps on talking, asking me what's wrong with my eyes.

My heart feels like it will implode inside of me. Then, the first shooter, the zit-kid is right in my face smiling.

"Duffy, you've gone crazy, you know," he says.

A piecing sound and a wet swipe across my eyes made me look up. Al is sitting on my chest telling me to stop dreaming. He looks like he's hyperventilating and concerned.

"I'm all right, Al. Take it easy."

Al flopped off of me and headed to his chair to keep an eye on the sparrows.

Nightmares suck. In fact, they suck so much that not sleeping is almost a better option. That is until you get about three days in a row without any sleep at all and you feel subhuman.

Subhuman or not, I needed coffee. Taped to the Mr.

Coffee was a note from Karl.

I'm going to make contact with Newstrom. Wish me luck. I can't wait until we get the bastard.

K.

That's great. I was about to go to war with a guy who has a lifetime of espionage and dirty military tricks up his sleeve. I bet he wasn't sleep-deprived or having creepy nightmares about zit-faced kids shooting him in the face.

The other great thing: my partner in all of this, good 'Ol Karl, who I kept kind of forgetting was certified Looney Tunes. Currently, he was supposedly out to make contact with an agent of worldwide terror and corruption. The fact Karl might be wearing his Redskins helmet didn't give me a ton of solace.

My coffee was only marginally better than the job's. Just not having to drink it within the proximity of the Michelin Woman probably accounted for the improvement in the coffee's taste. I called in again and said I would be faxing a doctor's note, which was a lie, but one I was confident I could get around. I flipped on the TV and went to one of the cable news networks. I could tell by the graphics and the reporters something out of the ordinary had happened.

A reporter who looked half-black and half-Asian tried to keep an earpiece in while he posed in front of what looked like a high school. The graphics underneath him said "High School Slaying Outside of Nashville–Three Known Dead."

The reporter got his cue to speak.

"This is Karl Bendorf, in Crawford, Tennessee, where there are reports of a Columbine-type assault on Crawford High School. Information continues to come in. Already there is conflicting information about what has occurred. One report is three students dressed in trench coats opened fire in a library filled with students, killing three and wounding several others. There is one confirmed death. A school employee named Elaine Fogarty was fatally shot in the face.

216

There are other reports that as many as ten students have been killed but the report has not been verified. I repeat, it has not been verified..."

Crawford, Tennessee? I didn't even know there was a Crawford, Tennessee. Did somebody get their information twisted and do the wrong crazy terrorist act? Is it just some sort of bizarre coincidence? I had no idea what to think.

Almost as if on cue, the phone rang. It was Karl.

"Where the hell are you?"

"I tried leaving messages for Newstrom with my contacts and left word for him to contact me. So far I haven't heard anything yet," Karl said.

"Have you been listening to the news? There's been some sort of shooting at a High school in Crawford, Tennessee."

"What?"

"You heard me." Silence came from the other end of the phone. After a long pause Karl came back on.

"That's a mistake, a coincidence. It just can't be Newstrom."

"How can you tell?"

"It just doesn't fit."

"You know, Karl, a lot of shit doesn't fit."

"Hang on Duffy, I'll be home in an hour, and we'll make a plan then."

He hung up. I looked at Al. He furrowed his brow and lay down to go to sleep. The whole thing didn't seem to make much sense to him either.

I sat around the house waiting for Karl to come back, wondering where the hell he would go to meet the elusive, ghost-like Newstrom. Karl wanted to keep this one to himself. For whatever reason–probably my looming insanity– I respected his wishes.

Around 1:30 he pulled up in the El Dorado.

217

"Okay, I've given it a lot of thought and it's one of two things," Karl said the second he walked through the door. It was like we were already in mid-conversation and with Karl, who knows, he might have been talking to me his whole trip back. Just the same, it confused Al who got excited about a human coming through the door. He began to go into his attack-as-greeting thing, but stopped and spun around three or four times.

"I'm listening," I said.

"Either Newstrom switched plans and is sending us a message by having it in another Crawford or he's trying to confuse us."

"I thought he wanted both of us dead."

"He definitely does, or at least wants us to believe it."

"Why?"

"If nothing else, to remain unpredictable." Karl walked past Al and sat in the sparrow lookout chair. Al raised his eyebrows, closed his eyes again.

"So what the hell do we do with our own little McDonough trench coat mafia?"

"We keep our surveillance up," Karl said while he thought of what to confuse me with next, the phone rang. It was Jamal.

We exchanged Salam Alekums and Jamal got right to it.

"Duff, I'm probably gettin' as crazy as the paper says you are, but you know those kids your friend was sure were up to something no good?"

"Yeah?"

"All eight of them are out today."

"Is that unusual?"

"Hell yeah."

"Jamal, we followed them the other day and I found some serious assault rifle shell-casings near their hang out."

"You what? Never mind—did you tell anyone?"

"I called Kelley and by the time he showed up the

casings were gone." I waited while Jamal went silent. He was quiet in the way people are when they're pondering the sanity of the person they're talking to.

"Duff, I don't know what to make of that, but you should know about this next thing 'cause you'll probably hear something about it on the news."

"What are you talking about?"

"The school is in lockdown while it is searched. There was a message scrolled in blood in the second floor boy's bathroom. They're not taking any chances."

"What did it say?"

"You ready for this–it's a bit deep. Here goes: 'Tomorrow the blood will flow from the hypocrite warriors. The true warriors of the city will rain down from the mountain top and they will die.'"

"Jamal–what the hell does all that mean?"

"No one fuckin' knows. Maybe they just have a social studies test they didn't study for."

"Must be one hell of a test," I said.

38

The next morning Karl, Al, and I went to McDonough High at six. There were police on every corner and if you weren't a student or a parent you weren't allowed within two blocks. Police ran wands over every student as they entered the building. The closest we could get was three blocks away.

By the time the bell sounded, it seemed like everything was under control. Police remained at every door and on the four corners surrounding the school. We waited until ten and then drove to the bowling alley to check out the hangout. We parked in the empty bowling alley lot and walked around the corner. No one was there, but as we walked to the center of the area we could see something had been painted on the back wall of the bowling alley building.

The blood will spill down the warrior's mountain. Their Abercrombie and Fitch will be stained forever!

"What the hell does it mean?" Karl squatted down and picked something up. "More shells."

"I'd feel a whole lot better if I knew where these punks were," I said.

"Yeah. I say they hit McDonough after lunch."

"And what do we do?"

"We wait, watch, and pray," Karl said.

That was exactly what we did, in the El Dorado, after we parked by McDonough. Al kept it interesting by farting a lot and Karl gave me long explanations on UFOs, Bigfoot, and the conspiracy that got Malcolm X killed. We talked about hydrogenated fat, Oreos, and the use of pesticides. We talked about social work, the military, and whether or not the

Yankees pitching would hold up. Al would flip over on his back, eventually get restless, clear his intestines of gaseous build up, and flop over again. Elvis did Gospel and then the *Elvis is Back* album from when he returned from Germany.

Nothing happened at lunch and at 1:37 p.m. Jamal spotted us as he walked to his car. I gave him a faint beep and he squinted in our direction. Once he realized it was us, he came over.

"They never came in," Jamal said.

"Everything normal in there?"

"If you call everybody being petrified, cops all over the place, lockers being searched, dogs, and metal detectors normal."

"Jamal, what's your gut tell you about these kids in black?"

"I don't know, Duff. I've been doing this a long time. They're goofy white boys who banded together to do goofy white shit your people do–watch *Star Trek*, laugh at *Seinfeld*, play Dungeons and Dragons–that shit."

"Could they be killers?"

"I don't know, Duff. Hey, I read *Psychology Today*. They're angry, disenfranchised and their parents aren't around. Shit, describes most of the student body."

"What about the shit written in the bathroom?"

"Don't know. Creepy shit, but whether or not it was just stuff to get out of school or genuine warning I don't know."

"It said something about mountains, warriors and the Gap?"

"Abercrombie and Fitch. C'mon Duff, the cool white kids stopped goin' to the Gap."

"Hold it!" Karl startled us with the yell. Al sneezed and cleared his jowls from the outburst.

"What's up Karl?" I said.

"Mountain, warriors and a reference to rich clothing?"

"Yeah, so?" Jamal said.

"VHS's nickname is the Mountain Warriors. The kids all wear Abercrombie and Fitch," Karl said.

The three of us got real quiet. Al sat up.

"And the kids we're looking for ain't here," Karl said.

I put the car in drive without saying goodbye to Jamal.

<u>39</u>

We flew down the country back roads to get to Vorhees Park. Karl talked a mile a minute and Al had picked up on the energy level and marched back in forth on the back seat, grumbling to himself.

"We could actually stop it this time, Duff. We can make it fail. It's never failed before," Karl said. His speech had trouble catching up to his thoughts. "I can't wait. I hope Newstrom is there in person. I want to look him in the eye when we stop him."

I didn't know what to think and decided to keep my mouth shut. In this up to my eyeballs, but not for a second did I get completely comfortable with whether it was true or if I was crazy. If true, me, a crazy guy and a basset, were about to try to thwart a guy with world class weaponry and a trained group of disgruntled Dungeons and Dragoners.

"Duff, this could make it all right again, do you understand? You gotta let me play it out. You gotta," Karl said. I could feel him staring at me while I kept my eyes on the road. I tried to deliver my body to where we went without doing a lot of thinking.

"Karl, I'm in this. I'll let you play it out," I said.

"Duff, I mean to the ultimate. I mean no matter what."

I looked at Karl.

"I mean I want to die doing this if the situation calls for it."

I looked at him for the first time during his rant. Our eyes locked for a moment.

"You gotta promise me, Duff, you gotta."

I looked at him for a long time.

"All right, Karl, all right," I said.

We pulled into the VHS parking lot. Despite our urgency, it looked like any other suburban high school on a late summer day. A bronze statue of the Mountain Warrior greeted us at the entrance to the campus. You could tell the statue was relatively new. The warrior no longer resembled a Native American like it had for years. Now, a Greek type mythological character with wings on its head and feet and somewhere, some old time Greeks were offended.

"All right Karl, what the hell do we do now?"

"Let's surveil the exterior and secure the perimeter."

Suddenly, he became Karl Schwartzkoff.

We parked the El Dorado in the student lot and headed out to the athletic field to surveil and seal off. Damn, people were right–I was nuts.

The place was huge. It dawned on me if we were at the freshman soccer field and the Dungeons and Dragons mafia entered from the JV girls field-hockey field, there would be no way to reach them by the time they got to the gym entrance. McDonough had a patch of dirt and a pavement basketball court with one broken hoop and the other hoop had no net.

We passed the freshman girls' softball field and headed toward the rock wall and obstacle course–yes, you heard me correctly–when I heard someone call to me.

"Please stop, Please stop." A smallish man with khakis and a blue button-down shirt headed toward us. He broke into a half trot and made it look like he tried to suppress a run. I was convinced he hadn't run since he got out of diapers.

"You are not allowed on school grounds. This is inappropriate!" It was Mr. Teters, the hall monitor, and he got worked up at the idea someone would break a school rule.

"I must ask you to leave immediately. No one is allowed on school grounds." Teters pushed his glasses up his nose. I know it's a nerd cliché, but he really did do it.

"Hey, Teters. My name is Duffy. We met a couple a weeks ago when I picked up the donated computer." I smiled but it didn't help. Teters remained determined.

"Neither of you have a green, orange, or yellow badge. You are not to be on school grounds." He didn't acknowledge our long friendship.

"Green, I thought there was just yellow and orange," I know it didn't make much difference, but I wanted to keep him talking, and I got genuinely curious.

"We have procedures here for when we identify an intruder. I will activate the Code Black procedure if you don't leave immediately." Teters was all business.

"Look Tetes we just…" I didn't get to finish whatever bullshit I was about to say. Teters reached into his khakis and pulled out his wad of keys and hit a button on a small plastic square thing. It was the kind of the thing the guys at Seven Eleven sometimes wore.

I didn't get to think much about 7-Eleven or anything else because a bunch of air raid horns went off and red strobe lights went off at every door. Teters started to sprint to the middle doors where a set of blue lights flashed. A sign there said "Student Emergency Gathering Area."

"Nice goin' Tetes," I said to no one in particular.

Amid the horns and lights, I could hear Al's distinctive baritone in the distance. He didn't care for lots of bells and whistles. Little by little, students started to file out of the exits, gathering in the different areas marked off for such events. The kids came out laughing and goofing off and got scolded for it, just like I remember at fire drills when I went to McDonough. The chance to get out of a lecture on Dickens or a discussion of the Holy Roman Empire was indeed cause for celebration. Still, this was not a fire drill, this was an emergency on the grounds, and no one took it seriously. I guess you can get used to anything.

There seemed to be a couple thousand kids gathering in about ten spots on the athletic fields. The thing that immediately struck me, the kids all, or at least mostly, looked the same in their outfits. The difference weren't so much in fashion, but in brand name and maybe they organized themselves according to the status of Old Navy, the Gap, and Abercrombie and Fitch. Don't ask me which one had the highest rank.

Sirens began to echo off the school and there were a lot of them. From the sound of them it was clear they were coming closer. I'm not exactly sure why this dawned on me, but I remembered the sound distortion had something to do with the Doppler Effect. Boy, put me in a school setting and in fifteen minutes I'm thinking old thoughts.

"Duff—focus!" Karl said. "Don't forget why we're here."

"Sorry, Karl. I guess I got mesmerized by all the activity."

Karl stone-faced, his head pivoting back and forth, systematically surveyed everything. The kids still filed out and horsed around, pushing each other and flicking each other behind the ears. Bobby, the fat kid from the nurse's office, got yelled at for making fart noises again. He desperately acted like he was unjustly accused.

"He's here," Karl said without inflection. "The son-of-a bitch is here."

I looked and saw Karl starring at a group of gym teacher types. Sure enough, there was Newstrom, the guy I met at the trophy case, and few other coaching types. They acted as bad as the kids, laughing and goofing around. One guy kept doing this forearm shiver move, gesturing about blocking or something.

"Easy, Karl, easy," I said. "He's not doing anything. He might just be visiting."

Karl didn't respond. I noticed he breathed hard and repeated 'focus' under his breath. The sirens continued and I

226

could see red flashing lights bouncing off the school bricks. A couple of administrative types carrying clipboards went from group to group checking things off.

"Look for the Goths, Duff. They're here, I can feel it."

I kept my mouth shut and looked. As my stare swept across the school-land I heard a voice yell, "New York State Troopers, freeze!" There were four guys in black gear and armor holding guns on us from a distance of about 200 feet.

"Are they talking to us?"

"Duffy, those three kids," Karl pointed to some kids, by a phys-ed obstacle course, that had drifted from the pack. "They look familiar to you?"

They were a couple of hundred yards away, but they looked like every other kid in front of us. Cargo pants, fake faded T-shirt, Nikes and carefully set hair to make it look like it wasn't.

"The one closest to us, has a tattoo on his forearm. It's in the same spot as the kid we saw behind the bowling alley."

"Yes, he does," I said. One of the other kids turned away. It was clear he had a tattoo on the back of his neck. Too close to be a coincidence.

"It's them," Karl said. Before I could do anything Karl took off, sprinting across the softball field toward the kids.

"Freeze! Freeze! Freeze!" came from the SWAT guy in charge.

Karl started to run in a random zig zag pattern, every few steps he'd roll and get up. The troopers opened fire and the dirt kicked up all around him. The crowd of kids and teachers were in shock and started to scream and yell, and some started to run. Enough got in the way of Karl that the troopers had to stop firing.

I took off, saw Newstrom heading for Karl, who closed in on the kids. Newstrom yelled something and the Goths in Gap clothes headed for the woods. It was tough to tell where everyone went. Karl sprinted, closed the gap on the Goths, and Newstrom closed in on Karl.

The cops no longer focused on us. They tried to corral the panicked mass of kids and teachers, who at this point had discarded any emergency plan. I reached the woods and saw the three kids, Karl, and Newstrom each pursuing the one in front of them as fast as they could. Karl closed in on the tattooed-neck kid. I saw him leap to do a flying tackle. The kid went down hard. Karl had him by the hair and he violently slammed the kid's head to the ground. Newstrom was within twenty feet of Karl and he had a gun in his hand. I had no weapon, but I gained on Newstrom who had slowed when he pulled out the gun.

Karl slammed the kid again and rolled off him in a tight ball like he had done it a million times, coming up in a shooter's stance, and holding a gun he must've taken off of the kid.

"Drop it Chip. I swear to God I'll put one in your forehead if you don't drop it!" Karl yelled.

I stopped 20 feet to the right of Newstrom. The kid on the ground rolled over, his face was a bloody mess. He grabbed for his nose, crying like a three-year-old. The absurdness of a terrorist crying like a toddler stuck with me for some reason. His buddies kept running through the woods to who the hell knows where. So much for loyalty.

"Karl, Karl, Karl…" Newstrom said. "You're still one hell of a soldier, I'll give you that." Newstrom kept his gun at his side while he smirked at Karl.

"Shut the fuck up," Karl said. "It's over. I got you this time. You're going to get what's coming to you." Karl paused and looked to me. "Duff, take his gun."

I walked toward Newstrom, who spied me from the corner of his eye.

"Karl, Karl, Karl, I know you're nuts, but you've never been stupid."

"Look asshole, it's over. You and your security company

228

assholes are done. I'm going public."

I walked toward Newstrom deliberately. I was hyper aware of what went on, but it almost didn't seem real.

"Get the gun, Duffy."

"Karl, don't be a fool. You've got nothing on me. I'm an old football hero and class president, here to visit the alma mater. You're the one who brought the troopers and threatened the school. You even beat up this poor high school junior."

"Poor high schooler with a gun."

"No one will ever know that part." Newstrom smiled. "In fact no one will know much about this at all. We've got too much behind us, Karl. I'm just going to drift away and no one will ever know any of this. You'll go to prison and I'll be on to the next thing."

"Not this time," Karl said.

"Oh yeah, Karl. You should've killed yourself when you had a chance. You were stupid enough to let those dead towel-head kids bother you–surely this shit will have you even crazier. And when you get to prison you'll find out the kind of connections I have there."

"Get his gun Duff."

I moved closer to Newstrom.

"You're a fool Karl. You could've been living my life and you pissed it away. There's no way you can stop me. You may have stopped me here, but I'll be on to the next mission and nothing will stop me." Newstrom's tone showed no sign of stress.

"Get the gun, Duff."

I stepped to Newstrom's side and reached for the gun very carefully.

In a split second, Newstrom caught me under the chin with the barrel, which forced the gun from his hand and knocked me down. I rolled over and sprang up a bit wobbly from the blow.

Newstrom was in front of me. He went to kick me in the face, but I caught his foot and twisted it until he went down hard on his back. My mind went dark and something went through me. It was like a waking nightmare–a panic attack in real time.

Now I kneeled on Newstrom's chest, throwing piston punches on his face, my shirt splattered with blood with each and every shot. His face was almost purple with blood; I noticed part of his nose had separated from the rest of his face. I wasn't in control; something else was. It came up through the center of me and wouldn't stop.

"Duffy, No! No! No!" I heard in the distance. "No! No! You can't!"

Something hit me hard like a halfback running into me. I came off Newstrom onto my back. Karl stood over me panting. My vision went in and out. Newstrom didn't move.

"I think you killed him, Duff," Karl said, looking down at the motionless body of Newstrom.

I was barely lucid as I got up on my knees to look. Karl knelt beside Newstrom doing chest compressions.

"C'mon, Chip. C'mon you motherfucker."

Newstrom spit up blood and moaned loudly. He rolled to his side and puked a mixture of blood and vomit. Karl started to shake and he looked terrified.

"Freeze! Hold it right there!" A voice from behind us interrupted whatever the hell was going on in Karl's and my heads.

It was one of the troopers, all in black, and he had three soldiers with him. I knew immediately they were the three guys who jumped me in the hospital parking lot. The four of them had their assault rifles fixed on us. From between them stopped a guy in a turtleneck and corduroy slacks.

It was Dr. Theodore Martin, Karl's psychiatrist in Germany, and now the trauma/grief shrink who showed up on television after each bit of terrorism.

40

"Karl, can't you just take your medicine and leave well enough alone?" the doctor said as he paced a few feet in front of his armed guards.

"That's what you would've wanted isn't it? Well fuck you, Doc," Karl said.

"Your friend nearly beat your old buddy Chippy to death. Corporal, attend to the Lieutenant." Two of the soldiers rushed to Newstrom's side, lifted him, and carried him back to where they had been standing.

"Get him in the Hummer. We'll need medical back-up," Martin said. Behind them, parked in the woods was a jet black Hummer. It must've been how they got in here in the first place.

"He's going to jail–you're all going to jail, you scumbags," Karl said.

"Karl, Karl, Karl. You really are insane. There will be no jail. There will be no media coverage. We don't exist, we don't answer to the usual sources. You watch; the papers tomorrow will report on the drill at VHS. There will be no mention of us or you or the stupid teenagers we trained. It all goes away. Just like it always does. It all goes away."

"I stopped you this time, you asshole, and I'll keep stopping you," Karl yelled at them.

"I'll give you this, Karl, you did indeed get in the way of this operation, there's no doubt. I'd have you killed if we hadn't already succeeded at well, how do I say this…keeping people from taking you seriously. Your friend there, he made it a bit more complicated, but after the debacle at Notre

Dame, not many see him as credible."

"So it's on to the next project isn't it, you fucking scum," Karl said.

"Karl, there's work to be done here, and where we are needed around the world. You don't see that."

"What I see are kids dying while scumbags like you line their pockets. You go to hell. I should've let Duffy finish Newstrom."

"Karl, forget it. You can't win. Nothing has changed. You have made no difference in this entire thing. It disappears, it vanishes." He smiled and paused. "You'll especially like our next…uh…event. It will have an explosive effect on the military." He looked briefly at the soldiers. "Let's go." The four of them headed to the Hummer, to who knows where.

"You want to tell me what the hell just happened," I said to Karl, who still stared at the Hummer as it pulled away. He didn't answer me. He looked to the sky and let out a bloodcurdling scream.

He sat on the ground and started to cry. When he sniffed away enough of the tears, he looked at me and said, "C'mon, Duff you get it by now. There's too many making too much to want to find peace. The money is in war. That's it, plain and simple."

I had no idea what to say. I just looked at Karl.

"People have too much at stake and as long as the machine has a way to make them fearful, the cash cow will get fatter and fatter. Martin's right. They're just on to the next project. Fuck!" Karl stood and kicked at the dirt.

"Karl, why did you pull me off him?"

"I've killed Duff. It takes its toll. I didn't want you to have to live it. Your nightmares are bad enough now." Karl looked up right at me. I didn't have a clue what to say. Karl kicked the dirt again and continued to curse.

Martin was right. The kids were back in school, the

troopers had gone back to their barracks, and I'm sure the papers would have nothing to say about anything.

"Karl, you were right all along and you saved a bunch of lives today." I put an arm around his shoulder. "C'mon, buddy let's get out of here."

We headed back through the woods to the fields, toward the parking lot. The drill over, the sirens silent, there was no longer any sight of troopers. I had no doubt the media would report a drill or a false alarm the next day. We walked along the edge of the woods by the soccer and softball fields to get back to the car.

Outside of one of the double doors a single teacher stood looking at us. A couple of hundred feet away, but she kept looking at us. I began to wonder if she would call another alarm and start this whole mess again.

"Duff, who's watching us?" Karl said.

"I've got no idea, but I think she's had her eye on us since the woods."

"You think she saw what went down?"

"We were off in the woods so I doubt it. I guess in the confusion she could've followed from behind and saw." I thought about it a little bit.

"She could be with Newstrom," Karl said.

"Yeah or she could be a teacher getting some air."

We came up on the Cadillac and Al, hearing us, got up from his nap and barked out the window. I saw Karl smile out of half his face. He got in on Al's side and Al licked him once while climbing on his lap.

"Duff, it's just like when I was over there. No resolution, no closure on shit. They got away with it there and they got away with it here." Karl punched the car door. We pulled out and away from VHS and headed towards Crawford.

"Still…"

"Still nothing, Duff. Face it, I'm still nuts, and now, so are you. You've been discredited and no one will ever look at

233

you the same way ever again. They won again," Karl said while he petted Al.

I didn't have an answer. He was right, though. I had become a crazy, punch-drunk fighter everyone laughed at behind his back. These fucking assholes went on to the next town to keep their own version of terror going, and they were still making millions. Karl and I sat in silence for a long time as we took the winding roads back home toward the city. We'd lost and had really nothing left to say.

Almost to the city line, Karl spoke. "Duffy, you promised me something."

I felt him looking at me while I drove. "I did?"

"Yeah. When we decided to do this I made you promise we could see something through to the end some time. That we could get to somebody doing something wrong and put a stop to it–a complete stop to it. No bullshit, no cover ups, no ifs, ands, or buts."

"Yeah, so. You got something in mind?"

Karl looked down at Al. His whole face changed.

"You bet your ass I do."

"You wanna clue me in?"

"We raid that no good fuckin' puppy mill and shut it down once and for all."

"Karl…"

"Duff, what the hell do we got to lose? Everyone thinks we're nuts already."

"But Karl I don't think they're doing anything illegal."

"Yeah–and technically neither are the security firms."

I didn't know what to say. I looked at Karl and I looked at Al. The idea started to appeal to me. It may not have been the guys we wanted, but it would be a chance to snuff out some evil shit. This might have been conclusive evidence I really was crazy but–you know what–I didn't give a fuck.

"All right Karl–let's do it."

Karl smiled and petted Al.

"We're gonna need some help you know," I looked at Karl.

"It would come in handy."

"There's probably good reason they all think we're crazy," I said.

"You don't think I know that?"

41

Karl could barely contain himself.

"Time for liberation and justice, liberation and justice, Duff!" Karl paced back and forth in the living room with Al watching him like a one-man tennis match.

"We need a plan Karl. Let's go over what we know about the place."

"Yeah, sure Duff, good idea. We know they got about 40 dogs and another 10-15 puppies ready to be sold off," Karl said.

"We saw those three guys pull in there, so we know there are three guys who live or work there. Hold it–"

"What is it?"

"The three guys we saw in the pickup who pulled in the gates when we went past on our way to Notre Dame…"

"What about them?"

"You remember I got a weird déjà vu feeling?"

"Yeah?"

"Newstrom's three guys, the same guys who jacked me in the head. Holy shit!" I felt as crazy as people thought.

"I wonder what the hell it means. Uh, Duff?" Karl scrunched up his face. "I didn't tell you this, but when I snuck in there, I found out there were more like 10-12 guys living or working in there. Sorry I didn't give you that detail."

"That's kind of an important detail."

"Yeah, sorry."

"Ten against two and forty or fifty dogs to rescue. Karl, how the hell are we going to pull this off?"

"And the guys running the place are all crew-cut, tough

guy types."

"Oh good."

We both got quiet for awhile. I began thinking as much as a mission like this might serve to exorcise both of our demons, it might do it by getting both of us killed. There was no way we could win against these odds.

The phone rang, jarring me out of my strategic thought.

"Duffy, for God's sake are you all right?" Trina said. She sounded desperate.

"Yeah, I think so–why?"

"You're in the news again. Something about interrupting a school emergency drill? They referred to you as delusional and disturbed or something like. Every one is worried about you."

"Great."

"Duffy, I'm worried about you."

"Yeah, I get that a lot."

"Duffy, I'm serious."

"Look, Trina, I appreciate your concern, but I don't really have time right now. Karl and I have to plan something."

"Karl–you and Karl are planning something. Oh my God…"

"Yeah, I don't expect anyone to understand. I don't care about that any more."

"What are you up to?"

"We're going to shut down the puppy mill I told you about. We're going to go in there and close it down."

"Duff–"

"Don't try to talk me out of it, Trina. We're doing it and I don't expect you or anyone else to understand. It is something we have to do for a lot of reasons."

"You think you're just going to go in there and take the dogs?"

"It might be a little more complicated."

"Complicated?" Trina sniffled.

"Well, there are about ten guys, who live there, we might have to deal with."

"Duffy, that's suicide!"

"We could use a few extra hands, but with my reputation I don't think we're going to find anyone. If we have to, we'll do it alone."

"Oh my God…"

She begged me to see her before we left and, like a sap, I said I would. She wanted to meet me at AJ's before we did anything and I promised her I would go. Hell, I needed a drink or two before I headed out to do something like this anyway. I wasn't looking forward to hearing the bullshit from the Foursome about my mental state, my beating up of a Notre Dame math student, or anything else. Just the same, going to AJ's was just something I did, almost like a bodily function.

I had been through some shit in my life, but this last month was something else, and at a whole new level. Life gets pretty weird when you're uncertain about what's real and what's illusion, and for me, I wasn't sure about much. I followed the impressions of a man I knew was certifiable. Shit–according to Rudy–I was certifiable. Newstrom, Martin, and those boys had told me they were untraceable and unprovable, and everything they do and did went unchecked.

My answer to all this? Raid a perfectly legal puppy farm that–oh, by the way–is also the local center for canned and dried goods for U.S. soldiers overseas. I've spent my life following my gut, and it's gotten me into trouble. I've lived following that gut, but now people let me know, in no uncertain terms, my gut was nuts.

"We ready, Duff?" Karl said.

"Karl I guess it's just me and you."

"And Al." Al's tail started thumping right on cue.

"Karl, before we head out there–is this really a good

238

idea? I mean besides the danger and all, will this really make things better?"

"It just might, Duff. It just might."

I told him we had to make a quick stop at AJ's because I promised Trina. He thought getting a drink and maybe asking the boys to come along might be a good idea. I told him I doubted the boys were likely to hitch a ride on our bandwagon, considering they thought we're both crazier than shithouse rats.

It was almost dark, certainly close enough to insure it would be dark by the time we got out to the puppy farm. On our way over to AJ's, things started to run through my head.

"Karl, how the hell are we supposed to get through the front gate?"

"We can climb it."

"How do we get 40 or 50 hounds out climbing a fence?"

"Er…uh."

"Geez…"

"What if they got guns and shoot at us?"

"We'll be sneaky."

"Great."

People were right. We were both crazy.

42

We pulled into AJ's, and the three of us headed in. AJ would give me shit about Al, but I've got used to that. The second I stepped in the place I knew something was wrong.

The place was packed.

Trina was waiting for me near the front.

"What the hell is going on?" I said. Trina forced back tears.

"I don't want you getting hurt. You may not care, but other people do." She started to sob and put her face in her hands. I wasn't quite sure what she was talking about. I looked around the room and realized familiar faces filled the place. I walked to my usual spot at the bar, dumbfounded.

Three rough-looking black guys with red bandanas sat on the first three stools of the bar. From behind them stepped a young black woman.

"Oh my God, Shony." The kid I kind of rescued a few years back came forward.

"Mr. Duffy, God bless you," she said and gave me a kiss and a gentle hug. "Miss Trina called and said something about you needing some help."

The three hard-looking black guys stepped around her.

"Who are you guys?"

The guy in the middle, with a Chicago Bulls hat and a toothpick, raised his eyes without raising his head and looked at me.

"Shony called us. I'm her stepbrother and these two are my…uh…associates. I do anything the girl say and she say some white guy named Duffy need help. Say it might involve some muscle. Shony say you the one…the only one… came looking for her when she got kidnapped. Said you saved her life." He paused a second and looked me up and down. "That's all I need to know. We here to help."

Next to the black guys sat Billy Cramer, my old karate student. He'd put on about 40 pounds of muscle. Next to him some other guy with cauliflower ears and a crew-cut leaned against the bar.

"What's up, Duff?" Billy got off his stool and hugged me.

"What the hell are you doin' here?"

"Trina said you needed a hand."

I didn't know what to say.

"Geez, you got big." I couldn't think of anything else to say.

"Duff, I'm doing mixed martial arts stuff and you gotta have some upper body stuff. I ain't the skinny, pizza-faced kid you stood up for a few years ago." He smiled. He had turned into a confident young man.

"This is Timo, we train together. Timo just likes to fight."

I shook hands with Timo, who barely acknowledged me.

"Mr. Duffy! The Frogman is here and at your service." Froggy took a night off from his park rendezvous. "Ms. Trina say Mr. Duffy need help. The Frogman doesn't forget."

The bewilderment shifted over. I had a lump in my throat and welled up.

Next to the Frogman, Doctor Pacquaio, the Philipino doctor I knew, stood. A few years back, I helped a guy get social services benefits by lying on some forms, and it turned out he was Philipino.

"Hello Duffy. Long time, no see you." Dr. Pac gave me a big toothy smile.

"What the hell are you doing here, Doctor?"

"You helped a friend of mine, a poor man with no home,

241

get a place to live. From my country, and I know for a fact he's still doing well." He looked me in the eye. "That's because of you."

Standing next to the doctor was Vinci, a boxer from the Crawford Y. Vinci, way past a-not-so-great prime, but he and I had been sparring partners since our teen years. Next to him Jamal, Angel, and Shaquan leaned against the wall

"Yo, Duff, this Trina says you're in trouble and need some back up," Shaquan said.

"Trina's a bit of a worrier," I said.

"She said somethin' about raiding a puppy mill. I ain't even sure what a puppy mill is, but it don't sound like this Trina is exaggeratin'," Vinci said.

"Yeah, well."

"We're in, too," Jerry Number One said. Jerry Number Two and TC both nodded along.

"I thought you guys thought I lost it."

"Oh, we're convinced you lost it," Jerry Number Two said.

I couldn't help but smile.

"Rocco will be along," TC said.

Next to them stood Mary Jo, a fellow Elvis fan, who lived out in the boonies. Someone once stole her Elvis scarf–one she got from the King. I found the scum who had ripped off her trailer on one of my bad-mood days. I gave the guy a beating and got her scarf, and some other stuff, back.

"I'm not good at kicking any ass, Duffy, but I barely got to thank you for what you did for me. I want to help you do whatever you want to do," she said, and a tear ran down her face. She had a baseball bat with her.

A short man came out of the bathroom tugging at a zipper on a pair of polyester sans-a-belts. I started to lose it at that point.

"You! Meshuganah, you know that," Hymie said. He had founded the clinic and kept Gloria from firing me a bunch of times.

"I don't know what mess you're in. You crazy schmeckle." He pursed his lips and shook his head in frustration. He dug into his pocket and got his roll of cash.

"Here's a grand."

"What's that for?" I said.

"Goddam it. I'm eighty-six years old and I can't go fighting some hooligans. I'd do anything else for you son." He waved a dismissive hand at me and walked away.

Trina wound her way back and stood in front of me with her hands on her hips. Her eyes red and her face puffy, she had the forceful look of a woman on a mission.

"I only had an hour to round people up. These people care about you, you know." She paused and wiped her eyes. "You don't have to do what ever fool thing you're about to do, you know." She stared at me. I stared back without saying a word.

She shook her head.

"You're going to tell me whatever it is you're going to do you have to do, and I won't understand. Damn, you're an idiot."

I just smiled

I called out and asked everyone to gather around. They all came here to help, but this thing needed to be organized.

"Look, everyone," I wasn't sure what to say. "I haven't been doing so good lately. As many of you well know, I might not be in my right mind. I'm pretty sure I'm a little nuts. I don't want anyone getting hurt or in trouble because I'm nuts and—"

The black kid with the bandana cut me off. "Shony said you crazy. She also say you the only motherfucker crazy enough to save her when she needed savin'."

"I know everyone called you nuts for teaching me karate and, uh, changing my life," Billy Cramer said.

"It was a crazy thing you did for my friend—you almo

lost your job. Beautifully crazy," Dr. Pac said.

"You got my scarf back and didn't even know me. We need more crazy people if you ask me," Mary Jo said.

"Look, Duff, everyone knows you're crazy and been crazy, so why don't you stop the bullshit and tell us what to do," Jamal said, speaking for the guys from the gym.

"All right, all right," I said. "Okay, here's the deal. You know this canned food drive everyone's been doing for the soldiers? Well, the place in this region that collects them is also what they call a puppy mill. They call it that because they breed dogs for profit like a mill and they mistreat the dogs. The dogs don't get exercise, they're fat but undernourished, unsocialized, and when they're done breeding, these bastards sell them to the cosmetic people to do awful tests on them. Our job is to go in there, steal the dogs, and get them out."

Everyone stared at me, but I had gotten used to that.

"Oh, and one more thing. Al's mom is in there and she's real sick and real pregnant."

"I just got a question," Billy said.

"Shoot," I said.

"How are we getting forty or fifty dogs out of there to wherever we're going with them?"

"That's a problem," I said.

The bar went quiet, except for the two Jerrys and TC, who whispered and snickered.

"What's up fellas?" I said.

"Uh, Duffy, I don't think transportation will be an issue," Jerry Number One said and the other two giggled.

On cue, while everyone tried to figure out what was going on, AJ's front door opened. Rocco came in wearing old army fatigues.

"Sorry, I'm late, Duff," Rocco said. "What's the problem?"

"Getting through the gate and getting all the dogs out," I

said.

"That won't be a problem," Rocco went back out the door.

"Excuse me everybody." I followed Rocco.

There, at the curb, parked in front of AJ's, sat the Deuce. Totally restored, tuned up, and humming like an engineering work of art.

"No, Rocco, not the Deuce, I can't. It's your pride and joy, man."

Rocco smiled and put a hand on my shoulder. "You know this friend of yours, Karl?" Rocco looked me in the eye.

I nodded.

"You know I did time in the service. I don't talk about it much, but this PTSD shit they talk about now didn't start in Vietnam. Some shit happened to me in Korea I don't like thinking about. It wasn't nice. So if I can maybe do something to help someone else make sense of that shit, maybe it will help me make sense of some old built-up shit in my life."

"But Rocco, the Deuce? Your dream?"

"Well, Duff, I got to thinkin'. Maybe she wasn't built to look pretty. Maybe she got built for a mission. Maybe for a mission exactly like this."

The big horn sounded. I looked up to see Karl behind the wheel, Al next to him. Al bayed along with the horn.

I guess it was time to go.

43

AJ's Army filed out and climbed in the back of the Deuce. Rocco drove, Karl went shotgun and Al sat between them. I stepped to the back with the troops.

The night had a chill and riding 55 miles an hour added to the cold. No one complained and no one talked. A certain tension existed to the trip that brought a bunch of people together who didn't know one another and didn't really have much in common. That is, except they liked me enough to do this, and they were crazy as shit for offering their services. The thirty-minute ride seemed a lot longer.

A mile outside the puppy mill, Rocco pulled over to the side of the road so we could mount a battle plan. Rocco looked at me to address the army. I shook my head and nodded to Karl. This was his show, and his chance to exorcise whatever demons haunted him. I thought it might be nice if he didn't get killed, or get the rest of us killed in the process.

"All right everybody listen up," Karl said his voice deep, his tone confident. It wasn't hard to picture him as an exemplary soldier. "This is what we know. A: The bastards who live here are right-wing whack jobs and we don't know what they are capable of. B: They're mistreating dogs, including a pregnant dog we've identified as Al's mom." Karl paused and looked at everyone.

"And C." His voice deepened and he turned the volume up a notch. "Their operation is fuckin' history the second we bust through that fuckin' gate." Karl yelled it at the top of his lungs and Rocco floored the Deuce.

Rocco had her up around seventy as we bombed down

246

Route 85. The puppy mill came into view about a hundred yards down the road. Rocco yelled, "Hang on tight, men."

The Deuce hit the gate, blasting it wide open. Sparks from the metal-to-metal violence flew and the gate splintered into a dozen pieces. The Deuce swerved, bounced, and for a second felt like it was going to roll over, but Rocco, like Lee Marvin on steroids, righted it and yelled "Yahoo! You Motherfuckers!"

Lights went on all over the compound and alarm sirens went off. Rocco didn't slow down and headed down the dirt road towards the kennels. When he got within fifty yards he slowed the Deuce down so everyone could jump out.

"Free the POWs," Karl yelled referring to the basset hounds.

The AJ's Army jumped out of the back of the Deuce and ran into the kennels. The hounds heard the noise and went nuts. A cacophony of barking, howling, and baying filled the night as the gang ran in.

Jerry Number One and TC were the first out, each carrying a couple of old hounds. Next came Vinci and Billy followed by the three gang-bangers all holding bassets. What a great sight.

Billy and Timo each had a fat lemon and yellow basset in their arms, running toward the Deuce. Jamal made a face trying not to inhale as his POW relieved himself. Mary Jo told a little guy to hush up, he would be all right. Dr. Pac tried to get an unruly barker into the back of the Deuce.

I heard Karl yell out for me. I ran to the back of the barn. He stood there with Al, who paced back and forth and wagged his tail.

"Duffy!"

I got back there as fast as I could and noticed what had caused the panic in his voice. Gladys moaned in pain and breathed hard. A little foam oozed out her mouth.

"She's in trouble, Duff. She needs help bad," Karl said.

He wrapped her in a tattered blanket he found in her pen and lifted her as gently as he could. "We gotta get her to a vet ASAP."

Ahead of us in the barn, there a flurry of activity continued as the gang rounded up the rest of the hounds. Karl walked with Gladys as gingerly as he could. Only a handful of hounds remained and the gang-bangers rounded them up.

"Damn these mutherfuckin' bitches smell!" I heard one say to the other. I didn't think he meant it literally.

I could hear the Deuce's engine. We had just loaded Gladys into the front seat when I heard Billy Cramer say, "Hey Duff, looks like we got some company."

Down from the hill came about twenty men, some skinhead types, others military types, heading right for the Deuce.

They didn't look happy.

"Hey Karl," I yelled, "I thought you said about 10 guys worked here."

Karl looked at the men running toward us.

"I was wrong," he said.

44

"Showtime!" Shony's cousin yelled.

"I was hopin' we were gonna get some action," his friend with the toothpick said.

Billy Cramer rolled his shoulders to loosen up and his buddy, Timo, just smiled out of the side of his mouth.

Shaquon cracked his neck, Angel hopped from foot to foot, and Jamal cracked his knuckles. I felt that twitch in my neck.

Rocco got the Louisville slugger from behind his seat. The two Jerrys and TC looked nervous and stayed with the dogs. It looked like they had us by about 10 men.

They were still at a disadvantage.

The first two to engage were Shony's gang-bangers. The three of them took on five skinny pale guys with shaved heads and tattoos. Two skinny bastards went down and out quick, and the other three found themselves in big trouble. Flurries of other punches flew and in seconds the skinheads went down on their backs desperately trying not to get stomped to death.

Over on the knoll to the right, Billy and Timo faced off against four body-builder types with flattops. Two charged Billy, who swung his left arm in a tight circle, wrapped up one guy, and turned him, using his bald head as a weapon. The head hit the other guy right in the face and blood exploded from it. Meanwhile, Timo had both guys down and screaming, as he had broken their pinkies with some sort of sick Brazilian Jujitsu shit.

Karl tangled with two guys and had his hands full. One

guy had him wrapped up while another got off the ground from Karl's kick, to work him over. The guy paused and reached into his pocket to slide on some brass knuckles. Karl was going to get really messed up. I headed over to try to get between him and the on-coming punch. I wasn't going to make it in time. Karl was going to take one hard and right in the face and I felt sick not being able to get there.

The skinhead smiled with his rotten teeth, and wound up to throw a haymaker right in Karl's face. He cocked his arm, putting everything he could into it. Suddenly he froze, his face turning into mask of horror. He.

Al had affixed his jaws to the guy's nads and he wasn't letting go. The guy screamed bloody horror. Al growled a sound I had only heard once before. His jaws bear-trapped on the guys' privates. Al's eyes bulged out of his head while he let out that horrible growl. The sound came from hell and Al let the world know he would not stand for Karl being fucked with.

The guy holding Karl got distracted just for a second and that was enough for Karl's training. Karl slammed the back of his own head into the bridge of the guy's nose, breaking the grip. Karl followed up with an elbow strike to the guy's temple. The guy crumbled face down.

To my left, the guys from the gym stood in a semi-circle. In front of the three of them, I counted seven guys on their backs. It looked like all held their faces or their midsections.

I surveyed the landscape, and it looked like the crew had done its job. Rocco shoulder-to-shoulder with me, yelled, "Let's load 'em up, and get out of here!"

The hounds in the truck, the opponents finished off, and everyone was in the process of running to the Deuce.

That was when the shotgun blast almost deafened everyone.

<u>45</u>

Ten feet in front of me, holding a shotgun, stood Luther Campbell.

"You piece of shit, what the fuck do you think you're doing, comin' in here and messin' with my hounds?" He looked down the barrel of his shotgun.

AJ's Army grew silent. Though we won the first battle, Luther held the great equalizer.

"I ought to blow your fuckin' head right off," Luther said.

"I–" I had no idea what to say.

"Point the gun at me you fat piece of shit," Karl said.

"Who you callin' a–"

"I'm calling you a piece a shit." Karl had a smile on his face looking as calm and relaxed as I was tense.

"Karl! Take it easy," I said.

"Duff, this is it man. This is where it stops. This is where the score gets evened. I'm stopping it right here."

"Karl, what the fuck are you talking about?"

"Get ready, fat man. I'm going to shove that shotgun right up your ass." Karl started to walk right towards Campbell. He approached unarmed and it looked like it was an act of suicide.

"Karl!"

"I'm sick and tired of being sick and tired and I've had it."

"I swear to God I'll shoot you if you come any further." Luther's voice cracked.

"Fuck you!" Karl responded.

"Karl!"

Karl smiled, walking without hesitation toward Campbell's gunsites.

"Don't come any closer or I'll–" Campbell said.

I sprinted toward Campbell screaming as loud as I could. Al charged with me and Campbell looked quickly toward us while Karl closed within five feet of him. He glanced back toward Karl and fired.

Karl went down.

The recoil sent Campbell backward and I tackled him a split second after the shot fired. The two of us rolled over and the fat bastard caught me in the temple with an elbow. I saw a flash of light and went a little woozy for a second, which gave him the time to get up and run toward the storage barn. Al was hot on his trail and I fell in behind Al. The bastard could run for a fat man.

I ran, gaining ground on Campbell. He went through the doors and around piles of canned goods. When I came through the doors he had disappeared. Mountains of filled pallets filled the corrugated steel structure.

"C'mon out, asshole," I yelled, but got no response.

Al sniffed the ground and I could tell he was looking for a scent. He worked his way around the giant pile of Vienna Sausages. Then he sat perfectly still and stared at the pile of cans.

"C'mon, Campbell, you fuckin' coward!"

A can of Vienna Sausages whizzed past my head and slammed into the corrugated steel wall behind me. It missed me, but not by much. I looked in the direction from where it came and heard movement. I noticed a sour gasoline smell and, turning, saw the wall ablaze.

A second Vienna Sausages can whizzed past my head. This one missed by a larger margin, but it made an explosion when it hit the wall. I heard Al bark. I had no idea what the hell was going on.

252

Three cans of sausage came from over the pile this time. I realized he wasn't even throwing at me. Al barked like a mad dog and stared at the mound of canned goods. Then it hit me.

Al recognized the explosives. The Vienna Sausages were mini-explosive devices!

Al ran around the pile. I followed the barking as it went from behind the pile, figuring Al headed in Campbell's direction.

I ran toward the corner of the cans where I could best estimate from Al where Campbell ran. Another handful of cans came over the pile and blew up where I had been standing. I dove as hard as I could over the corner of cans hoping Campbell would be on the other side.

I judged mostly correct and slammed into him, but I didn't get him right on and he bounced out of my way. He threw more cans at my feet and I felt the heat up my jeans as the fire climbed. I didn't stand around for them though and jumped Campbell and slammed him to the ground.

I hit the fat bastard with a closed fist right on the chin. I jumped on top of him and put both hands around his neck, choking him out. Campbell gagged from my hold and his eyes started bugging out. I've seen the face of a man dying before and this is what it looked like.

I squeezed tighter until I heard my name and a force knocked me off Campbell. Campbell rolled over and puked down the front off himself.

"Duffy, get out of here!" Karl's shirt was matted with blood from his shoulder to waist. He grabbed Campbell and pulled him up and the four of us ran out the side of the storage building. The storage building filled with three-foot high flames. We got out and slammed the door; though we couldn't see the flames, I knew they were climbing.

Outside the building, trucks and sirens and all sorts of cops fueled the confusion. I had no idea what was going on, but I knew we didn't have much time to get out of there. We all ran toward the Deuce.

"Duffy, Duffy–get over here!" I squinted toward the voice and saw Kelley.

"Kell–what the hell is going here?"

"Was that place filled with canned sausages?"

"What?"

"You heard me. Sausages–was it sausages that caused the explosions?"

"Yeah, yeah–how did you know?"

He handed me a piece of fax paper from the Department of Homeland Security.

"This came over our fax at around 10:00 p.m."

Intelligence reports point toward the use of small cans of VIENNA SAUSAGES as explosive devices. The plan appears to be that they are being sent to US soldiers in CARE packages and will be detonated in mass quantities when they arrive in Iraq and Afghanistan.

"What the hell?" I said. "That kid at Notre Dame had Vienna Sausages in his back pack."

"He got arrested two days ago and was found with a cache of weaponry in his dorm room," Kelley said.

"What the hell?"

"Yeah."

"Maybe I ain't as crazy as everyone thinks."

"Maybe," Kelley said.

Another cop guy came over to Kelley and grabbed at his elbow "We gotta evacuate ASAP. That whole place could blow. Hazmat fire personnel are on their way."

A flash of bright headlights ran across our faces, blinding us for a second. We could hear the rumbling of a large engine coming through what used to be the gate.

A black Hummer entered the gates, and it was pulling a trailer.

<u>46</u>

"Who the hell is that?" Kelley said.

"Holy shit."

"Duffy, who the hell is it?"

"Oh my God."

"Duffy!"

The head cop yelled instructions into a megaphone, telling everyone to evacuate ASAP. He repeated it over and over.

Meanwhile the Hummer and the trailer headed for the storage shed.

"Duffy, what the fuck is going on?" Kelley said.

"They're coming for the sausages. Holy shit. They're coming for the sausages."

"Who?"

"Newstrom! The guy no one has believed us about. The guy behind everything. He's part of this."

"He's headed for the shed?"

"He doesn't know about the fires. He can't tell," I said and watched Newstrom and his men file out of the Hummer. They had come to load up the trailer.

"We can't–" Kelley started to head toward the shed. I grabbed him by the arm.

Kelley looked at me with his mouth open. I shook my head.

"But Duff, it's going to blow–"

I just held him by the arm and shook my head.

I looked over to the ambulance taking Karl. They had him on the stretcher, but he was awake.

I looked at Karl. He looked toward the shed and then at me. We exchanged thumbs ups.

"Everyone outta here now!" Kelley's commander said.

"He can't see the shed from his angle," Kelley said.

"Kelley, get those civilians outta here now, and get your ass out right behind them!" the commander ordered.

"Duff–take care of Gladys!" Karl demanded before they pushed his stretcher into the ambulance.

Kelley broke away and ran to his squad car, hit the lights and headed toward the gate

Rocco yelled that the hounds were all accounted for and they were ready. I ran to the Deuce and jumped on board. Al stood in the front next to his mother, who moaned and breathed heavy. She didn't look good.

"Hold on tight," Rocco shouted. "We're out of here." He hit the gas hard and everyone lurched forward, which made Gladys let out a horrible sound. I looked in the back. The entire AJ's Army tended to the motley crew of bassets. The hounds howled and barked in a chaotic mess. I crawled through the opening to check on the dogs and I got to meet up close and personal with all the hounds Karl had told me about through their name tags. The hounds were wound up, but they all seemed okay except for Gladys. I climbed back through to the front seat and squeezed in next to Al.

Several cops and troopers fell in behind us with their lights on. We got out of the entrance seconds later and before my sigh of relief cleared my lips, the whole world shook.

A series of explosions cascaded and then one giant one kaboomed like Independence Day. The sky turned burnt orange and, for a moment, it was as bright as day out. Sparks, debris, hunks of storage building rained down on us. I looked back. Everything close to the storage building was gone. Through the smoke I could see a huge crater and then I realized something.

Just because somebody's crazy doesn't mean people

aren't out to get him.

The truck made a dramatic swerve, righted itself, and I snapped back in the moment. A very pregnant basset next to me made it tough to be totally relieved. Up ahead, I could see Karl's ambulance disappear and I hoped he was as all right as he acted.

A slew of fire engines passed us going the opposite way, heading towards the puppy mill. I thought they were going to be just a tad late.

The sky, still lit up, made me think of Independence Day.

47

Gladys moaned and the rest of the boys hooted and hollered from the back of the Deuce.

"Duffy, I got just one question." Rocco looked over at me while he drove.

"Yeah?"

"Where the hell are we taking 50 hounds, including this very-soon-to-be mother?"

"Uh…oh geez…"

"Forgot that detail, huh?"

I got so bent on my promise to Karl, I hadn't thought any further down the line. The top priority was to get Gladys to a vet. The problem, it was headed toward 11:00 at night and I didn't know the first thing about vets. The second thing, we needed a safe place to house the hounds while I figured out what to do with them. That meant I needed a big fenced-in area, medical attention and food for fifty dogs.

"Head to Rudy's," I said.

"You're kidding, right?" Rocco said. "Tonight's his big to-do, win-back-the-ex-night. Gourmet food, the string quartet, tuxedos."

"There's food, there's a big fenced-in area and there's Rudy–he's a doctor. It will be perfect."

"I'm not sure Rudy will think so."

"Yeah, there's that."

Rocco shook his head, but he hit the gas and headed toward Rudy's. It would take us about twenty minutes. I looked down at Gladys and I was not sure she could make it. She panted pretty bad, fussed around, and drooled excessively, even for a basset. Al whimpered and looked back and forth from me to his mom. This was tough.

"Rocco, speed it up a little. I think she might be ready," I said.'

"Ready? Like ready, ready?"

"I think so."

Rocco turned and yelled, "Hang on men, we're making the shift to light speed."

The Deuce lurched forward and I have to admit it got more than a little scary. Hounds barked, some bayed, and when I glanced back, it looked like my new best friends, the gang-bangers, were doing their best to avoid the basset induced fragrance.

"You get any thoughts for a strategy once we get to Rudy's?"

"Uh… Not really. I think this is just one of those Rudy things."

"A Rudy thing…" Rocco wasn't actually talking to me.

Rudy lived on the outside of town in a nice big old colonial. He had spent the summer getting it spruced up, having it landscaped, painted, the whole deal. This was all about getting Marie back. I didn't want to screw that up, but I had a pregnant hound on my hands.

Rudy would understand.

I thought he would.

Rocco made the turn down the private drive and we could see the white tent. Special lighting lit the road just for the party and I could see thirty or forty cars parked on Rudy's lawn. He even had a valet service for the night. The hounds reacted to slowing down, kicking their excitement up a gear.

"Park it right over there." I pointed to a spot about twenty-five feet from the tent.

"Rocco, I'm running in with Gladys to find Rudy. Can you direct the rest of the crew?"

"I got it Duff. Good Luck."

I scooped up Gladys, in her tattered blanket. She let out a sad half moan, half howl.

"Easy girl, easy girl."

I ran through the tent entrance, with its ivy-covered trestle. Fancy looking folks, some I recognized from the hospital, in fancy cocktail attire with their drinks in hand looked at me like I came from Mars.

"Rudy! Rudy," I screamed at the top of my lungs. The string quartet played on.

I madly looked from side to side. Partygoers cleared a path, mostly out of fear, as I ran through them. Finally, I saw him. He wore a white tuxedo jacket and black tuxedo pants. He was with Marie, who was dressed in a sharp looking black sparkly cocktail dress.

He caught sight of me and his eyes went wide, beyond what I thought was possible.

"Duff–what the hell–," he said. I don't know if I ever saw a man with a look of such intense horror and anger.

"Rudy, she's in trouble–I didn't know where else to go. She's pregnant and I think she's ready."

"I'm not a freakin' vet. I'm a–"

"C'mon Rudy!"

I laid Gladys down. Rudy took his coat off and got down on all fours. Marie had her hand on her chest and her mouth wide open with nothing coming out. Al sat next to me, whimpering.

"Okay…okay…easy girl…Duffy, get some napkins or a table cloth or something…" Rudy concentrated on Gladys.

I ran through the stunned partygoers who had now gathered around Rudy. The string quartet continued playing, giving everything a weird feel.

I gathered up napkins and supplies, rushing around all frantic, not knowing what the hell else to do. As I ran back towards the circle around Rudy, a roar of applause came up from the crowd. They clapped, hooted and hollered.

I pushed my way through the crowd with my stuff and there knelt Rudy. His tuxedo shirt covered in blood and his own sweat, his comb-over had flopped over his ear, and he was busy pulling out puppies. The partygoers continued clapping, the women crying and the men just had their mouths open.

"That's number eight," Rudy said, with a heavy exhale. He had some sort of creepy clearish fluid all over him. He ran his hand over Gladys.

"Easy girl…," he said.

"She okay?"

Rudy looked up at me and rolled his eyes.

"Yeah kid, she'll be fine." Rudy stood up, looking disgusted. "You have any idea what you've done or how hard I worked on this?" He looked around at what had become a less than glamorous affair. Covered in blood, dirt, sweat, and that creepy fluid, he had totally lost the Great Gatsby look.

"You know, Duffy I ought to–"

Marie didn't let him finish. She ran up and threw her arms around him. She cried really hard and shook.

"I'm sorry, so sorry Marie." Over her shoulder, he glared at me. I hung my head, knowing I had fucked things up for him again.

Marie cried and cried. The circle of partygoers around them got quiet and awkward. Marie pulled away and wiped her eyes.

"I'm so sorry, Marie. I wanted so much to–"

"The man I knew before never would've done something like this. This was so beautiful and so selfless." Marie and Rudy looked each other in the eyes, as if no one else existed. "God, I love you!" She threw herself into his arms and hugged him tight.

The partygoers cheered.

"God, I'm so glad you called me back," Marie said.

While they we're hugging, Rudy looked at me, shook his

head and rolled his eyes at me. I gave him a big thumbs up and I think I had a tear in my eye.

"Marry me–again!" Marie said to Rudy.

Everyone cheered like a bottom of the ninth home run at Yankee Stadium.

"Oh my God–you bet I will," Rudy said.

You couldn't ask for a better feel-good moment.

Then Rocco released the hounds

Suddenly fifty, or so, hounds descended upon the party. They ran, barked, and generally went nuts–until they found the caterer and the buffet.

A group of about six, including Lola Love, Sherlock, and Blake, knocked over the tenderloin carving station and pulled at the peppercorn-encrusted slabs. Arthur, Louie, and Sadie, and three of their best friends including that little Maltese-Pom, Tedward, had buried their heads in the gigantic shrimp cocktail bowl, slobbering all over the sterling silver.

All of AJ's Army joined in the party, chasing the hounds around. Quite a scene developed, and it dawned on me that my close friends weren't really the society party types. The gang-bangers ran after about six bassets that barked and howled and had a good time. Jerry Number Two tried to talk a big brown and white fellow out of eating the foix gras, but he appeared to be being ignored.

Billy chased Sally, Maui, and Guffy, who headed straight for the pool and dived in. Billy, having spent some time with Al and me, knew there was a good chance the dogs couldn't swim, so he went in after them. That started kind of a chain reaction and four or five hounds dove in to get refreshed. Billy's buddy, Timo, went in, and one by one he lifted the hounds out of the pool. Each hound got out and did that tornado basset thing to shake off the water before heading for the buffet table.

Somehow a bunch of bassets got into the caterer's portable kitchen and had a field day with the mini-quiches, eating them by the paw-full. A couple of other big fat red and whites had their heads stuck in an ice bowl, having a drink.

The society crowd kind of collectively gasped. Some of the women had their hands up around their necks in terror, while many others took it all in and laughed at the chaos around them. One couple sounded a little distressed over what they anticipated would be high dry cleaning expenses.

"Thanks for comin' Duff," Rudy said and put his arm around me.

"Did you hear?"

"Hear what? I've had my head in this party all summer."

"They found a weapons cache in the Asian kid's room at Notre Dame. The cans of Vienna Sausages were filled with explosives, headed to our soldiers."

"You're shittin' me."

"Maybe I'm not as crazy as people here think."

Rudy and I quietly watched fifty basset hounds run crazy all over his party, scavenging gourmet food, swimming in his pool, and dunking their heads in crystal serving bowls.

"Maybe, maybe not," Rudy said.

<u>48</u>

It wasn't long after that Kelley showed up and I got to meet his girlfriend, the conservation cop. He let me know Karl was fine; he'd lost a bit of blood but fortunately, he didn't take the full force from the shotgun. He also reported Karl didn't beat any orderlies up and seemed remarkably at peace during the whole process. Maybe the hospital staff ran out of tracking microchips.

"I know plenty of people in the dog rescue business," Kim said after we got introduced. She took out her cell phone. It was after two in the morning and the three of us stood at the entrance to Rudy's watching the hounds sleeping peacefully on his once finely manicured lawns.

"Kim, you do know it's after two in the morning, right?" I said.

She smiled. "You've never met people in the dog rescue business have you?"

Within an hour, five people had arrived, and each said they had two or three other folks that would 'foster' some hounds. Like some sort of canine UNICEF they came, rounded up the dogs, and let me know what a great guy I was for having the courage to storm the puppy mill.

I shook my head and smiled, mostly to myself.

"It wasn't me, trust me," I said.

They looked at me kind of funny, but they were busy rounding up the bassets.

The main rescue woman's name was Heather and she came over to shake my hand.

"You will not be forgotten in hound circles," she said.

"Somehow that fits," I said.

"Is there anything we can do for you?"

I thought for a second and although a voice inside me said I was nuts, I had learned to ignore that voice most of my life. Recently, I think I've gotten even better at not paying attention to it.

"Yeah, there is. Would it be okay if Gladys and her kids came home with me?"

"I can't think of a better home for them." She smiled and then spontaneously hugged me. I reached in my pocket and gave her the money I got from Heimi.

"What's this?" she said.

"For your expenses. You'll need it."

Kelley was smiling and so was Kim.

"You have some interesting friends, Mike," she said. No one called him Mike.

"Yeah, I know," Kelley said, looking at me. He looked down and lightly kicked at the grass. "Hey Duff?"

I looked at Kelley.

"I owe you an apology. I'm sorry for not believing you."

"Kell, you don't have to apologize. I was off my rocker and probably still am. Some of this shit's going to be with me for a while. Just because everything worked out doesn't mean I'm not a little–or a lot–fucked up," I said.

The next afternoon I got up, after sleeping right through to noon. I didn't remember dreaming and I barely remembered going to sleep. Gladys and the TCB Band–my name for the kids, after Elvis' backing group–slept on the floor. She seemed worn out, but otherwise okay.

I called Trina, after a couple of cups of coffee.

"I don't know if I said 'Thanks'."

"I'm just glad you made it okay," she said.

"Tomorrow she'll fire me for sure," I said. "But, you know, it might be time, and a couple of months with nothing to do might be good for the mental health."

"Duff, the place needs you and I think you need it. You could still get in there and get caught up on the paperwork. You've done it before, you can do it again."

"Not today, Trinie baby. Not after what I've been through. Not this time."

The other end of the phone got quiet and I heard a sniffle or two.

"Hey, you doing anything today? I could use a hand with something."

"You always need a hand with something," she said.

I told Trina to come over in about an hour and she did. She had on her 501s, a man's white T-shirt, and a pair of Adidas running shoes. Her hair, still a little wet, smelled of her plum conditioner.

I told her of my plan and she just shook her head.

"All of them?"

"Can you think of a better home for them?" I said.

"Well, actually, no."

We loaded the car up and Al sat in the back. At the hospital I commandeered a wheelchair and put the box on the seat.

"Looky who's here!" the world's cheeriest receptionist said.

Al walked with his mother and didn't sprint over to spelunk this time.

"This is Al's mom and his brothers and sisters," I pulled the blanket off the box. I put my index finger up to my lips. "No one has to know, right?" I gave her my best wink.

I got a wink back, and we headed up the elevator.

Karl was asleep. He had an IV in and a monitor kept track of his pulse and blood pressure. I was about to touch him lightly on the arm when Al shook the walls of the hospital with the world's most effective alarm clock sound.

Karl's eyes fluttered and he came around. He shook his

266

head a little bit and smiled down at Al and Gladys.

"She made it?" He grinned. "Thank God, she made it."

"Karl, I got something for you." He looked confused and I motioned to Trina.

She lifted the box onto his lap gently and took off the towel. The puppies peeped a little bit.

"Oh…oh my…oh my God." He started to cry. "They made it?"

"Every single one of them," I said.

Karl picked up each puppy, kissing everyone one of them. His tears ran into their mushy faces.

"Oh my God…" Karl kept repeating.

I looked at Trina. She was crying. I felt my eyes well up.

Karl sat oblivious. He just talked to his new friends. I let him do it without interruption for awhile.

"Hey Karl, buddy?"

"Yeah, Duffy?" he said without looking up at me.

"They're going to need homes, you know."

He finally looked at me.

"Gladys, too."

He stared at me and his jaw hung open.

"You mean…," Karl said

"I can't think of a more appropriate home."

"You mean…I get to…"

"Yeah, Karl, you do."

"But, I don't, I'm not sure…"

"You…and your family can stay at the Blue until you get your own place."

"You mean I can still live with you and Al?"

"…and Gladys and the entire TCB Band."

"Shit, Duffy, you really are crazy," Karl said.

"Takes one to know one," I said. The three of us laughed pretty hard while Al barked. Gladys, too tired to bark, purred a little bit.

"Hey, Duff," Karl said in a softer voice. "Newstrom and

267

his boys ran into that storage shed before it blew, didn't they?"

"Yeah."

"Their own evil blew them up."

"Yeah. I think the good guys won this time."

Karl and I looked each other in the eye for a long time. I'm not sure what I felt, but it felt good.

"Boy, we're some crazy motherfuckers, Duff," Karl said.

"Just cause you're crazy doesn't mean they're not out to get you, you know," I said.

I let Karl get some sleep and loaded up the hounds with a promise to look after them closely until he was released and back home with me.

Yeah, I know, it was nuts but what the hell?

<u>49</u>

Trina tried to talk me into heading to the clinic to do my paperwork, but I just couldn't see it. I can't say it felt like it was time to leave that job, but it just didn't seem right, after all I had been through, to worry about such trivial shit. Besides, I was exhausted. In fact, I was so exhausted I skipped AJ's.

That's exhausted.

Back at the Blue it was just me and my ten pets. I watched Gladys lay down, totally wiped out, while her babies went to town on her built-in milk truck. Al lay next to his mom and kept his eyes open. I cracked a Schlitz and watched.

I didn't turn on the TV and I didn't throw in an 8-track. I just watched, without thinking, just letting what was in front of me fill up my head. I did that for a long time, even sitting there with an empty beer, just watching.

I am at the clinic except I can't get in because the waiting room is jammed. The clients are all pushed together and barely able to breathe. I see Eli, Froggy, the Abermans, Sheila, and ones from the past like Sherry, and they're suffocating.

I can't get in because the door is locked and they can't open it from the inside. Suddenly Claudia is behind me and she's laughing. Trina is behind her with her back to me and Monique is there too, with her head hanging down.

Inside the lobby, sheets of paper start to blow out of an air vent and they're filling the lobby like water poured into an aquarium. The clients are drowning and I can't do anything about it. And then Karl is there peering out the window and he's in an Army uniform, except he's got on a Redskins helmet.

Then, Walanda, the woman I got Al from, steps in front of Karl and she's bleeding from the head. She's ranting and raving like she always did, but half her head is missing.

Then a loud bark...

...Wakes me out of it.

I'm on the couch, Al is at my feet, and the sun is up. The clock on the cable box tells me it's 5:15 a.m. Al won't shut up, his bark is in overdrive and he's getting on my nerves.

I blinked my way to consciousness and tried to clear my head. So much for the belief I had exorcised my demons. Maybe there were new ones to meet, Maybe Rudy was right and this shit was going to stick.

Al wouldn't shut up and there wasn't a chance of me going back to sleep.

5:30.

Fuck it, if I left now I'd get there by quarter to six and that would give me three hours to catch up on paperwork. It wouldn't be enough, but if I could get a signal to Trina, maybe she could stack the deck and together we could pull it off.

I got dressed to drive to the clinic. As soon as I picked up the keys, Al shut up.

I didn't stop for the red lights, and at this hour I don't think it mattered all that much. For the first time since the puppy mill, Saturday night, I realized the smell of smoke had gotten into something. It might have been my jeans or my running shoes or even my car. Thick, it made me a little nauseous and I opened all the windows wide which only made it worse.

I made the final turn down Central, and my stomach froze when I saw the parking lot. I saw the fucking Michelin Woman's car there. It wasn't even six yet and she was there

270

reviewing my shit to fire me.

Fuck me.

I turned into the lot, probably out of force of habit, because there was no way I was going in there to give her the personal joy of firing me to my face. The smell got worse and I started to get sick to my stomach, like my mind was really fucking with me.

Then I saw the dark grey smoke seeping out of the clinic roof. I stepped out of the El Dorado. As I did, I saw the lobby was filled with clouds of white smoke.

A ball of fire the size of a refrigerator appeared in the lobby and raced to the front door, doubling in size. It exploded into the entryway and blew out the glass all over the parking lot. I could feel the heat on my face twenty feet away.

Claudia was trapped in there.

I sprinted through the front threshold, holding my arm over my mouth as much as I could. I couldn't see a damn thing, but I knew the office and took the sharp left after the reception area, into the director's office.

"Claudia! Claudia!" No answer. I coughed like a son-of-a-bitch as I felt my way around her desk. I felt for a handful of curly black hair and found it.

The fat bastard weighed close to three hundred, but I got my hands under her armpits and pulled as hard as I could. I ran backwards through Trina's small office, which was filled with smoke. I wheezed and hacked but I wasn't on fire, at least not yet. The back of my head slammed into a wall, sending a wicked throb through my head. I dropped Claudia and had to find her underarms again.

Her body was limp.

I got a hold on her and drove my legs as hard as I could. I grunted and yelped with the effort and then I had to stop to hack out more smoke. One last pull and I dragged her out to the smoke-filled sidewalk. I pulled harder toward my car, dragging her to the front of it. I was out of breath, and began puking from the smoke.

I could hear sirens. When I looked down Claudia wasn't breathing.

The one in-service I think I actually attended covered CPR. I straddled her, swept her mouth clean and pressed my lips to hers and blew. I did it several times and then shimmied down her body, and compressed her chest. I went back up and puffed a few more breaths and repeated the compressions.

"Come on you fat bastard!" The trucks pulled into the lot.

Claudia wretched and spit something up, part of it hitting me in the face. She coughed and coughed and moaned and started to rock from side to side. The next thing I knew there were two firemen pushing me out of the way and taking over.

I took a step backwards and fell down.

I heard the roof cave in the clinic, creating a loud *whoosh* of air that sent billows of smoke and flames to the sky.

"Get back, you've got to get back," someone yelled. Whoever it was helped me to my feet and we ran together toward the back of the lot. As we did the clinic collapsed on itself.

Seconds after, the ambulance carrying Claudia sped past me.

<u>50</u>

I sat there and watched the place burn. Trina was the first one there, and Monique came by shortly after. We didn't say much; it just felt really weird.

A crowd of onlookers gathered. The fireman had the thing under control, but they continued to spray water on charred hunks of what used to be the clinic. I guess that's what they have to do to stop it from starting up again.

I walked up to a fireman who was changing his coat at the back of one of the trucks.

"The lady they took away–is she going to be–"

"You the guy who went in and got her, and did CPR?"

"Yeah."

"Well, pal, you'll never forget today. She was gone–flat lined and you brought her back. She was responsive and talking in the ambulance. How does it feel to save a life?" he said with a big grin.

"There's no way I could explain it to you."

I walked back to my small circle of co-workers.

"What do we do now?" Trina said.

"I'm taking a personal day," I said. Everyone laughed.

I started to head toward the El Dorado, which had its finish singed. I didn't know what fucking universe I was in, but I knew one thing. When AJ turned the knob on his front door at 12:01 I would be behind him.

"Hey, Duff!" A voice came from the other side of the lot, a little down the street. I couldn't make out who it was, but it looked like some guy walking his daughter. I walked towards the two of them while they walked toward me. As we got closer I noticed it was Sparky.

"Hey Duff, hell of a thing," he said.

"Yeah, unbelievable," I said.

"Kristy," Sparky looked at the little girl. "Say hello to Mr. Duffy."

"Hi Mr. Duffy," Kristy had two little ponytails and blond hair. She could've been the Sunbeam bread girl.

"That's my daughter, Duff," Sparky said with a big smile.

"But, I thought Paula said—"

"Weird, Duff. Last night I got my first call from Paula in years. Asked me if I heard about some drill at the school. Then she says it was no drill and she saw some stuff no one else did. Said she didn't know why, but she followed you and your buddy out into the woods and saw what really went down. Said she heard all sorts of scary shit. Said she saw my counselor doing some sort of heroic stuff, and she changed her mind about me and Kristy." Sparky smiled.

I looked at him with my mouth open.

"So when they get the clinic open, you'll still be my counselor, right?"

"Well, I don't know if I'll be around. Remember—"

"You had some paperwork trouble." Sparky nodded to the clinic. "Doesn't look like there's any paperwork for anyone to check, if you ask me."

"Sparky—"

"Paula says she's callin' the clinic and rescindin' her complaint about you breaking that confidentiality shit. Gonna say she made it up to get me in trouble," Sparky said.

"I think the files are kept in metal file cabinets so they are fire protected. They're probably in that mess somewhere," I said.

"Duff, my experience tells me that the right incendiary device combined with the right accelerant will raise the temperature of a fire sufficient enough to incinerate metal and reduce it and its contents to cinders." Sparky looked me in the eye.

"Say 'thank you' to Mr. Duffy," Sparky said to Kristy.

"Thank you, Mr. Duffy," Kristy said in the absent-minded way kids repeat things.

"Sparky–"

"I'll call for an appointment, Duff," he said. "We gotta go. We're going to the zoo and then the movies." He waved as he walked down Central Avenue.

51

I was on Schlitz number three, watching the local news report the fire at Jewish Unified Services was caused by a faulty electrical outlet. Jerry Number Two came in, but focused on his laptop, and AJ loaded the coolers.

I didn't mind.

Number four slid in front of me as the door opened and Trina came in. AJ asked what she wanted and she ordered a Jack and Diet Coke.

"You saved Claudia's life?"

"Don't remind me," I said.

"With CPR and mouth-to-mouth."

"Talk about nightmares."

"And there are no clinical records left. None to be reviewed, no treatment plans, no discharge summaries…nothing."

I shrugged.

"Welcome back."

She leaned over and kissed me, ever so lightly, on the cheek. I could feel her brush up against me as she did.

"And you're not getting married any more," she said looking me right in the eye.

"Geez, I haven't given that much thought lately. I guess I've had some other stuff on my mind."

"You feel like getting out of here? I got a twelve pack of Schlitz in my fridge."

"The way to a man's heart…"

I threw some money on the bar and followed Trina out. We took my car to her apartment and Elvis sang us there with

Dylan's *Don't Think Twice, It's Alright.*

We got to Trina's front door and I took her into my arms.

"Did I say 'Thank you' to you."

"You did."

"Not enough," I kissed her. We kissed for a long time and for the first time in a long time I didn't think of anything but how good it felt.

Trina broke the kiss.

"I'm glad Claudia wasn't the only woman from the office you wanted to kiss," she said.

"Talk about nightmares," I said as we headed inside.

The End

Tom Schreck writes on topics as broad as boxing, business, pets, fitness, psychology, relationships, golf (which he despises), diners, drive-ins, and prison for publications that include *The Business Review, Westchester Magazine, Professional Counselor, Referee,* and *Catfancy,* among others

He directed an inner city addiction clinic, earned a black belt, boxed with amateur and pro champions, judged world championship boxing, taught college in prison and has been a therapist, a bouncer, and a bad guitar player. He considers waiting on his three hounds while protecting the three cats they torment as his chief responsibility.

Tom graduated from the University of Notre Dame and holds a masters degree in psychology. He is communications director for Wildwood Programs, a nonprofit agency that serves people with developmental disabilities and he teaches at Hudson Valley Community College. For fun he boxes, listens to Elvis, walks his dogs, and drives his big old Lincoln (because today's Cadillacs are too small.)

He lives in Albany, NY.